The Relentless Pursuit of
the Cosmic Awareness

Michael Gary Wirth

Published by Leafen Egg Creations
Edison, NJ 08817

ISBN: 0692591931
ISBN-13: 978-0692591932

For my wife, Lauren, who always inspires me to keep going, especially when I lose all drive to do so.

CONTENTS

MICHAEL GARY WIRTH

ACKNOWLEDGMENTS

As I cross the finish line towards yet another completed novel, I need to look back on the journey that brought me to this point. What started as a NaNoWriMo endeavor has included plenty of other work that went into the finished product. And plenty of people that helped along the way.

Firstly, I need to acknowledge my wife, Lauren, without whom I would have foregone the entire ordeal. She has been there to encourage me and to remind me that talent isn't the only thing that makes a writer; writing also requires a buttload of hard work. And I thank her for putting up with all of those lonely nights to allow me to put that work in.

Also, to the other women in my life: my mother and sister. They are always there when I need help and I wouldn't have been able to get through life without them.

In addition, I'd like to share my appreciation for those that have encouraged me in my writing career. From my writing buddy Ben Jacoby to former colleague Robb Orr, you guys helped inspire me to keep doing my thing. And I can't forget Jack Chambers, David Vandervliet and especially Toby Miley for showing interest in my latest work, which became a huge push towards actually completing it.

Last but not least, my two long-time friends, Jay Amabile and Adam Szabunia, both of whom were present for the birth of Bastion Dagger. Though the character came around through some off-the-cuff brainstorming, I found him interesting enough to flesh out and make real (so to speak). And that wouldn't have happened without you two.

So with that, I'd like to take a moment and thank you, reader, for purchasing or downloading this book and, most especially, reading it. I hope you enjoyed it and that you stick around for the final chapter. (You didn't think I was going to end it like that, did you?)

PROLOGUE

Despite its vastness, the universe is an incredibly delicate thing. It doesn't take much to throw it off balance; even the tiniest flaw is enough to cause immense damage. Take, for example, the black shard of stone floating across the galaxy, unseen by anything, its existence all but forgotten. Through it flowed one of the most powerful forces ever controlled by a living being but out here, it was little more than a paper weight. Actually, it wasn't even that seeing as how it spun weightless through space.

It had been moving for months, unhindered by the lack of air resistance and gravity that is normal for deep space, spinning its way across the cosmos. But out of nowhere, with no explanation, it stopped spinning, its sharpened point snagging something. Some kind of microscopic hole in space.

Stuck, it hung a few minutes before the shard vibrated and pulsed wildly. It jerked back, pushed away by some invisible force, its edge leaving behind a tiny tear in the fabric of reality. Bright purple light flowed from the tear, casting over the black shard, its tiny white dots twinkling a pale, violet shade.

The purple light went dark as a black, wiggly digit erupted from the tear. It searched around the edges of the rip, like a periscope cresting the ocean water. The finger hooked and yanked downward. The fabric of reality relented to its coercion and tore open wider, allowing the bright purple light to flood out from the abyss.

Belial poked his head through the tear and looked around.

He'd been trapped in that other place for almost two millennia and was a little cranky. He didn't question how the tiny tear in reality appeared. In fact, it didn't quite matter to him at all. He was just happy that it did, and happy isn't an emotion that he expressed too often.

Placing his massive hands on both sides of the opening, the demon pulled himself through the hole and into our reality. He floated in space for a moment to get his bearings. As he looked around, the hole behind him closed, slowly stitching itself back up. He turned to find only open space, a galaxy of bright white stars smiling at him.

He stretched his arms wide, his joints releasing a barrage of popping and cracking beneath his flesh. A slight buzzing raged at the back of his skull. He ignored it, his only interest in exacting his revenge on his captors.

He pushed himself through space, moving like an Olympic swimmer in a pool of gelatin. His imprisonment left him drained and he moved sluggishly, at a pace that annoyed him. In his weakened state, it would take him centuries to get where he was going. With any hope, his travels would take him past a small star that he could drain to restore his lost strength. After that, he could begin his search to reclaim his power, restore his kingdom, and most importantly, have his revenge against the Angelic High Military.

After fifteen hundred years in Limbo, give or take a century, Belial had plenty of pent up rage to release and he planned on focusing that anger on the angels. But his last assault against the AHM hadn't gone as planned, leaving him unarmed, embarrassed and banished to a different plane of existence. So he at least realized that he couldn't just follow blind rage into battle; he'd need a plan.

As he trudged through the cosmos, Belial mentally worked out the steps of his revenge. First, he would bring the Angelic High Military to its knees, tearing it down brick by brick if he had to. Then he would find Lucifer and that wench sister he kept tied at the waist. They would pay for their betrayal. He would feed off their Hellfire, supping on the energy that he gave to them. Belial licked his lips at the thought of draining the life from them both, smiling at the image of them begging and pleading for their lives.

Rousing himself from his reverie, Belial felt a strange

vibration in his skin. It was very faint but unmistakable. He turned in place, his eyes scanning the inky blackness of the universe around him. As he moved, the vibration shifted, sliding from his right side to his left. He inched forward and the vibration increased. Something was calling to him, summoning him. It was a familiar feeling, one he couldn't place through the fatigue of his struggle but he wasn't about to ignore it.

The shrill buzz pierced his skull, causing him to roar in pain. The noise assaulted him and dulled his senses. He grew nauseated as he floated in the vacuum of space, limp and vulnerable. Closing his eyes, he concentrated, forcing the pain from his head. As he did, a picture popped into his mind, a sight that he recognized. Belial looked around at the millions of tiny white dots twinkling before him. His eyes fell upon one, off in the distance but closer than all the rest.

The white light called to him, beckoning him; he could feel it in his mind. Belial pushed himself toward it, his eyes never leaving the twinkle. As he drew closer, the buzzing in his head intensified. He tried to ignore it, told himself that the attack was just a tiny irritation but it grew stronger and stronger with every foot that he traveled. Shaking his head, he looked back toward the spot in space. He was close.

Reaching out, Belial wrapped his fingers around the black shard. A frozen coldness ran through his hand as he grasped it, the stone much colder than even the recesses of space. He pulled it closer and stared at the jagged, two-foot fragment. He watched as the tiny white dots flickered in the dim light of a nearby star. The dots swirled around each other as a galaxy does, moving in unison.

It looked so small, nestled in the folds of his palm. Small and powerless. But he knew that wasn't the truth. As he held the a piece of his Onyx Blade close to himself, Belial could feel its energy running through his veins, up his arms and throughout his body. His sluggishness quickly disappeared and he became more alert of his surroundings. He could hear the voices in his head returning, the ambient thoughts of nearby minds being picked up by his natural telepathy. It had been a long time since his brain listened to other conversations, being cut off from civilization entirely as he was.

The discovery of this one tiny piece in the vastness of space wasn't an accident; it sought him out, led him to its location.

Reaching out to him for his help to be healed. Which he was more than obliged to do. Once he had reassembled his sword, his mighty Onyx Blade, he would rise to his true power, and find the Angels.

But what could have shattered his sword? It was one of the most powerful weapons in the universe, tempered by pure Hellfire. The angels themselves didn't have the power to commit such an act, at least not the power the Belial knew them to possess. Could they have discovered a significant weapon during his exile? If so, they could prove to be more trouble than he imagined.

Closing his eyes, he channeled his power through the shard, reading the ambient energy it contained. He clutched the fragment against his chest and images formed in his head. Moments of time replayed before him, revealing the sword's secrets. A woman with blue hair standing with two men against an army. A large, writhing creature, tentacles thrashing, looking to sate its appetite. The angels.

Belial opened his eyes, a low, guttural growl emanating from his throat. The power of the Leviathan destroyed his sword. If the Leviathan had been conjured, that meant the angels were involved. But as the fragment showed, the beast was destroyed in the process, which meant the angels no longer controlled the power to combat his Blade.

Belial smiled again. Raising his arm, he funneled his vision through the fragment, scouring the universe for other pieces of the sword. A small quiver in the shard caught his attention. Turning, he looked out through space and pinpointed the location. A small blue and green world in the far off distance of a tiny, forgotten solar system. He propelled himself through the galaxy, allowing the vibrations of the shard in his hand to lead him to his destiny.

CHAPTER 1

Twilana's eyes watered as a cloud of dust enveloped the room. Tears rolled down her cheeks and pain engulfed her eye sockets but she refused to blink. Refused to look away from Aaron. In the short time she'd known him, this strange man that fell into her life through some fluke, cosmic accident, she developed deep feelings for him. There was a connection with him that she'd never felt with anyone else. The burning in Twilana's eyes intensified but she knew it wasn't just from the dust. They burned with the fear of loss. She knew that she would never see him again and that pain hurt her deeply. But she at least took solace in the fact that he was returning home. Safely. And that he'd have his life ahead of him.

Her eyes flicked to Matt, Aaron's friend and travelling companion. A man that she had considered a friend as well. One that'd she'd risk her life for.

"Go!" she shouted. Through the chaos and smoke, she watched as Matt grabbed Aaron's arm and pulled him toward the vortex. Twilana trusted Matt's logic, that he would not make an emotional decision. And as she watched Aaron disappear into the swirling purple miasma of the beyond, she was thankful for that trust.

Twilana squeezed her eyelids shut and a torrent of tears dribbled down her cheeks. Inhaling deeply, she swiped the back of her hand across her face, leaving wet streaks on her skin. The flood of emotions filling her chest made her uncomfortable, forcing her to face feelings that he'd never faced before. Being a captain in the

Janian military never afforded her many opportunities to care for somebody else. She'd dealt with death plenty of times and lost people she'd never see again. But this was different.

She balled her fist and shook her head, pushing the emotions to the side. Looking down, she watched as the beast undulated beneath her feet. She felt the sword in her hand, the heavy onyx blade that shone with the light of a million twinkling stars, and tightened her grip on the hilt. Lifting the blade above her head, she spun the sword in her hands, leveling the point at the creature. The Leviathan: a mythical being whose presence summoned the end of the world. Given the last couple of minutes, Twilana had to believe that there may be some truth to the myth. Not that she was going to simply stand by and let it happen.

Closing her eyes, she threw her head backwards and jammed the sword into the Leviathan's back. Thick, pink blood oozed from the wound as the monster shrieked in pain. Dropping to her knees, she dragged the blade through the Leviathan's flesh, splitting its hide as she inched her way down its back. Blood sprayed from the gash, bathing everything in a warm, pink goo.

The Leviathan released a piercing threnody as it bucked wildly. Twilana slid down its side, her boots kicking up a spray of blood as she landed on the floor and stepped back as the creature entered its final death throes. Her head hung limp as she listened to the wet slapping sounds of the Leviathan's dying tentacles all around her. The exhaustion of the past week finally caught up to her. Her body ached. Her soul ached. Her heart ached.

Turning from the bloody, pulsating corpse, Twilana looked up, her gaze meeting Metatron's. His gentle face stared at her, his eyes showing a mixture of relief and pity, knowing that, for her at least, the victory was bittersweet. She could feel her cheeks tingling from the trail of tears. All she wanted to do was scream out to relieve the pressure in her chest but as she opened her mouth, all that escaped was a yawn. Metatron smiled at the revelation of her humanity.

Seeing Metatron's smile eased Twilana's nerves. Her heartbeat slowed as she returned his smile, vowing to herself to find some place small, warm, and quiet to fall asleep for a few days. But a rumble in the floor disrupted that fantasy. She turned toward the body of the Leviathan and saw the quivering in its lifeless flesh. Slightly at first, almost imperceptibly but as she stared at it, the shaking became more pronounced, more intense. Placing her hand on its hide, she felt waves flowing throughout its body. She had no idea what was causing it but she turned from the Leviathan's corpse and sprinted across the room.

Twilana pumped her legs as hard as she could to put as much distance between her and the Leviathan. Behind her, a warm blast of air and a flash of bright, pink light ripped through the room. Her body grew heavy as the light engulfed her. Her muscles fought against her will, dragging her down. She dropped to her knees as every cell in her body grew cold, the light sapping all warmth from the room. Looking up at Metatron, she watched as his mouth moved. He was shouting to her but no sound passed his lips. He raised his hand, reaching out to grab her. She tried to lift her arm but the light had her trapped, unable to move. She watched helplessly as a grimace of fear spread across Metatron's face.

The light became brighter, washing away the details of the room around her. Metatron seemed to dissipate, disappearing slowly from reality. As the light grew brighter, Twilana suddenly realized that it wasn't Metatron that was disappearing. It wasn't the Ocularium fading from reality.

It was her.

Twilana bolted upright in her bed, sweat pouring down her face and chest. Her stomach roiled and her throat contracted. Leaning over the side of the bed, she retched, a splash of vomit erupting from her gullet. Her chest heaved a few times, forcing the contents of her stomach up her throat. She sat upright for a minute, staring at the wall across from her, waiting for another wave of sickness. Satisfied that it was over, she wiped the bile from the corner of her mouth and lay back in the bed.

The same dream plagued her every night for weeks. But it was more than a dream. It was a memory. A recollection of the event that changed everything.

Feeling a chill run through her body, she wrapped the bearskin blanket around herself and rolled over onto her side. She closed her eyes but images from the dream continued to flash through her brain. She knew she wouldn't be going back to sleep. Hopping out of the bed, she dropped the blanket and grabbed her clothes, the dirty, ragged uniform of her military days. It had long since outlived its usefulness but Twilana couldn't bear to part with it.

Sentimental attachment was only part of the reason she kept the uniform; she had no skills to sew new clothes. The dark blue outfit had been repaired many times over, cuts and tears sewed up with whatever she could find. The outfit looked terrible but as she slipped into it, it made her feel good. Powerful. Like her old self.

Crouching down, she grabbed her dagger. Like her clothing, it was cobbled together from whatever material she could find, repaired numerous times over the last few months. But one thing had always remained the same about the weapon. Wrapping her fingers around the cold black hilt, she dragged the edge across her fingertips, feeling its sharpness. The old stone she found had been quite useful, retaining its edge for quite some time, but she knew that she would need to find a new one soon. She pulled on the vines that attached the stone to the hilt.

Looking down at the handle, she remembered her dream, remembered the pain of leaving Aaron and Matt. Every time she looked at the weapon, she was reminded of that moment. The sight of the blade was directly attached to that memory. Besides the clothes on her back, the hilt was the only piece that remained of her time on that world.

It was the handle of the Onyx Blade of Belial.

CHAPTER 2

Ducking low, Twilana emerged from the mouth of the cave into the clearing. She righted herself and inhaled deeply, the sweet scent of the jungle air filling her lungs. A cool breeze brushed over her skin and flittered her hair. Twilana smiled, the air seeming to chase away the remnants of last night's horrific dream.

The sun peeked over the horizon far off in the distance, casting a few thin tendrils of light through the trees. Twilana looked out into the semi-darkness and reveled in the tranquility of the morning. The only downside was that with the sun came the heat; beads of sweat formed on her forehead. Wiping them away, she slipped the dagger into her belt and stepped from the rocky outcrop. She lowered herself down the sloping hill and quickly surveyed her surroundings, listening to the crinkling of the leaves as they rustled in the breeze.

The air was heavy with moisture. Twilana tugged at her shirt, fanning the sweat that dripped down her chest. This type of humidity was new to her; the buildings in her home city of Janus all contained self-sustaining bio-systems, each carefully maintained to create a comfortable climate. All of her life she was surrounded by air conditioners, heating units and dehumidifiers, making sure that she never suffered from unsightly perspiration. Even though she'd gotten used to the heat over the past few months, that didn't mean she liked it.

She stepped into the morning light. Skulking slowly between the trees, she kept her eyes focused on the ground, searching the dirt for a trail of animal prints that may lead to her breakfast. The humidity wrapped itself around her, causing her clothes to cling to her body. She was fanning the sweat on her chest again when she spotted a line of hoof prints leading over a small hill. She knelt next to the tracks and examined them.

Rising to her feet, she made her way around the tall trees surrounding her, pushing aside the curling vines that dropped from the branches. The area was awash in large, green, bushy leaves sprouting from the treetops. Bright yellow moss grew along the sides of the trees and down to the ground, feeding on the damp bark and jungle detritus. Every so often a breeze would shake the leafy canopy overhead, sending a flurry of leaves tumbling down to the jungle floor. Up above, puffs of flowers dotted the branches, breaking the monotony of green with balls of blue, pink, and purple. Reaching up, Twilana plucked a pink flower from the tree. Tilting her head back, she held it above her mouth and squeezed the nectar from the pistil. The juice flowed over her tongue, its sweetness invigorating her.

Pausing for a moment, she listened to the rustling of leaves, catching the undertones of something else. She turned her head and listened to the wind, holding her breath so she could hear better. Finding the source of the noise, she dropped to her knees and crawled over a large boulder, peeking down on a stream beneath her.

A scrawny brown fawn stood at the edge of the stream, its pink tongue lapping up the cool, clear water. Twilana watched the drinking deer, transfixed by the ripples that erupted in the water beneath the animal's mouth.

Sliding the dagger from her belt, Twilana inched her way toward the edge of the boulder, moving cautiously to stay as silent as she could. She grabbed the underside of the rock and rolled herself over the side, landing on a mound of moss directly beneath it. The muted thud sounded like a clap of thunder to her, forcing her to pause, breath held as she waited for the deer to bolt off into the brush. The deer lifted its head and sniffed the air a few times before turning back to the stream to continue its drink.

Gripping the handle of the blade, Twilana stepped closer to the fawn, slowly placing her feet in the soft, loamy dirt, moving like a cat on shag carpeting. Steadying her breathing, she pivoted the blade in her hand, resting the cool stone against her forearm.

She shifted her weight to her front foot, bracing, waiting for the perfect moment to pounce.

An orange blur passed before her. Stumbling backward, she turned her head and blinked rapidly. When she looked back toward the stream, the deer was gone. She spotted the fawn farther downstream, kicking and bucking as a tiger stood on its flank, its jaws clenched tightly around its neck. A heart-wrenching wail escaped the deer's mouth as its flailing grew weaker and weaker. Thick, red blood oozed from its throat, draining the life from its body.

"Oh no, you don't," Twilana muttered under her breath. Spinning on her front foot, she lunged at the tiger, swiping the blade at its hind quarters. The tiger roared in pain as the stone slashed its thigh. It kicked at Twilana, hitting her square in the chest. She flopped to the ground with a *thud*, the blade tumbling from her hand.

The tiger stepped back from the deer and limped toward Twilana. It sniffed at the air as it drew closer to her, fires of anger burning in its big, blue eyes. She looked up at the tiger, its low, throaty growl prickling her skin, questioning the intelligence of her attack. Her hand frantically patted the ground beside her, searching for her weapon.

Twilana's fingertips brushed the cold stone of the hilt of the knife. She rolled onto her belly and lunged for the blade as the tiger pounced on her, its massive paws pinning her shoulders to the ground. Grasping the hilt, she reached back and slashed at the animal's face. The blade tore open the animal's cheek and blood trickled down its maw. It roared again as it stepped back from her, giving her the chance to hop to her knees and turn toward the beast. Twilana leaped and buried the knife into the tiger's leg. It growled viciously, pawing at her. Tears formed in her eyes as the razor-sharp claws raked across her ribcage. She twisted the blade and the tiger's roar grew more pained as it pushed her back with its massive paw.

Twilana tumbled to the dirt, the pain in her chest almost unbearable, her vision blurry with tears. She wiped her eyes clear and ignore the pain in her side, struggling to rise on shaky legs. She clutched the blade so tightly the tips of her fingers turned white. The tiger circled around, limping on its injured foot, huffing loudly. It sprang but Twilana ducked out of its way. The tiger fell to the ground, kicking up a wave of leaves and dirt. She jumped onto the tiger's back, jamming the knife into its side. It reared up on its hind legs, throwing her into a growth of bushes and weeds.

Shaking her head, Twilana lifted herself up on her elbow and waited for the tiger to attack. She watched as it looked back at her, curled its lip and growled. It huffed loudly through its nose before turning to the woods and loping off between the trees, disappearing in the tall grass.

Twilana lay back on the dirt, a deep, throaty laugh breaking the silence. Her shoulder hurt, her side throbbed and she'd lost her breakfast. She sat up in the grass and wrapped her arms around her knees. Despite all of the bad luck she faced that morning, she somehow felt more alive than she had in months.

Pushing herself to her feet, Twilana felt a strange pulsing in her hand. Cradling it against her chest, she massaged the back of her hand to calm the nerves. A moment passed before she realized that her hand wasn't tingling because of an injury; the pulsing came from the blade.

Twilana held the weapon in front of her and watched as tiny vibrations moved through the hilt. She turned, facing the stream and noticed that the strength of the vibrations increased, growing more pronounced. Giving the blade a confused look she took a step backward. The vibrations weakened. She shook her head and smiled to herself, contemplating the strangeness of the weapon. She stepped forward again and, as expected, the vibrations returned. Twilana sighed, dropping her arms to her side and tromped through the tall grass. With each step, she felt the trembling of the blade grow stronger but she ignored it. She was hungry, she was tired, and her ribs hurt like hell. The hilt of the blade was crafted by some sort of ancient, magical demon. She stopped trying to understand it a long time ago. At this point, its only purpose was to help her hunt.

A sudden pulse shot up her arm, so strong and abrupt that it caused her drop the knife. She bent over to grab it, rifling through a clump of dried grass. As she grasped the hilt, a strange object caught her attention. Dark black, spotted with thousands of twinkling white dots. She reached through the grass and picked it up, holding it up to the light to examine it.

Her breath caught in her throat as she realized she was holding another shard of the Onyx Blade.

CHAPTER 3

The fluorescent light flickered over Lauren as she leaned against the stainless steel countertop, staring at the long strand of red hair she twirled between her fingers. Bored and disinterested, she contemplated her current situation. She looked down and scowled at the blue polo shirt covering her chest. The stiff polyester made her skin itch and just felt downright gross. She hated having to wear that shirt but she had no choice. According to Section III, Paragraph B, Sub-section 2 of the Employee Handbook, "*Arthur Treacher's employees are to dress in a manner that reflects the company culture and, as such, all manner of dress shall be in the form of a blue Polo shirt (to be provided by your manager) and khaki pants*". How the notion of "blue polo" and "khaki" reflected the nature of fried fish Lauren hadn't a clue. She tugged at the shirt and continued to snap the wad of pink chewing gum between her teeth.

"Would you stop that, please?"

Lauren grunted, her attention placed firmly on the strands of hair between her fingers and the gum in her mouth. Lucifer reached up and pulled her hand away from her hair.

"And stop that while you're behind the counter. The last thing I need is for someone to complain about hair in their food."

"Sir, yes sir," Lauren said, mocking him with a salute. Sighing exasperatedly, she strolled to the register and leaned her elbows on the counter.

Lucifer was dressed as the model associate. Khaki pants neatly pressed and wrinkle free. Blue polo shirt tucked into his

13

pants, secured by a shiny black belt. His hair, though well-coiffed, had lost the sheen he was used to but he managed to adjust to the new look. Even his nametag, which introduced him as "Lou", was pinned proudly to his chest at a perfect 90 degree angle.

"Are you bored?" he asked, straightening his back. He shifted down the counter and pulled a sleeve of drinking cups from the shelf. "Because if you want, you can count all this stuff for me." He bent over to get a look at the cups in the back of the shelf, eyeballing each one and taking a mental count. Looking down at the inventory spreadsheet clipped to his brown clipboard, he checked a box next to the entry for *Medium Cups* and scribbled a legible *94* on the line for *Count*.

"Yeah, OK," Lauren groaned. "Like you'd let anyone take the reins of your precious inventory."

"You're right," Lucifer growled, placing the clipboard on the countertop. "I won't let anyone do this. You know why? Because I believe in doing things right. Meanwhile all you seem to do is mope. Do you think I like being here? Having to hide away from everything? Not to mention this." He pointed to his nametag which, beneath his name, exclaimed 'Assistant Manager'. "You think I *like* being an 'Assistant' Manager in a place like this? Hell, there's no reason I shouldn't be a District Manager. But I deal with it because I know. We just need to give it time and when we return to New Eden, things will be different."

The fall from power was the most frustrating part of their exile for Lucifer. Back home in New Eden, he enjoyed a lofty position of being the head of the underworld, a virtual kingpin of the vices and sins of the city. If someone needed a fix, had some itch that needed to be scratched, Lucifer was sure to profit from it in one way or another. But when he tried to release the Leviathan in the middle of the Angelic High Military building, a plan that failed spectacularly, he and Lauren had been forced to hide out on the nearest planet, blending in with the population by getting low profile, low paying jobs.

While Lucifer eventually grew into his new role, Lauren hated it with every fiber of her being. She pushed up from the counter and faced him, leaning her hip on the dented stainless steel. Though she couldn't stand what they were reduced to, she trusted Lucifer completely. He took her in when she was at the lowest point of her life and showed her what it was like to have someone care for her. He told her they needed to lay low so she would do what he asked. But that didn't mean she wouldn't have a little fun with him in the meantime. She blew a large pink bubble with her chewing gum, letting it pop loudly. Her smile widened as Lucifer gave her a side-long glare.

"Go clean out the grease traps," he muttered. Lauren's smile faded. She turned and skulked back to the kitchen, picking clumps of gum off her lips.

CHAPTER 4

Twilana dropped a handful of leaves into a small, hollowed stone and crushed them with the pommel of the dagger. The oils from the eucalyptus leaked from the leaves. She placed a few rose petals in the bowl and drizzled some water on top before muddling the mixture even more. Satisfied with the consistency, she scooped the mush with two fingers and spread it across the gash on her ribcage, slowly rubbing it into the wound. The stench of the salve burned her nose but she felt the relief penetrate her skin almost immediately.

Massaging her side gently, she smiled as the pain slowly dissipated. She slathered more of the ointment on her chest and tore the sleeve from her shirt, tying it around her abdomen. The idea of destroying one of her few pieces of clothing annoyed her but she knew it was better than leaving the wound untended. She sighed and crawled to her bed, laying on her side in the pile of leaves.

Twilana winced as a sharp pain shot up her leg. Reaching into her pocket, she dug the black shard from her pants. She sat up on the leaves and crossed her legs in front of her. Turning the shard over between her fingers, she felt the tiny vibrations flow through her hands. She reached down and grabbed the dagger, feeling the vibrations in both arms intensifying as she brought the pieces closer. She held them side by side, looking from the small black shard to her dagger and back again. The shaking started to tickle her fingers.

Inhaling deeply, she placed the shard in her lap and gently tugged at the twine wrapped around the hilt of the dagger, letting the sharpened stone fall to the floor. Dropping the twine next to her, she picked up the shard from her lap and held it close to the hilt of the sword, feeling a strong compulsion to touch the shard to the handle. Like some sort of inexplicable tic. But after everything she'd seen, everything she'd experienced, she was willing to put logic on the backburner and follow those instincts when they appeared.

Staring down at the two pieces of the Blade, she felt the pulsing shoot up her arms and evaporate into her shoulders. Closing her eyes, she held her breath and tapped the tip of the shard against the hilt.

A flash of blue light erupted from the pieces of the Blade. Twilana's eyes shot open and her head snapped back. Visions danced on her eyeballs, beamed directly into her brain from the weapon in her hand. Figures she didn't recognize replaying moments in time. Two winged men wrestled in the air, shouting to each other, the beating of their wings drowning out their words. A tall, dark creature looked out over a burning field of death and destruction, his red eyes flaming in approval. The dark man stepped heavily across an ornate tile floor, his shadow slowly engulfing a still body lying before him.

The visions disappeared as suddenly as they began. Twilana stared at the ceiling, her breathing ragged. She was afraid to move. Afraid to blink. Her stomach roiled, the nausea from the morning returning. She breathed through her nose, steadying her heart, willing herself to not throw up again. She blinked twice and slowly lowered her head. Her eyes fell on the hilt of the blade in her hand. The shard was gone, completely vanished from her grasp. But her blade was larger than it had been before, though now lopsided and badly balanced. The shard had fused to the hilt like a cosmic jigsaw puzzle. A tiny smile lifted one side of her mouth. This wasn't the strangest thing she'd experienced but it certainly ranked high on the scale.

Pushing to her feet, Twilana gently massaged her ribcage. She felt no pain. Not just the dull sensation of the salve numbing the wound but more like the pain had completely vanished. Untying the bandage from her chest, she lifted her shirt. Shock registered on her face to find that the wound was completely healed, replaced by three long, white scars. Twilana eyed the Blade. Pulling her shirt down over her belly, she dropped her arms.

Closing her eyes, she focused on the weapon. On the coldness of the stone in her fingers. On the weight of the blade as it hung limply at her side. A tingle jolted through her body and her pulse quickened, a surge of excitement running through her.

Twilana's arm shot outward, slashing the air in front of her. She raised her other arm, assuming a defensive position, a Kata she learned in the Janian military. Slowly, Twilana circled around, eyes still pinched closed, remembering the fighting exercise. The Kata was developed to increase the reflexes and flexibility of soldiers in hand-to-hand combat. As Twilana flowed through the long-forgotten motions, she felt her body relax.

That feeling wouldn't last very long.

A gentle breeze fluttered across her face, brushing back her hair. She opened her eyes and a wave of goose bumps prickled her skin.

A glowing purple gash hung in the air before her. Twilana stared at it, her mouth agape. She stepped back as the wind played from the lips of the slit, an eerie smell permeating the room. Like mud and fresh strawberries. She felt the roiling in her stomach return. Again.

The sight would have been shocking had it been the first time she'd seen it. But portals like this were all too familiar to her. She'd fallen through quite a few of them less than a year prior. This was a void between worlds. A dimensional passageway.

Holding the blade at her side, Twilana reached out, her fingers brushing against the edges of the tear in space. A slow heat swirled around her fingertips. She wiggled them and the heat quickly turned cold, then warmed again. She thrust her hand into the gash and a numbness engulfed her fingers, as if her hand had been cut off from the rest of her nervous system. She stepped backward, pulling her arm from the rift and rubbed her fingers against her chest. The feeling returned, no harm done. Cradling her arm, she looked up at the gash and cocked her head to the side.

Twilana inhaled deeply. She crept forward, raised the blade and placed the tip into the rift. She wrapped the fingers of her other hand around the pommel of the hilt and slowly forced the blade down. The rift resisted at first but she pushed harder against the handle and little by little, the gash widened, revealing more of the swirling purple miasma beyond it.

The blade of the dagger *tinked* against the rocky floor of the hut. Straightening her back, Twilana stepped back and looked at the rift, watching as the two sides flapped in the breeze like sheets on a dryer line. Her arms hung limp at her sides. She closed her eyes again, rolled a kink out of her neck and exhaled deeply. Opening her eyes, she stepped forward and passed through the flaps, disappearing into the space between worlds.

CHAPTER 5

Lauren dragged herself down the cramped hallway toward the back of the kitchen, shuffling her feet along the old, dingy linoleum. She dreaded the idea of cleaning the grease traps. It wasn't busy work; it was punishment, and Lucifer knew that. Cleaning the traps was dirty, stinky, and having to hunch over for that long made her back hurt. She hoped he would change his mind about the task at the last minute, though she knew that wasn't likely.

Mumbling a string of expletives aimed at Lucifer, Lauren grabbed the doorknob of the supply closet and gave it a yank. A mop handle flew from the closet, knocking over a half-filled bottle of cleaner from a high shelf. The bottle landed on Lauren's foot, causing a new string of cursing to erupt from her mouth. She hobbled on one foot and tripped on the mop handle, falling backward into the wall behind her. The impact knocked the wind out of her but she mustered enough energy to kick the bottle of cleaner back into the closet and slam the door petulantly.

Catching her breath, Lauren slowly opened the door and stepped inside, reaching up to the top shelf to grab a pair of heavy rubber gloves. Tucking the gloves under her arm, she picked up a rusty metal trowel from a lower shelf and slipped it into the handle of the wheeled 32-gallon garbage tub that sat in the center of the room. Rolling the tub from the closet, she hip-checked the door closed and shambled back down the hallway.

Stopping at the tiny alcove that housed the grease trap,

Lauren grumbled her displeasure again, hating the thought of manual labor. Being a ward of Lucifer, Lauren had been endowed with the ability to tap into Hellfire, the mystical force that imbued him with his powers. Hellfire allowed Lauren to do amazing things like alter reality by bending the rules of probability. A task like cleaning the grease traps could be completed with a quick thought and the flick of her wrist. That is, if she was allowed to use her power. But Lucifer put a moratorium on Hellfire usage, claiming that the Angels could track it and pinpoint their location, and he didn't want to attract any "unwanted attention". She *could* use her powers, and in fact, *should* use them. But she knew that if Lucifer found out, he would find a punishment worse that cleaning the grease trap.

Lauren looked down at the gunk-covered box nestled in the floor. She shook her head and grabbed the gloves from under her arms, sliding her hands into them. They were much too large for her, ending mid-forearm and flopping around as she moved. Lauren didn't care, though; when it came to cleaning the grease traps, she'd rather have bulky gloves than no gloves at all.

She bent down and unlatched the cover, struggling as she pulled it up from the metal box. It released with a stomach-churning *schlorp* and the stench of old grease, cooking oil, and congealed fat wafted up from the box, slapping Lauren in the face. She turned her head to the side and retched.

Taking deep gulps of clean air, Lauren managed to regain control over her gag reflex. Her stomach settled and she turned back to the grease trap. She imagined herself inflicting horrific, terrible revenge against Lucifer. The thought of him sitting in a Judas Cradle in particular brought a smile to her lips. Pushing the image to the side, she reached up and pulled the trowel from the handle of the garbage tub. She stabbed the blade into the grease and pulled up a pile of the sludge, carefully dropping it into the tub.

The work was long and boring, just as she'd expected it to be. Every few scoops, Lauren would turn her head and suck in a few quick breaths of fresh air before returning to the box. Minutes passed and she felt the small of her back tightening from being crouched for so long. Placing the trowel on the floor, she rose to her feet and leaned backward, stretching her back muscles. She twisted, working out the kink. Her flexibility returned and she leaned down and grabbed the trowel. As the blade disappeared into the lard, the stench of the grease wafted up and sent her reeling. Lauren dropped the trowel and shot to her feet, turning away from the trap.

Her stomach rose up in rebellion and she started to gag again. She leaned over the garbage tub, unsure if she would be able to control her vomiting a second time, and noticed the splotches of grease across her new sneakers. Anger overpowering sickness, Lauren braced herself on the edge of the tub and bent down to wipe the grease from her shoes, alternating between coughing and cursing. As she scrubbed the leather with the rubber glove, the tub shifted, rolling a few inches down the hallway. Lauren reached out to grab the corner of the wall, trying to catch her balance but the grease from the gloves slipped and she fell on her butt.

Lauren yelped as a sharp pain raced up her back. Leaning to the side, she felt around the floor under her bottom and discovered a small, hard object. She picked it up and brushed the grease from it, wondering how a rock had gotten into the grease trap. As she wiped the filth from the stone, Lauren noticed the dark, black rock was flecked with tiny white dots. She stared at it, feeling a strange sense of familiarity, like she had seen it before.

"Hey, Lou! I think you better come see this."

CHAPTER 6

Alison Swift stormed through the hallways of the San Francisco Historical Museum, her stiletto heels clacking against the brown marble tiles. She brushed the curl of hair that dangled in her face behind her ear and crossed her arms in a half-hearted attempt to mask her irritation. She failed completely at this task, however, since it made her look even more annoyed. She spent weeks planning the grand unveiling of the museum's newest exhibit, carefully orchestrating the entire event. And naturally it only took one man to ruin all of the work she put into it.

A smile spread across her face as she pictured herself wrapping her fingers around his neck, watching his cheeks grow blue as she choked the life out of him. Not like she'd ever do anything like that but sometimes the fantasy made her feel better.

She stopped in front of a glass-pane door. The lights inside the office were off, casting the room in near darkness. Alison pressed her face to the glass, shielding her eyes from the ambient light of the hallway to look inside but she could see nothing. Grabbing the handle, she threw the door open, the glass rattling as it slammed against the adjacent wall.

"Bastian!" she shouted into the darkness. "Are you in here?" Hearing no reply, she walked to the far end of the office, arms reaching out to guide her. Her hands slapped the wooden venetian blinds hanging over the window. Groping around in the darkness, she found the blinds' pull string and gave it a tug. Warm, harsh sunlight flooded the room.

Bastian Dagger's body jerked as he shielded his eyes from the sudden onslaught of light. His chair toppled backward and his arms shot out for the desk in an attempt to catch himself but all he managed to do was knock a stack of papers from the desktop. They slowly fluttered to the floor as Dagger rolled from the upturned chair onto his back.

Alison watched Dagger as he struggled to his knees, her body convulsing as she stifled a laugh. She placed a hand over her mouth and looked out the window, taking a moment to compose herself. Back in control, she sidled closer to the man, reaching down and grasping him under the arm. She helped him to his feet as he brushed the dust from his pants. Alison looked him up and down, the irritation on her face intensifying.

"You're hungover again, aren't you?" she asked curtly.

"No, no," he said, shaking his head slowly, turning his face away from the window. "Still drunk, maybe, but not hungover." He squinted at Alison through the tousled hair hanging in his face. His cheeks were covered in three days' worth of stubble. His body went rigid as he stared at her, taking in the sight of her black satin ballgown. Blinking wildly, he wiped tears away from his eyes.

"You do realize the unveiling is in ten minutes, don't you?" she asked. "Why aren't you ready?"

Dagger turned and leaned against the corner of the desk. He looked up at Alison dumbfounded, his brow furrowed. "The... The unveiling... Uh..."

Alison's irritation turned to anger. "Don't you dare tell me you forgot." She stomped across the office toward a large cabinet at the far wall. Throwing open the doors, she rifled through the collection of button-down shirts. "I've been planning this event for five months, Dagger. Five, long months. I've put all of my energy into making sure this is the biggest, most high-profile event this museum has ever seen, all to make you the center of attention." She pulled a dark blue shirt from the rod. Eye-balling it quickly, she shook her head and dropped it on the floor of the closet.

"This is the biggest find that we've had in years and it's all because of you," she continued. "That, unfortunately, means that you have to be there. And you need to be sober." She pulled a white shirt from the cabinet and tossed it at Dagger. She slammed the doors shut and stepped toward the corner of the office. Reaching down, she opened a small refrigerator nestled next to a filing cabinet and pulled out a can of Coca-Cola. She tapped the top of the can a few times before pulling the tab. The can released a loud hiss, spraying soda all over Alison's hands. She sighed loudly and walked back to Dagger, handing him the can.

"Ah, yes. The orb," he said, taking the Coke from her. He took a quick sip. "How's that going, by the way?"

"The *Sphere*," Alison corrected. "And it was going well, until I found my guest of honor passed out drunk in his office."

Dagger chuckled, placing the can against his temple. He always appreciated Alison's demeanor, her brashness to say exactly what she was thinking. His eyes now adjusted to the light, he looked at her face and gave her a smile. "Well, if you had to find me drunk, in my office would be a good place to do so."

Alison rolled her eyes at Dagger's attempt at levity, which was, unfortunately, one of his more endearing traits. In an effort to bring more attention to the museum and help drive attendance, Alison wanted to find more exciting exhibits, not just the standard "Egyptian sarcophagus" and Renaissance painting. Enter Bastian Dagger, the infamous archeologist. Dagger was well known in the field to do whatever it took to find what he was after.

And his reputation spoke for itself; his newest discovery, the Sphere of Ancaarta, was being hailed as the greatest discovery of the 21st century. The Sphere is the first item to be found to be connected to the ancient civilization of Ancaarta, a culture that was believed to have died out before the rise of Mesopotamia. Until Dagger, though, Ancaarta was only referred to as a legend of the ancients. The discovery of the Sphere made headlines around the globe and brought the attention of the world smack dab on top of the San Francisco Historical Museum.

Alison folded her arms across her chest and shifted her weight to one leg. She glared at Dagger as he took a sip from the can and placed it on the desktop beside him, growing impatient as he slowly worked the shirt from the old plastic hanger. "Christ, Dagger, what am I going to do with you?"

He slid his arms into the shirt and buttoned it. "You may be upset with me now but you'll forgive me when I show you what I have for you."

Alison raised an eyebrow. She tapped her foot impatiently and placed her hands on her hips. "Oh, yeah? And what, pray tell, could you have that would make me forgive this?"

Tucking the shirt into his pants, he grabbed the soda and drained it in a single gulp. Dropping the empty can on the desk, he released a belch from the side of his mouth. He looked up at Alison and reached into the pocket of his pants.

She watched Dagger intently as he held his hand out before him. Clutched in his fingertips was a small, black rock. The stone was about four inches long and sparkled as it refracted the dying sunlight. She reached out and took it from him, allowing him to return to the labor of tucking in his shirt.

Turning toward the window, Alison held the stone in front of her. The light filtered through it, casting her face in a pale, bluish-purple haze. Lifting her glasses, she squinted at it, marveling at its beauty. The edges were straight and clean, indicating that it had broken off of a larger piece. Alison replaced the glasses and rubbed the shard between her fingers. It was cold. Much colder than it should have been after being in Dagger's pocket for so long.

Bringing the stone closer to her eyes, she could see the thousands of tiny white spots embedded in it. She gently rubbed her fingernail against the shard, gauging the depth of the spots but she discovered it was completely smooth. The spots were a part of the stone, not painted on or engraved. She stared at the shard, transfixed, as it twinkled in the sunlight and thought for the slightest moment that she noticed a swirling mass in the center.

Alison turned back to Dagger, the words catching in her throat. "Where...where did you find this?"

"Tunisia," he replied as he clipped a black bow tie to the collar of his shirt. "I found it a few miles outside of the Byzantine dig." He pulled a tuxedo jacket from the cabinet and shrugged himself into it. "It must have been uncovered by a sandstorm or something because it was just kind of lying there."

"You have no idea what this is, do you?" she asked. The pitch in her voice rose, her inflection wavering.

Dagger stared at himself in the mirror that hung on the inside of the closet door. "Nope," he said, pulling the clip-on tie from his shirt and grabbing a necktie from the cabinet. "I was going to spend some time in the library and try to figure it out. After I sobered up, at least."

"No need. I know exactly what it is."

CHAPTER 7

Twilana tumbled end over end as she fell through the abyss, a familiar sense of uneasiness and anxiety gripping her chest. Her breath caught in her throat as she watched reality bend all around her. Objects appeared from nowhere, distorted and surreal, before dissolving into nothing.

The air here moved slower. It blew back the hair on her head but she felt no movement on her face. Each breath was a struggle, like trying to inhale maple syrup, complete with the same sickeningly sweet smell. The scent overpowered her nostrils and turned her stomach. She pinched her eyes shut and breathed as slowly as she could, forcing herself to ignore all of the sensual stimuli happening around her.

A rush of clean air blew across her body, flapping the loose shirt around her stomach. Looking down, Twilana saw a split open beneath her to reveal a carpet of bright green grass. It came closer, moving at incredible speed. She realized that she was falling, yet another sensation that she had grown accustomed to. Bracing herself, she landed on the ground with a jarring *thud* that knocked the breath from her lungs. A wave of pain assaulted her and every nerve in her body vibrated.

She lay on the grass motionless, allowing the cool breeze to play across her face. The crisp, cool air felt good against her skin, especially after being stuck in the dank, humid forest for the last eight months. The smell of wildflowers hung heavy all around her, mingling with the smell of ozone. The scent soothed Twilana, calming her and relaxing the nausea in her stomach. Sitting up, she leaned on her elbows and listened to the soft rustling of the wind through the leaves. A bird *cooed* from a faraway tree. A stream of water trickled nearby. The scene was so serene and peaceful that even a battle-hardened soldier like herself had no trouble appreciating it. She closed her eyes and smiled, enjoying the short break from the stress in her life.

Slowly, her body relaxed and her pain subsided. Pushing herself to her feet, she brushed the grass from her uniform and looked out toward the horizon at the setting sun saying goodbye to the day. Fog swirled in the distance and the cool breeze turned cold, prickling her skin. She glanced down at the rocky slope of a descending mountainside, remembering the last mountain she had encountered in her adventures. The one that rose above the plain-lands of China where she and Matt faced off against a squad of Japanese soldiers. They were overtaken and held prisoner, sentenced to death for crimes against Japan. Matt nearly died in that prison, Aaron was revered as a god and they were only able to escape that world through the interference of the Angelic High Military.

The memory sent a chill up her spine. The thought of her friends made her chest hurt and she felt the fingers of loneliness grab her. Closing her eyes, she let out a jagged sob, feeling a release from the flow of her emotions. Inhaling deeply, she held her breath for a moment before blowing the air out through pooched lips. Her thoughts lingered on Aaron and Matt for a moment longer, wondering if they made it home during the battle with the Leviathan, before shaking her head to focus on her current situation.

Squinting out at the horizon, she spotted a thin wisp of smoke rising up from the trees. She wasn't happy with the idea of trading a familiar jungle for an alien forest but she didn't have much of a choice. Bending down, she grabbed the Onyx Blade from the grass and tucked it into the belt of her uniform. She gave the setting sun one last glance before making her way across the grassy field toward the tree line, hoping that whoever was tending the fire would be willing to help her.

*   *   *   *   *

Twilana picked her way through the trees, ducking below low hanging branches. Each step she took made a resounding *crunch* as she crushed the fallen twigs and dried leaves that littered the thin path. She would be able to move quieter if she slowed her pace but the sun had nearly disappeared behind the horizon and she hoped to find help before the light was extinguished.

Pushing aside two scraggily ferns, she spotted a stout cabin a few yards off. The cottage was built of shoddy gray bricks and held together with a mortar of dried mud. The roof was thatched with tree branches and straw, tied together with sun-dried kudzu vines. A tiny stone chimney jutted up from the roof, belching a thin stream of smoke into the night sky. Though not much to look at it was a wonderful sight, the perseverance of human endeavor. Twilana smiled at the care that was put into the details and the turning of detritus into a home.

Next to the cabin stood a man chopping wood on an old tree trunk. He was dressed in a dirty white shirt that clung to him from a layer of sweat. His brown pants were well worn, the hems torn and frayed. A long-sleeved flannel shirt hung from a tree branch close behind him. He swung the axe downward with strength and precision, slicing a log clean in half with a single blow. As the two halves clattered to the ground, he took a step back and wiped the hair and sweat from his forehead.

"Excuse me," Twilana shouted, announcing her presence as she walked from the edge of the forest. "I'm hoping you can help me."

The man placed the head of the axe on the ground and leaned on the handle. He turned to her and squinted through the encroaching darkness.

Twilana watched as the man lifted his hand to wipe the hair from his face again. A shock of recognition spread through her body.

The man returned her recognition. "You!" he shouted. Hefting the axe handle in both hands, he stepped toward her, his face stern and angry. "How did you get here? Haven't you ruined me enough?"

CHAPTER 8

Lucifer stared at the shard lying in the palm of his hand, his eyes wide with disbelief. "How did this get here?"

"So you know what it is?" Lauren asked. She was happy that he finally moved past the incoherent ramblings about *power* and *rightful place in the universe* and was starting to make sense. Leaning against the counter, she pulled an emery board from her back pocket and began filing the edges of her fingernails. She held her hand out, inspecting their perfect, glossy sheen.

Lucifer lifted his gaze from the shard and shot her a look from beneath his brow. "How can you ask…?" He grasped the shard in two fingers and held it closer to her face. "Don't you recognize this?"

Lauren looked up from her fingernails at the stone. She shot the shard a quick glance before resuming the impromptu manicure. "Yeah, that's the thing I found in the grease trap," she replied, sarcasm dripping from her voice. "I gave it to you."

She watched as Lucifer's confusion slowly morphed into anger, his forehead crinkling the way it does when he gets annoyed. Dropping her arms to her side, she released an exasperated sigh. "Yes, it looks familiar but I have no idea why. Happy? I'm not a complete moron."

"Very good," Lucifer said, the anger draining from his face. "But I'm really surprised that you can't place it. After all, this is a piece of the Onyx Blade. The sword that belonged to Belial. The weapon that destroyed the Leviathan. The most powerful weapon in the universe." He punctuated each of his descriptions with a flick of his wrist.

Lauren's eyes passed between Lucifer and the stone a few times. She looked up at him and gave him a sly smile. "Doesn't look all that powerful to me."

Lucifer exhaled through his nose loudly, his patience quickly waning. "We can use this to get out of here."

Her eyes crinkled as her tongue danced around the corner of her mouth. She plucked the shard from Lucifer's fingers and held it up to the light. "Does that mean I can use my powers again?"

"That, and so much more." Lucifer crossed his arms and leaned against the counter. "This shard will *enhance* our abilities. Make us stronger. We don't have to pretend to be fry cooks any more. And once we find the rest of the pieces and put the thing back together, we can bring the Angelic High Military to its knees."

Lauren's eyes remained transfixed on the shard. "And what about the humans?" she asked, shooting Lucifer a glance. "Can we find them, too?"

"Oh, we'll do more than just find them, my dear," Lucifer said, taking the shard from her. "We'll make them suffer to the point that they'll beg us to erase them from existence."

Lucifer recalled the embarrassment they suffered at the hands of the shaved apes in New Eden. Those two worthless, powerless men made him look like an amateur. All of the planning he put into trying to destroy the angels was wasted because of Matt and Aaron's meddling. And that blue-haired whelp that was with them. Twilana. He snarled as he recalled the weeks it took for his hand to regrow after Twilana severed it back at the AHM building. He planned on making her suffer worst of all.

Lauren also fantasized about her revenge so many times. About the things she'd do to Twilana should their paths cross again. Tying her down with razor wire to flay the flesh from her bones. Slowly dripping battery acid onto her face, allowing it to eat away her eyes. Electrocution. Branding. Forcing her to listen to Air Supply's full discography. And only when she ran out of clever ways to inflict pain would she snap the bitch's neck like a twig. She didn't care about the angels anymore. She had a score to settle and that was all that mattered to her. The thought of finally exacting her revenge made her giddy. "So, how do we use it?"

Lucifer cocked his head and blinked. He heard her words but was unable to form an answer. A silent moment passed before he responded. "I...I don't know."

"What do you mean you don't know? You know all of this crap about this little piece of rock, but you don't know how to use it?"

He shrugged. "Being away from the Hellfire for so long has left me...depleted."

Shaking her head, Lauren stalked past him and through the threshold to the kitchen. Stopping at the back wall, she closed her eyes and held the shard out in front of her. She focused her thoughts on the stone, imagining all of her power flowing through her arm.

Lucifer peeked around the corner, a gentle breeze mussing his hair. He watched as a soft pink light emanated from Lauren's hand, spilling between her fingers. It grew brighter and brighter, spreading over her body. Lucifer shielded his eyes from the light and the intense wind that whipped his hair back. He looked at the stack of tray liners blowing off of the countertop and flying out into the dining room.

"Keep it up," he shouted, turning back to Lauren. "Whatever you're doing it looks like it's working."

A tingle ran up Lauren's arm and a coldness enveloped her body. She pinched her eyes tighter, ignoring the prickling sensation across her skin. She thought of Twilana and the pain she would inflict. She thought of going home to New Eden and getting the chance to sleep in her own bed. She thought of Nathaniel, Lucifer's second in command, and his ruggedly handsome face.

Lauren felt a surge of power flow from the shard into her. Her head snapped back and her eyelids fluttered open. The wave of energy engulfed her body completely, setting her nerves on fire. She opened her mouth to scream but no sound escaped her throat. Lauren could feel her hand stretching out, placing the shard against the wall. Slowly, her body dragged the shard downward, cutting the concrete with the jagged edge of the stone.

A long, glowing gash appeared in the wall. Reaching up, Lauren's fingers wrapped around one side of the gash and, like a curtain, slowly pulled it to the side. A gust of wind blew past her, snapping her from her reverie. Her body shook with fear and exhaustion as she glared out into the endless expanse of the bluish-purple abyss.

"Amazing," Lucifer whispered behind her.

Glancing over her shoulder, Lauren's shocked eyes landed on Lucifer. "What the hell just happened? What did I do?"

"I'll tell you what you did", he said, sliding gracefully next to her. He placed his hand on her shoulder and pulled her close to him, comforting her. Reaching up, he pulled the shard from her hand. "You've gotten us out of here." His arm moved to her waist and he escorted her into the gaping void. The light engulfed them and they disappeared into the abyss that was, just moments ago, a concrete wall.

CHAPTER 9

Michael placed the head of the axe on the ground and wiped the sweat from his forehead. His stomach rumbled, his arms ached, and he could barely stand the stench of his own body. He'd grown accustomed to a life in solitude, learning quickly to adapt to the manual labor of survival. He was in peak physical condition before; in the past few months, however, his body had become harder than iron, his muscle tone like chiseled granite. Not that his looks made any difference. He barely interacted with or even seen any other people for the last few months.

A rustle at the edge of the woods caught his attention. Looking up, he watched someone push themselves through the brush. He tightened his grip on the axe handle, the muscles in his arms tensing. The lack of human interaction put him on edge, especially when someone shows up without warning.

He squinted at the figure. Thin. Medium height. Hair trailing past the shoulders. A woman. That made him relax slightly. Until he recognized the details. A dark blue uniform with a yellow shield embroidered on the right breast. Hair a light shade of blue. Two deep purple eyes as shocked to see him as he was to see them.

"You!" he snarled through clenched teeth. His body tensed again and he lifted the axe from the ground. He sprinted across the grass toward Twilana, the blood pounding in his head and a growl rumbling from his throat.

As Michael closed the distance between them, he swung the axe downward, forcing her to leap out of the way. She pulled a blade from her belt and slashed at the axe handle. The stone grazed off the wood, leaving a small gash just beneath Michael's hand.

Michael dug his feet into the ground and pivoted to face her. Crouching low, he drew the axe backward, readying his muscles to pounce again. He watched as Twilana regained her footing and turn to him.

"How did you get here?" He allowed the axe handle to slide through his fingers so he could clutch it closer to the steel head. "Haven't you ruined me enough?"

"I didn't come here for you," Twilana responded, her voice flat and calm. She raised her hands in front of herself non-aggressively and toed slowly to the side. "I'm not here for a fight."

"Well, that's what you're getting." He jumped, swinging the axe again. Twilana ducked and rolled clear of the attack. Michael landed on the grass behind her and spun. She kicked out, catching him in the knee as he turned. He dropped to the ground onto his free hand. His head snapped sideways as her fist cracked against his jaw, stunning him for a moment. Twilana kicked his wrist, knocking the axe from his grip.

Michael lashed out and grabbed Twilana's wrist. He yanked her toward him, punching her in the ribs as she fell. She yelped in pain, the blow landing on the scars from the tiger attack. He flung her to the side. She struggled to stay up but tripped over her feet, tumbling to the ground.

He rubbed his chin, flinching at the tender spot on his jaw. "Getting me exiled wasn't enough, was it?" he asked, stalking toward her. "Now you're here to finish me off." A trail of bloody spittle rolled down his lip.

Twilana looked up at him, struggling to speak through ragged breaths. "Wait," she said, raising her palm to him. "Let me explain." She tried to inch away from his advances but the effort to speak exhausted her. Moving was nearly impossible.

"I don't need your explanations," he responded. Reaching down, he grabbed her by the throat and lifted her from the ground. Her hand flew to his wrist and held tightly, trying to keep the weight of her body from crushing her windpipe. As she struggled in his grip, Michael's gaze fell on the dagger in her hand. His eyes went wide as he recognized the jet black blade.

"Where did you get that?" He eased his grip on her throat and lowered her to the ground.

Twilana coughed and turned away, her free hand rubbing her neck. She cocked her head to the side to glance at him. "This?" she asked, lifting the knife. "I had it. Well, most of it. Since the Ocularium. It's what brought me here."

A grin spread across Michael's face. He folded his arms across his chest. "You don't even know, do you?"

"Know what?" Twilana managed between coughs.

"How powerful that blade really is."

CHAPTER 10

Alison rushed through the museum corridors, the *click-clack* of her stilettos reverberating against the marble floor. As she rounded the corner, the soft sounds of a cello and the murmur of conversation wafted through the air. She stopped and turned to watch Dagger trailing slowly behind her.

"You want to put a rush on it?" she asked sarcastically, her annoyed look catching Dagger's eye. "We're already late."

"So what difference will another few minutes make?" Reaching out, he grabbed her hand and pulled her closer to him. Wrapping his arm around her waist, he led her in a short, playful waltz. "Or we can just blow this whole thing off and spend some time in the library, pouring over some old, dusty books researching that shard."

Alison placed her hand on his chest and pushed him away, fighting back a smile. "Yes, I *would* rather be in the library," she said, grabbing his wrist and pulling him toward the oversized double doors at the end of the hallway, "but I put in a lot of time and effort to plan this unveiling so we will be in attendance."

Dagger sighed and resigned himself to Alison's control. The effects of the alcohol wearing off, he could feel a headache building in his temples. He was too tired to fight back; it would be much easier to just show up, schmooze with the stuffy museum donors to ensure that the funding continued to pour in and get the hell out of there as quickly as he could. He would rather be digging in the dirt in some far off desert somewhere than spending time in a climate controlled room surrounded by bad champagne, mini-quiches, and pretension.

Although he was kind of looking forward to the free booze.

Alison pulled the glasses from her face and stuffed them into the tiny black clutch she carried. Tucking the bag under her arm, she grabbed the handle of the door and gave it a tug. As the door swung open, they were assaulted by the dulcet tones of Mozart's *Violin Concerto No. 3 in G Major* played by the string quartet situation in the corner of the spacious ballroom. Dagger looked around the room, eying the men traipsing across the floor. Each was a carbon copy of the other, dressed in the same black-and-white tuxedo, same salt-and-pepper hair style, same growing paunch over the belt. The women, on the other hand, were as different as the men were the same, dressed in a variety of colors and styles. Ball gowns of every type floated about the room, each meticulously paired with different hairstyles and jewelry. Dagger also noticed that each woman wore a distinct perfume, which mingled in the air, making his stomach roil. His head pounded as he fought back a wave of nausea.

Alison grimaced as she spotted Dagger's gagging. "Don't be such a baby," she said, tugging his arm. "It's only a couple of hours. It won't kill you."

"Fine," he said, taking control of his gastrointestinal reflex. "But you owe me a drink."

A waiter dressed in a black vest and clip-on bow tie walked by carrying a silver platter. Alison reached up and plucked two tall champagne flutes from the tray, handing one to Dagger along with a sly smile.

"There. We're even."

Dagger curled his lip, mocking her. He grabbed the flute and held it in front of him. "*Salud,*" he said before draining the glass in a single gulp. A belch erupted from his throat, puffing his cheeks. He wiped his mouth with the back of his hand. Turning, he placed the empty flute on the rim of a potted plant next to the door, his eyes landing on a young woman in a gold V-neck ball gown as she walked by.

"Maybe this won't be as bad as I thought," he said with a grin.

Alison rolled her eyes and shook her head. Choosing to

ignore him, she looked toward the center of the room at the large glass display case holding the Sphere of Ancaarta. The case was covered with a dark red sheet with a fringed golden cord tied around it. She thought about the elaborate reveal she had planned for the Sphere, wherein she would make a toast to the museum and the patrons, invite Dagger up to say a few words about the find (which he would inevitably decline to do), and pull the cord to reveal the Sphere. The thought of it made her stomach flip. She wasn't used to being the center of attention; in fact, she downright hated it. But as the Sphere of Ancaarta was the highest-profile find the museum had in over a decade, she knew that it needed a larger-than-life spectacle.

Glancing out the window, she noticed the limousines and news vans lining the street. She smiled to herself, pleased that everything was coming together so smoothly. Turning, she watched as Dagger chased down a waiter holding a plate of hors d'oeuvres. The waiter stopped, allowing Dagger to select a few from his tray. He grabbed a small, fried, triangle the waiter called "crab rangoon" and popped it into his mouth. The waiter turned to leave but Dagger grabbed his arm and pulled him back. One by one, Dagger snatched each of the rangoons from the tray and stuffed them into his pocket. He smiled and gave the waiter a nod to dismiss him before taking a highball from the tray of another passing waiter. He slid a second crab rangoon into his mouth before spotting Alison watching him.

"What?" he asked, a spray of crumbs erupting from his lips.

Alison rubbed her temples, tilting her head down to hide her smile. "Can you at least try to be on your best behavior?"

Dagger swallowed and shot her a toothy grin. "Sorry. I haven't eaten in a while." He took a swig of the highball. "So, when are you gonna show this thing off so I can get out of here?"

"You better make yourself comfy, buddy, because it's not going to be for at least another hour."

He sighed. He could already feel himself getting antsy. In another hour he knew that he would start to whine. Even *he* couldn't stand himself when he got to the whiny stage. "I'm gonna need another drink," he muttered. Downing the last of his cocktail, he chased after the petite blond waitress carrying the highballs.

"I'm going to name my first ulcer after him," Alison said

to herself. Turning on her heels, she greeted a graying, plump woman in an olive-green dress.

CHAPTER 11

Lauren yelped as she landed on her butt in the dusty, arid desert. She lay back on the hot sand, a decision she regretted immediately. Shooting to her feet, she felt the harsh sunlight beating down against her skin, making her feel like she was submerged in the deep fryer in the Treacher's kitchen.

Brushing the sand from her clothes, Lauren noticed a faint purple bruise forming on her bicep. She poked it, sending a dull pain shooting through her shoulder. "Oh, great," she moaned. Placing her hand on the bruise, she released a pulse of Hellfire into her arm. The pain intensified before quickly dispersing. Moving her hand, she looked at the bicep and smiled at her blemish-free skin.

She tilted her head back and shielded her eyes from the sun, its harsh rays burning her face. Lauren waved her hand and a wide-brimmed hat with a tiny pink bow in the center appeared on her head. A twirl of her finger conjured a pair of white, heart-shaped sunglasses. She looked down at her clothes, particularly the poly-cotton blend of the Arthur Treacher's staff shirt already soaked with sweat. Brushing her hand down her chest, the shirt morphed into a white tank top and a sleeveless orange-checked button-down tied at the waist. Lifting a leg, she wiped her hand on her thigh, changing her khakis into a pair of cut off jean shorts. She extended her thumb and forefinger, making a gun-gesture with her hand and "*pew-pew*"ed her Nikes. A white light engulfed her feet and, as it dissipated, revealed a pair of orange and white striped flip-flops with a tiny plastic flower blooming from the center of the straps.

Feeling cooler, and cuter, Lauren smiled. "Much better."

A soft whine buzzed in her ear, catching her attention. She looked up and spotted a small, dark speck in the sky. As the speck grew larger, the noise became louder. She squinted through the dark lenses of the sunglasses and realized what the spot was. She stepped to the side just as Lucifer landed face down in the sand next to her.

Bending over, she placed a hand under his armpit and helped him up. She gagged as the underarm of his polo shirt grew steadily moister in the heat. Ignoring it, she lifted him to his knees, brushing the sand from his shirt.

"Are you OK?" she asked as she fixed his tousled hair.

Lucifer coughed, a cloud of dust erupting from his mouth. "Seriously?" he asked through ragged breaths. "You couldn't, like, catch me or something?"

Lauren smiled. "Sure, I *could* have. But I didn't."

Lucifer rolled his eyes and struggled to his feet, shaking the rest of the sand out of his clothes. He looked Lauren up and down, examining her outfit.

"I see you've had a moment to change."

"There was no way I was wearing that gross old uniform out here."

He nodded at her logic. He held his arms out and waggled his fingers to himself. Lauren sighed and waved her hand. A thick cloud of white smoke rose from the ground, hissing as it swirled around him. Lauren flicked her wrist and a gust of wind blew the smoke away, revealing Lucifer decked out in a pale blue, short-sleeved button down, a pair of khaki cargo shorts, and dark brown boat shoes. A thin pair of sunglasses rested on his nose.

Lucifer reached up and plucked a hat from his head, glaring at it. "A trilby?"

Lauren giggled. "You need something to keep the sun off of your forehead. Besides, it really does go well with your facial structure."

Lucifer shrugged, replacing the hat. He opened his hand and looked down at the shard in his palm, thankful that he was able to hold onto it after smashing into the ground. Balling his fist, he turned and looked out over the distance. The sea of sand spread out all around them, the horizon lined with a row of brown, stone buildings, all of varying sizes and shades. A few of the buildings were topped with semi-circular protrusions, jutting up into the sky. A lonely cloud floated overhead, doing little to block out the sun's rays. The landscape was devoid of most foliage save a small grouping of palm trees about fifty yards from the village and a few rows of low-growing bushes that lined the space between the buildings.

"Where are we?" Lucifer asked, rubbing his chest.

Lauren pointed to his hand. "You have the thingie. What does it say?"

Lucifer held the shard up to the sun. It refracted the light, creating tiny black spots across his face and along the ground below him. He stared at the fragment, squinting occasionally, trying to make out even the tiniest suggestion of where they were. Turning his head, he held the shard to his ear, listening to a low-frequency hum emanating from it. This surprised him as he hadn't actually expected to hear anything. Not that it mattered as it didn't answer his question of where they were. Dejected, he drooped his shoulders drooped and released a loud, disappointed sigh.

"It's not saying much. I don't even know how this thing works. It was so much easier when it was a sword. The whole…" He paused, jutting his arm sharply a few times. "Stabbing thing is pretty self explanatory."

Lauren grabbed the shard from his outstretched hand. As she closed her fingers around it, a faint purplish light began to radiate from the stone. It travelled up her arm and surrounded her face. Her eyes glossed over, her stare became vacant. Holding her hand out before her, she used the shard like a supernatural dowsing rod. It beckoned her to turn and to take a step, leading her northwest. She obeyed. She had no reason to trust it (which just sounded crazier the more she thought about it) but for some reason she did. She took a few slow, hesitant steps before growing comfortable enough to break into a brisk walk.

Lucifer watched as Lauren trotted off across the sand toward the village. Shrugging, he jogged behind her, sweat pouring down his skin as he struggled to keep up.

Lauren stepped carefully through the sand, the loose ground making the walk treacherous. Cutting sharp turns, she moved as if she was trapped in a wall-less maze. She could hear Lucifer's breathing behind her, growing heavier as the heat sapped him of his energy. After a few minutes, the shard beckoned her to stop. She dropped her arms and pointed at an innocuous spot in the ground.

"Here. Something was definitely here."

"What do you mean, 'was'? And what the hell just happened?"

Lauren shook her head, handing Lucifer the shard. "I don't know. I held it and let my mind go blank. All of a sudden, it started pulling me along. It felt like it was leading me to another part of itself."

"You mean another piece of the sword landed here? Well, where is it now?"

Lauren grimaced. Her full, pink lips twisted into a frown and her eyebrows dipped behind the large heart-shaped lenses that covered most of her face. "I don't know. But I don't think we should find it. I got a sense that something was coming. Something...not good."

CHAPTER 12

The fire roared in the hearth, belching thick, black smoke up the chimney. Michael placed a fresh log on the fireplace, sending a shower of glowing embers into the air as the fire enraged. He stood over the hearth for a moment, allowing the heat to chase the chill from his body. Turning, he watched Twilana as she sat wrapped in a blanket on his ratty old couch. A plate holding a few crumbs and duck bones lay on the floor next to her. Finally nourished, the color returned to her cheeks but she still looked tired. She nursed a cup of tea, smiling as the wisps of steam swirled up into her face.

He stepped toward her and hitched up the legs of his pants, slowly lowering himself to the floor. Grabbing his mug of tea from the side table, he took a quick sip and gazed up at his visitor.

"So…" he began uneasily. "The Blade of Belial. How did you end up with it?"

Twilana wiped the corner of her mouth with a finger and placed the mug on the floor. "After the…thing with the Leviathan, I blacked out and woke up in the middle of a jungle, still clutching the hilt. I kept it. It became useful. Then yesterday, it…I don't know…led me to another piece. The two of them recombined. Somehow."

"May I?" Michael asked, holding out his hand. Twilana drew the blade from her belt and placed it in his palm. He pulled it closer, holding it in both hands, twirling it with his fingers.

Grasping the hilt, he ran his finger across the jagged, broken edge.

"It's a remarkable weapon," he said. "One of the strongest in the universe. Wars were fought to get this sword. None of them were successful." He chuckled softly to himself. "It's definitely not what it used to be though, is it?" He sighed. Worrying the tip of the knife in between the floorboards, he carefully carved out a few slivers of wood.

"Wait," Twilana said. "I thought Belial was just a myth."

Michael's brow furrowed and he shook his head slowly. "Oh, no. Belial is most definitely real. I lead the battle against him. It took the full power of the Angelic High Military to take him down. More than that actually.

"Belial was a big deal, a long time ago. Head demon. Powerful. Sadistic. And he derived most of his power from the sword. They say that he cut out a piece of the universe and forged the blade in the heart of a sun. Or some kind of comic book nonsense like that. I never paid it much attention. All I knew was that he needed to be stopped."

"You said it took more than the angels to beat him?"

Michael nodded. "We had to ask Lucifer for help. That...wasn't my proudest moment but we needed his resources."

Twilana pooched her lips. For a proud soldier like Michael to ask for help from one of his biggest enemies? That goes lengths to show Belial's strength and fierceness. But then again, there must be more sides to Michael then she'd seen so far. After all, she never would have guessed this man who brought her into his home, fed her and warmed her was the same Angelic officer that called for her execution less than a year ago. He seemed calmer now. Maybe the exile from New Eden was the best thing to happen to him. Maybe he really was capable of change.

"And Lucifer really helped you?"

"Yeah, in a way. But of course, Lucifer can't be trusted. After Belial fell, we searched everywhere for the Blade. We never found it, though, since it seems Lucifer got to it first and hid it away."

"But what does it have to do with me? And how did I get here?"

Michael shrugged. "No idea. We've never had the chance to study its true power. It probably shattered with the blowback from the explosion of the Leviathan. But how you ended up on a different plane? Could be that the energy flux activated an oculus and sent you to some random world. If I had my contacts at the AHM, I could have them study this…"

Michael trailed off. "That's not going to happen, though. I can't tap into the Angelic Telepathy. They stripped me of everything. Power. Title. Even my wings. Besides, even if I could get in touch with them, there's no way they'd allow me to use their resources." He chuckled. "And to think I'm only the second Angel in the history of the AHM to get a punishment that severe."

Twilana reached out to him, gently squeezing his shoulder. Looking up, Michael caught her eye and smiled.

"Well, if it's any consolation," she said, "you deserve it for trying to kill me."

Michael's head snapped back as he released a loud, throaty laugh. "Yeah, I've had to work through some anger issues. And I'm sorry about the axe thing from earlier. It's clearly still a work in progress."

"Tell you what," Twilana said, returning his smile. "Get me an extra blanket and we'll call it even."

"Deal." Rising to his feet, he held the blade out to her. She grabbed it and rubbed the flat side of the knife against her palm, feeling the cold chill of the stone. She watched as Michael disappeared into the other room to rifle through a chest at the end of the bed.

"You know," she said loudly, "the funny thing about the Blade is that it vibrated. When I was in the jungle."

Michael's voice floated from the bedroom. "Oh, yeah?"

"When I got close to the other fragment, the hilt just started to buzz. Like it could feel the other piece. And the closer I got, the stronger the vibrations got."

Michael emerged from the bedroom carrying a gray, woolen blanket. He placed it on Twilana's lap. "It could be that it was pulling you towards itself. Like it has a need to be reassembled. That might be how you got here."

"What do you mean?"

"If the Blade can call out to itself while in close proximity, maybe that extends beyond worlds. When it opened the portal, it might not have been a coincidence that it opened to this world. Could mean that another piece is here somewhere."

Twilana placed the blade on the floor and grabbed the

edges of the blanket. She tossed it open, allowing it to float down over her body. "Can it do that?" The words barely past her lips, she broke into a massive yawn, so intense that it rippled through her body.

Michael shrugged. "I've witnessed stranger things. And with that sword, I can't even begin to imagine the kinds of things it can do. But for now, get some sleep. If something is here, I'll help you find it in the morning. I've grown pretty accustomed to the landscape around here."

"Works for me," she said, laying her head on the arm of the couch. She pulled the blanket up to her chin, closed her eyes and inhaled deeply. A moment later, a tiny snore rose from her nose.

Michael walked toward the window at the front of the cabin. Looking up at the night sky, he watched as the stars twinkled down at him. He thought about the incident on New Eden, the attack that caused his exile from the Angelic High Military. He thought of his soldiers, the men that he had disappointed through his actions. He thought of Gabriel, a thought that quickly turned to guilt after realizing that it had been months since he thought about Gabriel. He would still be alive if it wasn't for Michael.

Shaking his head, he turned back toward Twilana, watching as her chest rose and fell in her sleep. His eyes cast quick glances to the blade lying on the floor. Striding over to the bookshelf next to the fireplace, he shuffled around the shelves, picking up the jars and examining their contents. He uncorked one and sprinkled a pile of dust into the palm of his hand. Crouching down, he tossed the dust onto the fire. The flames roared, their colors shifting from orange to yellow to green to blue. Swirling and spitting, the fire spilled from the hearth, forcing Michael to step back from its grasp. He watched as a man's face slowly took shape in the flames.

"I have new information about the Onyx Blade," Michael said, staring at the fiery face.

CHAPTER 13

Lauren managed to find the correct path rather quickly considering she had no idea what she was doing. From the moment Lucifer handed her the shard, a barrage of images flooded her mind. Snapshots of time. To Lauren, these images seemed to last forever but in reality, each glimpse was over in a fraction of a second. A man in a black, leather jacket. A black cap with an interlocking "SF" embroidered in orange on his head. A black stone unearthed from a pile of yellow sand. Lauren could feel the man's excitement at the find, even across time. The ordeal made her feel strange, as if she had tapped into the pleasure centers of a complete stranger. But she managed to glean something else from his mind.

A name. Bastion Dagger.

She told Lucifer what she saw, allowing him to use his skills in deciphering the information. They trudged into town, finding a Starbucks where they each filled up on Java Chip fraps and iced lemon pound cake, with an extra marshmallow square for Lauren. Lucifer was able to convince a man in the café to allow him use of his computer, though Lucifer's method of "convincing" entailed wiping his mind and leaving him a vacant, drooling mess. A quick Google search for the name "Bastian Dagger" yielded only two results. They easily ruled out the Honda salesman from Toledo and discovered that the second was the Director of Archeological Discovery for the San Francisco Historical Museum. Pulling up a different website, Lucifer booked two plane tickets to California (made possible by the gold American Express card Lucifer found in the wallet of the catatonic Starbucks patron) and he and Lauren were soon on their way.

* * * * *

They exited a yellow cab outside of the museum and quickly got lost in a wave of activity. The limousines lining the street belched out an unending stream of well-dressed couples, all of whom sported gowns and tuxedos. A news crew stood right outside of the entrance, stopping people as they approached the doors to ask questions about the event.

Lucifer looked up at the banner hanging from the building. "Premiering Tonight: The Sphere of Ancaarta". He read the words over and over, seeing them but not quite believing them. He'd known about the Sphere for years. Millennia, really. And had spent most of that time trying to find it and add its power to his own. His stomach flipped with the excitement of the possibility of finally obtaining it. He turned to Lauren and looked her up and down.

"I don't think we're properly dressed for this party."

She smiled at him and raised her hand. With a snap of her fingers, a bright flash engulfed them and changed their clothes, giving them the appearance of the cookie-cutter aristocrats all around them. Lucifer's blue button-down shirt and cargo shorts melted into a black tuxedo with a dark red shirt and black bow tie. He sported a new set of cufflinks in the shape of serpent's heads. Lauren's tropical outfit morphed into a long, blue-sequined, off-the-shoulder gown. A matching pashmina draped her shoulders and her hair was tied up high on her head. She even managed to disguise the shard of the Onyx Blade as a pendant hanging from her neck.

Lucifer looked down at his suit with a smirk. "Not bad."

"I always was the one with the good fashion sense."

He nodded, extending his elbow. She placed her arm in his and they climbed the stairs, gracefully gliding through the door.

Getting into the party was easier than Lucifer expected. Usually events like these are Invitation Only, boasting the appearances of famous actors, well-connected politicians, and the occasional intellectual. When the guards at the door didn't recognize him or Lauren and asked for their invite, he simply waved his hands, making them convulse with seizures.

Lucifer looked around the ballroom as he stepped over the

flailing guards. *Not bad at all*, he thought, noting the dark wood and velour Queen Anne chairs at the far corner. He admired the immaculately polished hardwood floor (*birch, most likely*) and eyed the hand-carved crown moulding that ringed the ceiling. As far as museum ballrooms go, this was the most impressive that Lucifer had seen.

Ignoring the interior decorating for a moment, Lucifer watched each of the party-goers as they flitted around the room, trying to spot Dagger in a sea of red and bloated faces. He stopped a waiter and took two glasses of champagne from her tray, handing one to Lauren.

"Anything?" he asked, taking a sip. Even the quality of the champagne impressed him. He wouldn't have imagined that a backwards planet like this one would be capable of producing a decent beverage.

She touched the pendant hanging at her neck, rolling the shard between her fingers. Sipping her champagne, she closed her eyes, concentrating on the images in her mind. After a moment, she looked over at Lucifer and shook her head.

"Just a lot of stuffy old people. No Dagger. No shard."

He sighed loudly and drained the rest of his Veuve Clicquot. "OK, well, let's split up." His eyes fell on the drape-covered display case in the center of the room. "There's something I want to check out anyway." He walked off without waiting for a reply.

Lauren watched him leave before turning her attention to the guests. Sipping her champagne, she tried to act nonchalant. To blend in. She wound the pendant's chain around her fingers, shifting her weight from foot to foot. Her nonchalance quickly degenerated into boredom as her fidgeting grew more pronounced.

"Hello, there," a deep voice announced from behind her. The noise startled her and she spun around so quickly that her drink spilled over her hand.

She looked up into the dark eyes of a scruffy-faced man. His brown hair was tinged with gray, giving him the look of age and experience without making him look old. His chiseled jaw bulged as he gave her a wide toothy grin. The only imperfection she could see on his face was his crooked nose, but even that added an air of mystery to his countenance.

"Oh, I'm so sorry about that," he said, pulling the pocket

square from his jacket. He exchanged the cloth for her empty champagne glass.

"No, no it's OK," she said as she dabbed her hand dry. She looked up at him, her eyes locked on his, her face turning a telling shade of pink. The moments passed as they stood transfixed by each other. He reached out and took the pocket square from her.

"Again, here I am forgetting my manners. My name is Bastian..."

"Dagger," Lauren finished abruptly. "Yes, I recognized you from the...um...news. About the..." She motioned to the display case.

"Ah, yes. The Sphere." He was both surprised and flattered that she knew who he was. "Well, I really can't take all of the credit. I did have a team out there with me, but it does seem that my name is being used the most."

Lauren tilted her head back with a laugh. It was one of her "high-society" laughs, the kind that she used to fit in with the pretension that comes from affluence. High pitched and throaty, it lasted a second longer than it should have. Dagger cocked his eyebrow at her as the laugh floated away.

"And you are..."

She extended her had to him, which he lifted gently in his fingers. "My name is Lauren."

"Lauren," he repeated, placing his lips against the back of her hand. "That is lovely. So tell me, do you attend many of these unveilings?"

CHAPTER 14

Lucifer circled the room, getting a feel for the environment. He enjoyed parties like these as they gave him the chance to extend his power. Being in a room full of rich people meant that he could glean some pretty impressive information from them; sometimes he'd get a hot stock tip that he could use later to make a quick bundle. Sometimes he'd hear a juicy rumor that would make for some good blackmail. With everything that he was overhearing, he was kind of hoping to spend a little extra time on this world to plant the seeds of a revival.

As he brushed past his fourth statesman of the night, a woman in the corner of the room caught his attention. He immediately appreciated her dynamic fashion sense, noting that her black dress with the red rhinestone swath around the hips matched his color palette perfectly. She held a cell phone to her ear and spoke quickly, her eyes pinched and a vein throbbing in her temple. He watched as she tucked the hair behind her ear and turned away from the crowd.

Stopping a waiter, Lucifer grabbed a second glass of champagne, stepping confidently toward the woman. As he approached, she hissed something into the mouthpiece of the phone before clapping it shut. She slid it into the clutch purse and turned, jumping at the sight of Lucifer.

"Sorry to startle you," he said calmly, handing her the fuller of the glasses. "I noticed you were having a pretty intense phone call. I hope everything is well."

Alison gave him a smile and brushed the tangle of hair away from her face. "Just a miscommunication with the caterers," she said, taking the glass from him. "Nothing that should affect your evening."

"I'm Lou," he said, taking a sip of his champagne.

"Alison." She extended her hand to him. He shook it professionally.

"So, an argument with the caterers? That must mean this party is your doing."

"Yes. I'm the museum's curator. I...put a lot of effort into tonight. I had *hoped* everything would go as planned but..."

"Things don't quite work out that way. I am well aware." They shared a laugh. Lucifer could see Alison relax. Her shoulders dipped slightly and she dropped her arm to her side. "This really is a lovely affair."

"Well, thank you. It's nice to know that the work I put into it is marginally appreciated." She sipped the champagne. "So, Lou. What is it that you do?"

"I'm in the art business. Import, export, that kind of thing. But I've always been a history buff. A passion of mine. I was very excited to hear about the discovery of the Sphere of Ancaarta."

Alison mentally ran through the list of invitations. She remembered there being a Len, a Lee and even a Laird, but she didn't recall inviting anyone named Lou. Despite the fact that she wondered how he got into the party, she found herself mesmerized by his conversation. And his charm. And his looks. "So you know the Sphere?"

"For quite some time, now. When I was a boy, I used to play a game pretending that I had the Sphere and I would remake reality to my will, pitting all of my toys in a battle against each other." He chuckled to himself. Not because he was impressed with a lie but because it was the absolute truth. He abandoned the search once he took possession of the Onyx Blade but he never forgot about the Sphere.

Alison smiled at him, the glass pressed to her lips. "That's, of course, only a legend. The Sphere doesn't actually contain any power."

Lucifer nodded politely. "Of course it doesn't. That would just be silly. There's no such thing as magic." *Now Hellfire, on the other hand...* "Would you mind if I..." He cocked his head to the side, squinting his eyes innocently. "Got a little sneak peek?"

Alison looked up at a passing couple, one of the state Senators and his trophy wife, Mindi. Or was it Candi. It didn't matter; she'd be gone by the end of the year. She leaned closer to Lucifer and lowered her voice. "I'm really not supposed to."

He placed his palms together, pleading with her playfully. "Please? You'd make the little boy inside of me very happy."

Alison smiled at his innocence and thought for a moment. "Well, I could push the time table of the unveiling up a bit." She curled her finger to him as she turned toward the draped pedestal. "After all, I'm the one who made the schedule."

CHAPTER 15

"All I'm asking for is a chance."

Michael knelt on the floor in front of the fireplace, leaning in as close as the heat would allow him. He wiped the sweat from his forehead with the back of his hand.

"I told you your appeal needs to go through the proper channels. There's nothing I can do until it reaches my desk." Lamechial's voice echoed through the tiny room, causing Michael to grit his teeth with each word. He looked back at Twilana asleep on the couch, worried that his conversation would wake her. He watched as she curled onto her side, kicking her foot over the arm of the couch. She let loose a curt snort and smacked her lips a few times. Michael sighed with relief before turning back to the hearth.

After Michael's exile, the Tribunal chose Lamechial to lead the Angelic High Military. An older angel, he gained the admiration of the high council for his ability to discover dishonest angels in the ranks. It was Lamechial who brought word of Lucifer's treachery to the Tribunal, news that eventually led to the Archangel's dismissal. The AHM recently experienced an upsurge of corruption and the Tribunal felt that Lamechial was best suited to flush out the bad seeds. He accepted the role, discovering and excommunicating more than twenty dirty angels in his short time as leader. Needless to say it didn't win him any favors with his peers, who labeled him a snitch, but it won him the respect of the Tribunal, a relationship Michael was now hoping to exploit.

"This has nothing to do with my appeal," Michael said,

shifting his weight. "Well, maybe a little. What I'm asking is what if I can win back some esteem with the AHM. What if I had something to offer?" Michael's legs began to tingle as he felt his toes go cold.

"What could you possibly have to offer us?" The flames in the hearth flickered as Lamechial spat the words.

"I have a lead on the Onyx Blade of Belial."

Lamechial's eyes narrowed. "The Blade was destroyed with the Leviathan, Michael. You know that. You were there. There's no use trying to build a case on trickery."

"It wasn't destroyed. Not completely. It was..." Michael's words trailed off. He held up a finger. "Wait."

Michael pushed himself to his feet, groaning at the crackling of his knees. The blood finally flowing, his legs were assaulted by a wave of pins and needles, his feet taking the brunt of the onslaught. But Michael ignored the pain and hobbled over to the couch. Bending slowly, he grabbed the Blade that lay on the floor next to Twilana. As he rose, she grunted and turned over onto her back. Michael froze, his eyes fixated on her, careful not to breathe or make even the slightest noise. A moment passed, then two. Twilana smacked her lips a few times and grumbled something about a deer but remained asleep. Satisfied, Michael shuffled back to the fireplace, wincing at each creak of the floorboards.

Squatting down in front of the fire, he held the blade before him. Lamechial's eyes went wide as he spotted the dagger. What Michael held was much shorter than the Onyx Blade of Belial but Lamechial recognized the distinctive swirling of the galactic bodies the Blade contained. He shook his head, causing the fireplace to sputter. The angel cleared his throat, his face returning to its original stoicism.

"Where did you get that?"

"It was brought to me. By Twilana."

"The woman who vanquished the Leviathan?"

Michael nodded, placing the Blade on the floor next to him.

"That's not even the sword," Lamechial protested. "Just a fragment. You try to win me over with nothing."

"The Blade wasn't destroyed by the Leviathan. It was shattered. From what Twilana tells me, it can be repaired. I can use this piece to find the others and reassemble it."

Even from the awkward construction of Lamechial's face in the flames, Michael could tell he was stroking his beard. It was his tell, showing that he was contemplating his options. Michael took it as a good sign. "This is definitely an interesting development."

"Will you take this news to the Tribunal? At least see what they have to say?"

Lamechial gave it a thought, pausing longer than he had to. It was worth it to make Michael apprehensive. Besides, he didn't want to seem too eager at the prospect of helping an excommunicated angel. "I will. Though I will not make any promises. Please keep me apprised of the situation. If you comply with the requests of the Tribunal concerning the Blade, I do not see how this can hurt your appeal."

"Understood." The fire surged once more before calming, settling back into its natural red-orange color. Michael sat back on the floor and wiped his forehead with his sleeve. Looking down at the Blade, he sighed. A smile spread across his lips as he pictured himself being brought back into the fold of the Angelic High Military.

CHAPTER 16

Belial clenched his fist, tightening his grip on the shard in his palm. He could feel its power coursing through his flesh. Vibrations rippled through his skin as he grew closer to his destination. He had been rocketing through space for what felt like days, allowing the tiny piece of his Blade to lead him to another fragment of itself. And all of that time afforded him the opportunity to plan his revenge.

His mind focused on the sword. It was what fueled him, what kept him moving. Even at his peak, this long journey through the galaxy should have drained him but this one, tiny shard had imbued him with enough energy to keep going. Could the energy flux that destroyed the Blade have bolstered its power?

The thought made Belial smile. He was nearly unstoppable with the Onyx Blade before. If its power really had been augmented...

Closing his eyes, Belial reached out across the galaxy, fixing his mind on his destination. Slowly, an image began to form. A small blue and green world, an inconsequential planet floating out in a forgotten segment of the galaxy. He wondered how a piece of his sword could find its way to a world like that one.

Belial opened his eyes and smirked. *No matter,* he thought to himself. *Once I reassemble my sword, I'll raze the entire planet.*

He would make this "Earth" his new home, altering it to fit his needs. The inhabitants would become his willing slaves, anointing him as their rightful deity or be destroyed by his power.

The strongest among them he would turn into demons, using them to rebuild his horrific army with which to conquer other worlds.

A stiff buzz in the back of his skull pulled him out of his fantasy. Belial stopped, floating high above the tiny planet. He stared down at it, squeezing the shard tighter, using it to pinpoint the second piece. Moments passed slowly. Deciphering the fragment's location, Belial swooped down through the planet's atmosphere. The intense heat he generated tearing through the thermosphere reinvigorated him, amplifying his psychic connection to the shard.

Sweeping east, the demon rocketed across the vast ocean, cutting through the crest of the water. The buzzing in his brain grew stronger, which he concentrated on and used as a guide. Looking up, he spotted landfall, a skyline of buildings quickly coming into view. He slowed, climbing toward the sky, using the cover of clouds and darkness to mask his arrival.

Belial watched as a flock of creatures gathered around a squat brick building in the center of the city. Columns of light shone upward, sweeping across the clouds and illuminating the sky. Every now and then the light would cut across his face, blinding him for a moment but it made no matter. The buzzing had reached a crescendo and he knew he was in the right place. Opening his fist, he looked at the shard lying in his palm.

"It's time to reclaim my throne."

CHAPTER 17

"That's a beautiful pendant you have there," Dagger said. He stuffed one hand into his pants pocket and leaned against the buffet table. The stone was nestled just below Lauren's suprasternal notch, its pitchy blackness superimposed against her creamy white skin. From the way it stood out, he wondered how he hadn't noticed it when he first saw her, but a quick glimpse into her piercing hazel eyes was all it took to remember why. Now that he had seen it, however, he couldn't take his eyes from it. "May I?" he asked, pointing to her neck. Lauren gave her consent with a quick nod and Dagger lifted the pendant gently in his fingers.

Lauren placed her hand on his forearm as he examined the pendant. "It was a gift from my brother. I...found the stone and he turned it into a necklace for me."

Dagger nodded as she spoke, barely hearing the words. He turned the pendant over in his fingers, watching as the stone refracted the soft, incandescent light that shone from the ceiling. The stone was speckled with tiny white dots that twinkled as it moved. It felt familiar to him, like he'd seen it before but for the life of him he couldn't place where.

"Ladies and gentlemen, can I have your attention please?" Alison's voice called Dagger back to reality as it boomed above the thrum of the conversation. The music lulled to a stop and silence fell across the room, all eyes turning to her. She stood in front of the covered case holding a small microphone to her lips. Lucifer stood a few feet from her, looking like her twin, as if they'd color coordinated their outfits for the evening. Seeing most of the room was watching her, she gave them a small bow.

"Thank you. Now I know why you're all here. You are excited to see the Sphere of Ancaarta, a mystical artifact that hasn't been seen by human eyes for 5,000 years. And I also know that, according to the schedule, we weren't planning on showing the Sphere for…" She stole a quick glance at her watch. "Another twenty minutes. But I have to say, my anticipation is just too much to bear and I imagine it's the same for a few of you." Alison cast a sideways glance at Lucifer and gave him a playful smile. "So, I've decided to push up the time table and unveil the Sphere now."

A round of applause thundered through the ballroom, amplified by the high ceilings. Alison's smile widened, showing more of her perfectly white teeth. She pushed her glasses up the bridge of her nose and cleared her throat, waiting for the ovation to die down.

"So if you would, please gather around closer." She leaned over and handed the microphone to a squirrely looking man in a rumpled suit. The crowd gathered around the case as Alison grabbed the golden cord. Lucifer slipped between the throngs of people, putting himself within shoulder-width of Alison. He placed his hand on her elbow and gave her a reassuring squeeze. She looked up at him with a smile.

"May I present to you…" Alison's arm stiffened as she gave the cord a stiff tug.

As the curtain dropped to the floor, a deafening *BOOM* ripped through the room. Alison looked up at a massive hole torn through the ceiling. Lifting her arms, she shielded herself from the shower of falling concrete. She felt a pair of arms wrap around her waist as her body was shuffled away from the debris. Craning her neck, she looked at Lucifer's face, inches from hers.

"What…what's happening?" Her voice cracked with fear.

If Lucifer answered her, she couldn't hear him over the screams of terror that ripped through the room. Alison watched as people clawed and pushed their way through the chaos. Bodies fell to the ground, trampled under the waves of terrified partygoers racing toward the exit.

"Go," Lucifer's voice whispered in her ear. She could feel the warmth of his breath against the side of her face. "Get out of here."

She nodded and pushed herself from his grip. Making her way through the crowd, she threw herself through the side exit toward the Museum annex.

Lucifer watched as Alison disappeared through the small doorway before turning back to the display case. He placed his hand on the glass, Hellfire throbbing through his fingers. Thin wisps of smoke rose from his palm as the energy melted the plexiglass enclosure. Reaching in, he grabbed the Sphere from atop the pedestal and stuffed it into his blazer pocket. Stepping back slowly, he looked up and stared at the gaping hole in the ceiling.

A tall, black figure appeared high above the room. As it slowly descended into the ballroom, a cold chill ran down Lucifer's spine. The figure's eyes glowed green, its head and face covered in bony protrusions. Two long horns erupted from the sides of its skull. Spikes grew from its shoulders and ran down its arm, ending at its black, gauntleted hands, one of which clutched a black, jagged blade. The creature floated just above the screaming, terrified crowd, showing a row of razor sharp teeth as it smiled at the chaos.

Lucifer recognized the creature immediately, and the recognition scared the hell out of him. Turning, he scanned the faces of the panicked crowd, frantically searching for Lauren, locating her at the back corner of the room, huddled behind a tall, dark-haired man in a cheap suit. Lucifer pushed his way through the people rushing past him like a salmon swimming upstream, keeping his head low to avoid being seen by Belial.

*   *   *   *   *

"We need to get out of here," Dagger shouted over the din of the chaos. His fingers were wrapped around Lauren's wrist as he shielded her from the waves of people running for the exit. He looked around, spotting Alison ducking through the side exit. He slung his arm around Lauren's waist, ushering her toward the door.

"Let go of me," she growled, pulling away from his grip. She stood on her tip toes, looking over the tops of the heads of the frightened crowd. She reached up, grabbing the pendant around her neck and gave it a sharp tug. The chain snapped and she held the shard out in front of her. Hellfire engulfed her hand, spreading out across the room. Arms and legs thrashed as the throngs of people were pushed to the side by a bright purplish haze. She spotted Lucifer near the display case.

63

Dagger stared at Lauren, wide-eyed and slack-jawed. "What the heck was that?"

She gave him a sly smile as Lucifer appeared next to her, grabbing her elbow.

"Time to go," he said. She nodded and sidled next to Dagger. Cupping his chin, she pulled his head down to her face and placed a kiss on his cheek.

"Thank you so much for tonight," she said sweetly. "I had a wonderful time. Call me, 'kay?" She let go of his chin, wound her arm through Lucifer's and they rushed toward the door. They took two steps before the dark figure of Belial swooped down in front of them, his deep green eyes falling upon Lucifer's face.

CHAPTER 18

"Why, if it isn't my old friend Lucifer," Belial's voice snarled, the corners of his mouth curling into a sneer.

Lucifer stopped dead in his tracks, frozen in place by Belial's ominous stare. He tilted his head back, his eyes slowly moving up the dark figure. A feigned look of surprise passed over his face as his gaze landed on the demon. "Belial! How have you been? What are you doing here?"

Belial growled at Lucifer's flippant response. Landing on the floor with a thud, he stepped heavily toward him and Lauren, his footsteps echoing through the silence of the near-empty ballroom.

Images of their last meeting swirled through Belial's mind as he stalked toward Lucifer. Of the deception Lucifer showed him on the battlefield. When Lucifer was cast out of the AHM, stripped of his title and power, it was Belial who took him under his wing. Gave him access to the power of Hellfire. Restored him when he was at his lowest. But when the time came for Belial to face the angels, Lucifer provided them his aid, leading to the demon's defeat. With a childish prank, at that. It was a memory he recalled over and over as he sat in Limbo.

He stopped before Lucifer, placing his hands on his hips and fixed his glowing green eyes on him. Belial towered over Lucifer, standing a good two feet taller. Lucifer stared up at Belial's face, readily cognizant of just how sweaty his body had become.

"Don't mess with me, Lucifer. I know you have it."

Lucifer loosened his tie and swallowed hard. "Sorry, I don't follow." He shifted his weight from foot to foot, his anxiety making him fidgety. Slowly, he inched his way backward, trying to put some distance between him and Belial. He barely realized that Belial's hand had grabbed the front of his shirt and yanked him off the floor. Belial pulled him close, holding him inches from his face.

"I won't ask you again. Where. Is. My. Sword." Smoke billowed from his nose and the rank odor emanating from his mouth made Lucifer's eyes water.

Lucifer coughed and turned his head to the side. He looked back at Belial with wide eyes. "Wait...You mean... Oh! Your sword! OK. Yeah, I remember the sword. Onyx Blade, right? That's what you called it?"

Belial shook his head, the sound of Lucifer's voice grating on his nerves. "Yes, the Onyx Blade. You had it. Actually, you took it from me. And now I want it back."

"I did have it, yeah, you're right. But, see, there was this thing and... Well, it broke."

Belial drew his arm back and tossed Lucifer through the air. He landed on the hard tile, the impact knocking the breath out of him. Lucifer scrabbled across the floor, struggling to breathe as he pushed himself up on his arms. Wheezing, he looked up to find Belial extending his arm and opening his fingers, exposing the two-foot shard of stone in his palm.

"Yes, I know it broke. I'm trying to put it back together. Now where is the rest of it?"

"Well, see...This...uh..." As Lucifer stared at the shard in Belial's hand, he found himself at a loss for words. He lifted himself up onto his knees and glanced up at Belial's smoldering green eyes, trying to find a way to schmooze himself out of this predicament. "Rest of it? I'm not sure I know what you mean."

"Oh, you do," Belial said, his voice rumbling in the back of his throat. He closed his fist and crossed his arms. "This shard led me here, to this backwater planet where, lo and behold, I find you. I truly doubt that's a coincidence."

No, not at all, Lucifer thought to himself. "Listen. If I could help you, would you consider a truce?"

Belial stared down at him, pondering a moment. "Sure," he said, his voice curt and booming.

Lucifer smiled and clapped his hands together.

"Wonderful," he said. "Lauren, can you come here for a minute?"

Lauren slinked across the room, her eyes wide with terror, black mascara streaking down her cheeks. She crouched behind Lucifer, using his body as a buffer between her and Belial.

"Can I have the shard, please?" He held his open hand out to her. She lifted her shaking hand and gently placed the pendant, chain and all, in the center of his palm. With his other hand, Lucifer grabbed the end of the chain and held it up to Belial.

"See? Here it is. Just like I promised. Take it."

Belial's eyes followed the black shard as it swung back and forth from Lucifer's fingers. He reached down and grabbed it, the tiny piece engulfed by his enormous hand. Turning, he walked across the room, his massive footfalls echoing in the cavernous ballroom. As he held the two shards, he felt the buzzing flow through his arms. The fragments of his sword called out to each other, thrumming with the need to be reunited. Closing his eyes, Belial tapped the pendant with the larger shard and felt the surge of galactic energies through his body. A bright, purple light exploded from his hand.

Lucifer draped his arm around Lauren, allowing her to help him to his feet.

"What do we do now?" she whispered.

Lucifer patted his breast pocket. "I have a plan."

"Is it a good one?"

He shrugged. "We'll find out."

The light subsided and Belial opened his eyes, looking down to find that the shards had melded. He turned back to Lucifer and smiled.

"I'm glad to see you've used your head for once," Belial bellowed. "Maybe, just maybe, I'll have a use for you once I've dominated the universe."

Lucifer brushed his hands across his pants and straightened his blazer. "Thanks. I just hope you have a good medical benefits."

Belial sneered. "Always with the jokes." Without another word, Belial flapped his wings and rose from the ground. He hovered in the air, glaring at Lucifer for a moment before rocketing upward and crashing through the ceiling. Lauren jumped to her feet and released a spray of Hellfire from her hand to create a dome over them, protecting them from the shower of concrete and metal left in Belial's wake.

CHAPTER 19

Alison peeked through the crack of the door, watching the creature as it floated down from the ceiling. Her heart raced and her hands shook. She could hear the shouts of terror bleeding through the walls, bolstering her own fear. Most of the people had made it out of the ballroom but she spotted a few unconscious bodies on the floor. Some were hit by the falling debris, others trampled by the ensuing mob.

Her heart skipped as she spotted Dagger lying on the floor, pulling himself across the tiles on his hands. His legs scrabbled behind him, giving himself some momentum but his smooth, leather shoes kept slipping on the floor and offering him little help. She opened the door wider and waved him in, goading him to move faster. His eyes fell on her and he redoubled his efforts, pulling his body harder. Alison reached out and grabbed him by the forearm, pulling him the last few feet and closing the door behind him.

Dagger rose to his feet and brushed the plaster dust off his pants. He looked over at Alison huddled against the door, hugging her knees and rocking back and forth on her bottom.

"Are you OK?" he asked.

She nodded quickly, then stopped, shaking her head slowly from side to side. "What the hell was that?" she asked.

"You mean you didn't book that as part of the entertainment?" He shot her a playful smile. She looked up at him and furrowed her brow, a complete lack of amusement on her face.

Dagger extended his hand and she stared at it for a moment before taking it in hers. Lifting her to her feet, he wrapped his arm around her waist.

She turned the knob and opened the door slightly. Her eyes went wide at the sight of Lucifer dangling from the creature's enormous hand. "What is that thing doing to Lou?"

"Lou?" Dagger repeated incredulously. "You know that guy?"

Alison shrugged. "Not really. I met him tonight but he seemed really nice. He said he was a fan of the Sphere. Had been since he was a boy. How sweet is that?"

"Adorable," Dagger answered sarcastically. He ducked below Alison, pushing his face closer to the door and squinted through the crack. "Wait... That's Lauren. What is she doing?" He watched as Lauren crouched down behind Lucifer and placed something in his hand.

"How did she get a piece of it?" Alison whispered.

"Piece of what?"

"The Onyx Blade. That necklace she had was made from the same material as the Onyx Blade."

"*That's* what that was," Dagger said, finally realizing the missed connection from earlier. "I saw it around her neck but had no idea why it looked familiar."

Alison titled her head down and frowned at him. "Really? You saw a piece of it an hour ago, held it in your hands but you didn't recognize it right in front of you? Are you sure it was the *necklace* you were looking at?"

Dagger shook his head and ignored the jibe, focusing his attention on the conversation in the ballroom.

"What is it...? Is it trying to reassemble the Blade?"

Dagger felt Alison shrug above him. "Is that possible?" he asked. "If that thing wants the pieces of the sword, should we do something with the one we have?"

"Yes, I think that's a good idea." Alison stepped back from the door. She hiked the black dress up around her ankles and hurried down the hallway, the *click-clack* of her heels echoing in quick succession.

Dagger watched as she disappeared around a corner before turning back to the ballroom.

CHAPTER 20

Sunlight spilled through the cabin's front window, falling across Twilana's face and rousing her from her sleep. Her eyelids fluttered and she stretched her arms wide. Wiping the sleep from her eyes, she watched through the window as the tree tops bent in a gentle breeze, a few stray leaves being swept away on the gust. The cabin was silent and still, the only noise coming from a group of birds calling to each other outside.

Kicking her feet over the edge of the couch, she sat up and surveyed the room. It took her a minute to remember where she was, the events of the previous day having worn her down so much that she barely recalled falling asleep.

Turning, she looked down at the old, brass candlestick that sat on the end table next to her. Piles of melted wax collected around the rim, dripping down to the table below. Next to the candlestick was a stack of leather-bound books. Twilana leaned over and lifted the cover, glancing at the sloppily hand-written notes scattered across the pages.

Dropping the book cover, she rose from the couch and twisted her back, her spine making a series of *pops* as she stretched her muscles. She strolled over to the extensive bookshelf that ran the length of the wall, her eyes scanning the book spines and knick-knacks that cluttered its shelves.

Most of the books were of the "How To" variety, covering topics that a lone survivalist would need to know: gardening, hunting, woodworking. Interspersed were random novels, fiction written by men she'd never heard of. She pulled one from the shelf and flipped through it, smelling the dusty, musty scent of the yellowing paper.

Replacing the book, she moved down to a shelf that held a collection of glass bottles. A few of them were empty, containing little more than dark sprinkles at their bottoms. But most held different things: leaves, powders, and something that looked like a desiccated animal paw.

She picked up a translucent-green glass bottle filled with a fine powder. Shaking it, she turned it upside-down, then righted it, watching the powder as it settled on the bottom.

"Sleep well?" a deep voice boomed from behind her. She jumped, dropping the bottle on the shelf, knocking two others over in the process. Her hands flew to right them, craning over her shoulder at Michael as he sauntered through the door, a basket of strawberries in one hand and a dead rabbit slung over his shoulder.

"I didn't hear you come in," she said, leaning against the bookshelf. She brushed the hair back on her head and crossed her arms.

Michael pulled the rabbit from his shoulder and held it before him. "I went out to get us some breakfast." He placed the basket of strawberries on the end table, pushing the candle to the side. "Why don't you get started on those while I prep this guy?"

Twilana's stomach let out an embarrassingly loud growl as her eyes fell upon the basket. She cleared the distance to the couch in two long strides, plopped herself down and reached for a berry. Biting into it, she savored the sweet juice as it trickled down her throat. It had been a long time since she had a good strawberry; the jungle she'd lived in was devoid of strawberries, even though it was completely overrun with bananas (and she really never wanted to see another banana again). Dropping the berry stem on the table, she reached for a second.

Michael slung his knapsack from his back and let it fall to the floor. Crouching, he poked at the glowing embers in the fireplace to stoke the fire, placing a few pieces of tinder to reignite it. The flames jumped and licked at the wood. As the fire grew, Michael turned back to the rabbit, rolling out a rubber mat on the floor. Pulling out a long, serrated knife, he began to skin the animal.

"So," he said, tugging the pelt from the carcass, "I figured we could go out looking for the shard. After we eat, of course."

"Of course," Twilana repeated, her mouth full of berry.

"You said that the blade buzzed when the pieces got close," Michael said, his eyes fixated on the rabbit

Twilana nodded and swallowed. "More like vibrated, but yeah, pretty much." She wiped a drop of strawberry juice from the corner of her mouth.

"Then we can use your dagger to find the other piece. Like...a divining rod. The closer we get, the more it will vibrate."

"We're assuming that there is a piece here," she said, wiping her fingers on her pants. "What if there is no other piece? What if there is no reason the sword brought me here?"

Michael slid the rabbit on a long, wooden spit and placed it between the prongs that protruded from the floor of the fireplace. He watched as the flames tickled the rabbit, listening to the low sizzle of the cooking meat.

"Then I guess I'll have myself a new roommate." He shot Twilana a toothy smile.

*   *   *   *   *

They ate in silence, Michael taking bites of the meat from the bone as Twilana tore the food into small bits and chewed them slowly. Their short conversation had prompted her to think. Mostly about her journey but also her past. Her friends. She was happy that Michael was willing to help her look for the other piece of the sword but scared of what they would find. Or, more accurately, what they wouldn't find. What if there was no purpose for the Blade to bring her to this place? What *if* she was just the punchline to one big cosmic joke?

She thought of the possibility of them finding another shard. It *had* brought her here, there was no denying that. If they found another piece, would she be able to control it? Use its powers to open a portal home? She left Janus under...stressful circumstances. After she discovered that Magistrate Rek had offered the surrender of her people to the Lacertidae, a race of vicious Reptillianoids who wanted to exploit their mines. She opposed Rek's plans by enlisting the help of Aaron and Matt to disrupt the signing of the treaty. Even if she could control the Blade, she couldn't just go home. She would be sure to incur Rek's wrath, be a fugitive.

So where would she go?

"Oh, before I forget." Michael's voice snapped her from her thoughts. She watched as he dug through his knapsack. Glancing down, she looked at the plate of rabbit bones in her lap and placed it on the floor as Michael pulled out a bundle of cloth and handed it to her.

"I went down to the market today, traded another rabbit that I caught."

She untied the bundle, revealing a fresh change of clothes. A blue tunic, soft and well worn. A pair of light brown pants made from a rugged material. The waist looked to be the right size but the legs seemed a bit long for her, as if they were made for a man. A very thin, lanky man, but a man nonetheless. The final item was a heavy wool sweater with a very tight weave of purple and red threads. It was tough and felt almost waterproof. All of the clothes look well used, like they withstood quite a bit of abuse in their time, but they were still in better shape than her uniform.

"You got all of this for a rabbit?"

Michael nodded. "I'm a good negotiator," he said with a wink.

Twilana rose from the couch and shuffled into Michael's bedroom, dropping the bundle on the bed. She peeled her old, gnarled uniform from her body, happy to be rid of the rotting material but sad to see it go. Dropping it on the floor, she slipped into the pants, tying the drawstring around her waist. She reached down and cuffed the excess fabric of the legs around her ankles.

She pulled the tunic over her head, cinching the tie strap that hung in the center of the blouse. It held the shirt snuggly against her body, offering no play in the material. Though tight, it was no more form fitting than her Janian uniform, so she imagined she'd get used to it.

Picking up the sweater, she weighed it in her hands. She looked out of the window, judging the day. The sun was out and shining bright, with very little cloud cover in the sky. It seemed warm, making the sweater unnecessary. She tied it around her waist, just in case she might find a need for it later.

"How does everything fit?" Michael shouted from the other room.

Twilana walked from the bedroom and picked up her boots from the corner. She padded over to the couch and sat, digging her feet into them. "Pretty good, actually." She laced up one boot and began working on the second. "So, any idea on where we should start looking?"

"No, not really," Michael said, wiping the empty bones from his plate into small piece of cloth. "I figure the best place to start should be where you came through. Think you can find your way back there?"

Twilana nodded. Grabbing the blade from the floor next to the couch, she rose to her feet and slid it into her pants pocket.

Michael picked up his knapsack and slung it over his shoulder. Reaching down, he grabbed a second sack and handed it to Twilana. He took his axe from the corner of the room and rested it on his shoulder.

"Ready?" he asked with a grin.

CHAPTER 21

Twilana stepped from Michael's cabin into the fresh, morning air. The sun was rising in the distance, casting everything in a bright, yellow pallor. About a hundred feet ahead was the thick, lush forest that led her to this place, a journey that felt so long ago even though it had been just a few hours.

She turned and looked out across the plain at the mountaintops jutting up from the horizon. The mountain peaks rose so high that they disappeared into the swirling clouds, the fluffy, white puffs melding into the snow that ran down the mountainside. It was a breathtaking view. Twilana began to understand how Michael was able to overcome his hubris after his exile. Was able to soothe his anger. This sight was enough to calm anyone, showing just how majestic the world could be.

Closing her eyes, she tilted her head to the sky. The sun shone down on her face, bringing life to her cheeks and making her skin tingle. She inhaled deeply, taking in the rich scent of the wild juniper as it started to blossom. For the first time in months, Twilana felt happy.

"Do you remember which direction you came from?" Michael's voice called out to her. She looked over at him, watching as he stepped from the cabin and closed the door behind him. She simply nodded and waved toward the forest.

"Then let's get going," he responded and trekked toward the treeline.

She followed him down the trail as it wound them deeper

into the forest, taking them up a short incline before leading to a steep drop-off. Twilana inched her way along the hill, taking each step with care.

The forest opened up into a wide, grassy enclosure. She looked up and spotted the snow covered hilltops off in the distance, recognizing the bubbling sound of a nearby stream. Taking a few steps out into the warm sunlight, she crouched low to run her hand over the top of the tall, soft grass. Turning back, she watched as Michael stepped out of the shade of the trees.

"This is it," she called out to him. "This is where I came through."

Michael unslung his knapsack and settled onto a fallen log. Pulling a canteen from his bag, he took a deep swig. "What does the blade say?" he asked, splashing a bit of water on his face.

Twilana reached into her pocket and pulled out the dagger. Holding the hilt in one hand, she carefully gripped the jagged stone with the other and closed her eyes. She focused on the Blade as moments ticked by. A short pulse spread through her skin and quickly dissipated.

Her eyelids snapped open and her gaze shot to Michael. "I think I felt something." She took a step to the right and waited. Nothing.

She stepped backwards. Nothing.

She jogged thirty feet from the treeline. Pausing, she squeezed the Blade, feeling the rough edge dig into her skin. A pulse ran through her hand, stronger than before. "Definitely something here," she shouted. "This way." Stuffing the blade into her pocket, she rushed off across the plains. Michael sighed, shoving the canteen back into his knapsack and chased after her.

*   *   *   *   *

They walked for hours, moving slowly as the ground became uneven and treacherous. At one point, Michael stepped into a hole hidden by a patch of grass. He fell, twisting his knee and forcing them to take a short break. Twilana was fine with this, despite it delaying their journey, as it gave her a chance to enjoy the cool weather. Being stuck in a muggy jungle for months left her longing for the breeze.

Having massaged the twinge out of Michael's knee, Twilana led the way, holding the Blade tightly, stopping occasionally to verify they were going in the right direction. This wasn't much of a consolation, though, as the Blade offered little more than a few faint vibrations.

The sun kissed the horizon as they came upon the edge of a cliff face. Twilana dropped her arms to her side and looked out into the valley below, engulfed by the sheer beauty of this world. She saw the outline of a small village situated in the center of the valley, a row of buildings lined along the river cutting through the mountains. A sudden surge rocked her arm, a tingling running all the way up to her shoulder. Her eyes widened as she looked down at the dagger.

"I think we got something."

Michael stepped next to her, carefully peeking over the edge of the cliff. "Please don't tell me..."

Twilana nodded and smiled as she watched the anxiety spread across his face. "Don't tell me you're nervous about climbing?" she joked, dropping to her knees. She kicked her legs over the edge and turned onto her stomach. Her feet searched the wall for purchase as she inched her body down the rocky wall.

"Not really the climbing," he replied. Slipping the knapsack from his back, he tied the strap around the axe handle, securing it tightly.

The axe handle banged against his leg as he slung the bag onto his back. "It's the possibility of falling that worries me."

Twilana chuckled. During the last few hours, she grew to appreciate the man Michael had become. She was grateful for the change he'd gone through. Grateful for the softness that entered his heart. Grateful that she was able to forgive the past and move on.

"It'll be easy. Once you find your hold, test it before you shift your weight. It may not be one hundred percent foolproof, but it is certainly helpful."

Michael nodded and watched Twilana as she descended down the mountainside. Taking a calming breath, he lowered himself onto the edge of the cliff. He paused a moment, stealing quick glances down at Twilana, watching eagerly as she climbed step by step, her attention focused on making sure she wouldn't fall. Satisfied, Michael reached over and worried his finger in the dirt, digging out a small hole. He slipped a hand into his pocket and pulled out a small glass bottle half-filled with a sparkly blue powder. Uncorking it, he sprinkled a little of the powder into the hole. He placed the bottle on the ground and pulled out a book of matches, tearing one free from the rest. He struck it against a rock and touched the flame to the dust. Tiny green flames shot up from the ground and swirled into the face of Lamechial.

Two green-flamed eyes settled on Michael. "Anything yet?" the older angel barked.

"We've got a bead on another piece of the sword," he said, stuffing the bottle and matches back into his pocket. "We are en route to its location."

Lamechial sighed loudly, the noise translating through the flames with a shower of sparks. "Please contact me when you have something useful." The irritation in his voice was evident.

"Yes, sir," Michael said sheepishly. He brushed the loose dirt over the fire, extinguishing the flames.

Placing his hands on the edge of the cliff, Michael closed his eyes. "They better appreciate this," he muttered.

CHAPTER 22

Alison's body shook uncontrollably, the adrenaline coursing through her veins with such intensity that all she could hear was the blood pounding in her head. She bolted down the hallway, rounding the corner sharply. Her foot slipped out from underneath her and she lost her balance. Grabbing onto a water fountain, she managed to pull herself up onto her trembling legs. She pressed her back against the wall. Her heart pounded and her chest hurt. She closed her eyes and took three deep breaths to calm her nerves. Slowly, she began to relax, the shaking in her body subsiding. Pushing herself from the wall, she continued toward Dagger's office.

Shoving the door open, she bound through the threshold. Headlights from passing cars streamed in through the open blinds, mingling with the flashing red and blue emergency lights of the approaching police cars. Alison ignored the ruckus of the panicked screaming from the crowd in the street and bee lined across the room. She tugged the corner of the framed reproduction of Van Gogh's *Starry Night* and revealed a small safe embedded in the wall behind it. Alison turned the dial, leaning in close to see the tiny lines in the dim flashing light. The poor visibility and anxiety wracking her body forced her to enter the combination four different times but she eventually heard the *click* of the lock disengaging. Pulling the handle, she opened the safe door and reached in, grabbing the cloth-wrapped shard that lay on a stack of papers. Stuffing it into her purse, she turned and rushed from the office, leaving the safe door wide open.

* * * * *

Alison's heels echoed in the silence of the empty museum hallways. As she neared the side door for the ballroom, she spotted Dagger hunched over and peeking through a crack in the door. She toed her way toward him.

"Anything happen?" she whispered.

Dagger jumped at the sound of her voice and the door closed with a *crack*. He turned to her with wide eyes and stared, holding his hand against his chest. Stifling a smile, Alison brushed past him and placed her hand on the doorknob. Unclipping the purse, she pulled out the shard and cradled it in her palm.

Dagger's eyes fell on the shard and his mouth opened slightly. "What are you doing with that?" His voice was ragged.

"Giving it to that...thing."

"Are you out of your mind?" Dagger shot to his feet and placed his hand on the door, slipping between it and Alison. "You can't give that to him! You saw what he did in there. There has to be a reason he wants it and it can't be good for us."

Alison shook her head. "I don't care," she said. "I just want that thing out of here." She pulled the door handle but Dagger gave it a shove, slamming it shut. Alison's face grew stern as she glared up at him. "Get out of my way, Sebastian."

"No. Give it to me." He wound his arm around her waist and pushed her away from the door.

Alison pushed back but her high heels slid along the slick floor. "Let go of me, Dagger. I need to do this." She smacked at his shoulder and placed her hand on his chest, trying to shove free from his grip.

A crash within the ballroom caught their attention and their heads snapped toward the door. Dagger's arm dropped from Alison's side and she pushed past him. Grabbing the knob, she gently eased the door open. Her breath caught in her throat and her skin prickled with goose bumps as she peered into the room.

CHAPTER 23

A large chunk of concrete crashed onto Lauren's dome of Hellfire, cracking in half and fell to the floor. Lowering her arm, the dome slowly dissipated, allowing a shower of plaster dust to rain down on her. Lauren stared up at the holes in the ceiling, feeling pangs of fear in the pit of her stomach.

"What are we going to do now?" she asked Lucifer. She waved a cloud of dust away from her face as a cough erupted from her throat.

Lucifer brushed the plaster from his jacket. As he reached into the inside pocket of his jacket, he noticed a flicker of movement from the corner of his eye. Turning slightly, he caught a glimpse of the crack in the door. He ran his hand down the front of his shirt, casually smoothing the wrinkles in the fabric and gave the door a chin-cock to let Lauren know that they weren't alone.

"It's OK," Lucifer shouted, shuffling past Lauren. "He's gone."

The door swung open. Alison hesitated a moment, her gaze drifting up toward the ceiling. Dagger brushed past her into the ballroom, staring up at the holes as he neared the center of the room.

"Guess we can install those skylights now, huh," he said with a chuckle.

Alison frowned at Dagger and stepped into the ballroom. Her eyes swept the room, assessing the damage the creature had caused. Though the ceiling took the brunt of the attack, the falling debris destroyed many priceless works of art that decorated the room. A few of the paintings that hung on the walls now sat in crumpled heaps on the floor. She spotted the Babylonian clay tablet in the far corner smashed to pieces. But the worst was the unconscious bodies of the partygoers who were too slow to escape the panicked rush. Anxiety flooded her chest as she realized the amount of money this would cost the museum in repairs and bad PR.

Lucifer looked Dagger up and down, extending his hand. "I don't believe we've met. I'm Lou."

Dagger grabbed Lucifer's hand and opened his mouth to introduce himself but was cut off by Lauren. "This is Bastian Dagger," she said. "He's the one who found the shard."

Alison turned to face Lauren, her brow furrowed. "How do you know about that?"

Dagger cocked his head to the side and eyed Lauren carefully. "Yeah, how *do* you know about the shard?"

Lauren grimaced, realizing her mistake. "What? No, I didn't say 'shard'. I said 'Sphere'."

Alison shook her head and stepped closer to Lauren. "No. You said 'shard'. I heard you clear as day. There's been no announcement about the shard. No one knows about the shard. So what is it that you're not telling us?"

Lauren stammered as she retreated from Alison. Lucifer held his hand up and stepped between them. "Time to drop this charade," he said, looking at Alison. "This is my sister, Lauren. She's not an international fashion model. I'm not in the import/export business. And that thing..." He pointed toward the ceiling. "Was not a rep for Amway. He's a big, bad cosmic entity bent on the destruction of...well, everything. But for now, what he wants most of all is to reassemble his sword."

Dagger placed his hands on the sides of his head and massaged his temples. "Wait. 'His blade'?" He looked at Alison, pointing to her hand. "You said that thing was a piece of the Onyx Blade of Belial." He turned back to Lucifer. "If what you say is true, then that thing was Belial?"

Lucifer nodded slowly. "In the flesh. Or, mystic incarnation of flesh, anyway."

"I think I'm gonna be sick." Dagger placed his hands on his knees and leaned over. He breathed deeply a few times before starting to dry-heave.

Alison looked down at him and shook her head. "Pull yourself together," she whispered. Cocking her head back, she frowned at Lucifer. "How do you know about all of this?"

Lucifer sighed, shoving his hands into the pockets of his pants. "You wouldn't believe me if I told you."

Crossing her arms over her chest, Alison shifted her weight to one leg, narrowing her eyes on him. "Try me."

Well, I'm the basis for the Biblical version of the Devil and I stole the sword from Belial and helped to confine him to imprisonment in Limbo for a few millennia. I need to make sure that I get the sword because it's the most powerful artifact in the known universe and with it, I can use it to rebuild my base of power and destroy both him and the angels that cast me out of New Eden. Reciting it in his head made Lucifer realize that the truth may not be the best track to take. He slid a glance at Lauren.

"My sister and I are...demon hunters. We've been tracking Belial for years and learned the truth about the Blade. Because of how powerful it is, we clearly need to keep it out of his grasp. It's also the only thing in the universe strong enough to stop him so we need to find the pieces ourselves and rebuild the sword."

Moments passed as Alison stared at him wordlessly. "OK, now you're just fucking with me."

Lucifer chuckled at her bluntness. "I knew there was a reason I liked you." He could hear the sound of Lauren exhaling, her patience beginning to wear.

"Can we just kill them now and take the damn thing already? We've already spent too much time here."

Dagger shot upright, his eyes wide with shock. "Whoa, whoa, whoa. Who's killing what? Let's all just settle down now."

Lucifer waved his hand at Dagger, easing his worries. "Relax. No one is killing anyone." He turned and glared at Lauren, his lip curling into a snarl. "You hear me? No one. Is killing. Anyone." Placing his hand on his chest, he looked over at Alison. His shoulders relaxed and a smooth smile spread across his face. "Please, just give us the shard." his voice was flat and calm. "It's not safe here."

Alison fixed her eyes on him, the tapping of her shoe the only noise in the room. He was right in one regard; the shard wasn't safe here. The destruction of the museum and possible fatalities proved that. But she knew that Lou was lying to her.

'Sister'? 'Demon hunters'? What kind of idiot did he take her for? That sounded like the premise of a cheesy prime-time television show.

"I don't think that's the best course of action." Slipping the shard back into her purse, she clutched the bag in her hands behind her back and slowly stepped away from them. "I think we need to find somewhere else for this thing."

Rolling his eyes, Lucifer sighed and dropped his hand to his side. "I didn't want to do this but you've brought it upon yourself." He twitched his hand and tendrils of energy emerged from his fingertips, lassoing Alison's arms and legs. She struggled against their grasp but the tendrils pulled tighter, immobilizing her appendages. Lucifer pulled his arm, tugging Alison closer to him. He watched as the fear slowly rose to her face, draining the color from her cheeks.

"Let her go, you son of a bitch," Dagger shouted as he lunged toward Lucifer. Lauren stepped between them and raised her hand, releasing a blast of Hellfire. The flames hit Dagger in the chest and he spiraled backward, landing flat on his back. Lauren chuckled as she watched him pat at the orange flames spreading across his shirt.

"Thank you," Lucifer said, his eyes never leaving Alison's face. Reaching up, he grabbed her chin and lifted her face to his. He stared at her, studying her features. The creases in her dark red lips. The yellow flecks in her eyes. The freckle on her right cheek.

"I like you, Alison. I really do. Which is the only reason you're not dead yet. But I need that shard. And I will stop at nothing to get it." He traced his hand around her waist, his fingers tickling her wrist as they slid down her arm. Grabbing the purse, he snatched it from her hand and pulled it closer to himself. Unclipping the clutch, he pulled the shard from the bag and held it in front of her face.

Lucifer palmed the shard and stepped back. With a twitch of his hand, the energy tendrils melted into smoke and released Alison. She dropped to the floor, rubbing the circulation back into her wrists.

"There are forces at work here that your feeble minds can't possibly comprehend," Lucifer continued. "It's best that you just stay out of it. Go on with your insignificant lives, reach whatever your average life expectancy is and just be happy with being completely ignorant of the grand scheme of the cosmos. It's really the best thing for you."

Lucifer stretched his arm out to Lauren. She stepped next to him and grabbed the shard. Looking over at Dagger, Lauren gave him a wink and a flirtatious smile. She clutched the shard tightly and focused her Hellfire, channeling it directing into the piece of the Onyx Blade. Rays of purple light erupted from her fingers, engulfing her and Lucifer. The light pulsed and flashed, forcing Alison and Dagger to cover their eyes. A gust of wind blew through the room.

Alison's eyes watered as the smell of sulfur burned her nostrils. Peeking out from behind her hand, she looked up to find that she and Dagger were alone, her clutch purse lying where Lucifer and Lauren had been moments ago. She glanced at Dagger, spotting the large char mark in the center of his shirt. "Are you OK?"

He sat up and nodded. "That was one hell of a party," he said with a smile.

CHAPTER 24

Twilana leaped from the rocky wall, dropping the last few feet to the loamy ground below. Her boots made a deep *thump* as they landed in a mound of moss. She rubbed her hands together, soothing the raw, red fingertips. Her biceps and thighs burned and she was out of breath but somehow she felt good, relishing the chance to flex her athletic muscles, literally and figuratively.

She inhaled the crisp clean air, the aroma of dirt, decaying leaves, and burning wood filled her nose. The temperature had dropped since they left the cabin, chilling the sweat that dripped down her back. The cold invigorated her, providing her with the energy to press on.

Looking back up the mountain, she shielded her eyes from the late day sun and watched as Michael struggled to find proper foothold. He climbed well for someone who had never done it before. She thought about shouting a few words of encouragement but decided against it. She didn't want to startle him and cause him to lose his balance. Or worse, insult him and have him try to kill her again. Instead, she settled herself on a large boulder alongside the path and fished a canteen from her knapsack.

Twenty minutes passed as Twilana watched Michael work his way down the wall. He was a few feet from the ground when she finally lost her patience and convinced him to jump the rest of the way. He shot a few looks toward her, wary of her advice. But even he was tired of climbing so he closed his eyes and counted to three before pushing himself from the wall.

He hit the ground and his ankle went out from under him, causing him to tumble across the moss. Twilana looked away, covering her mouth with her hand. Michael pushed himself up from the dirt and dusted off his clothes. He watched from under his brow as Twilana's body shook with silent laughter.

"I'm glad you found that so funny," he said, his forehead crinkled.

"I'm sorry," she said, wiping the tears from her cheek. "Are you OK?" She reached down and picked up his knapsack, handing it to him. He slung it over his shoulder, giving her a curt nod and reached out for her canteen.

"So, where to now?" he asked, taking a swig. Wiping the corner of his mouth, he looked around at the valley. The land was mostly flat save for a few hills rolling along the distance. Trees dotted the countryside sporadically, offering little protection against the wind. Michael felt a shiver rocket down his spine.

Twilana pulled the blade from her pocket and held it in both hands. The vibrations grew stronger; not considerably but just enough that she noticed the change. She squinted out into the distance, pointing the tip of the blade to the southeast. "Feels like it's that way."

Michael looked out across the valley. "If I recall, there's a small town out there. It's as good as any place to start. At worst, we can at least get something to eat." He took a step but his leg gave out on him, the muscles screaming with fatigue after the arduous climb. He looked up at Twilana sheepishly. "Mind if we take a break first?"

She smiled and grabbed him under his arm, helping him over to the boulder.

*　　*　　*　　*　　*

The feeling returned to his legs, Michael pushed himself up from the boulder and headed down the hill toward the town in the distance. The sun kissed the horizon, casting the sky in a luscious array of red and orange. A cold breeze blew across the countryside and Twilana decided it was a good time to slip into the sweater.

They walked along a clear dirt road, the easiest leg of the trek they'd faced so far. As the sky darkened even further, the deep red turning to a dark purple, a wave of shouts and jeers rose from the distance. Twilana jogged toward the sound of the ruckus as

Michael hobbled as closely as he could.

Twilana crested a hill and the village came into view. It was much sparser than she imagined, consisting of little more than rows of squat wooden houses. The hamlet was enclosed by a long wooden fence, just enough of a marker to determine where the town limits ended. Beyond the fence, a large stage had been assembled and all of the townspeople were gathered around it.

A trio of men appeared from behind the stage. As they approached the stairs the sounds of the crowd increased, their yelling drowning each other out and melding into one long, raucous buzz.

Twilana watched as the two larger men dragged a third up the stairs to the stage platform. The smaller man's head lolled back and forth on his neck, his feet dragging lifelessly behind him. They dropped him on the center of the stage and erected a long, wooden post. A thick rope noose dangled from a perpendicular beam.

Twilana didn't know what was happening but she knew she didn't like it. Not long ago, she and Matt were brought out to a similar stage in front of a similar crowd shouting similar epithets. They were held prisoner by a Japanese tyrant, charged as spies for the Chinese army. Their trial was a sham but their execution would have been quite real had Aaron not arrived in time to save them. Revisiting the memory angered her and she felt the heat flushing her cheeks. She pushed through the crowd to get closer to the stage when someone grabbed her elbow and pulled her back. Turning, she looked up at Michael's face. His eyes were serious and he shook his head slowly.

"Let go of me," she snarled, her bright, violet eyes shifting colors, mirroring her emotions. Michael watched as her irises changed from purple to a dark blue, to a deep, blood red. Despite the frightening sight, Michael held her arm tightly.

"No," he said, stepping closer to her, his fingertips digging into her flesh. "We need to be smart about this. We can't rush headlong into something that doesn't affect us without knowing what's going on."

She stared up at him. He was right, of course. There could be a perfectly good reason for this spectacle. The logic overpowered her emotion and her eyes swirled back to their original color. Seeing her relax, Michael released her arm.

"Let's find out what's happening," he said, inching his way

through the crowd.

A well-dressed man appeared just off-stage and sauntered up the stairs. He took each step slowly and deliberately, walking with an air of pretension. He wore a dark brown suit, his jacket tails hanging down to the back of his knees. The suit was well worn, the fabric around the elbows and knees beginning to thin. Tiny threads danced at the edges of the cuffs. Beneath the jacket was a dark red doublet with a golden chain hanging from the breast pocket. A black tricorne hat sat on his head. Looking out at his audience, he raised his hand. The din of the crowd settled. Twilana turned her attention to the man as he spoke, his words flat and emotionless.

"We took this man into our ranks," he began, his hand tracking to the man lying on the stage. "But he betrayed us. He brought death and fear into our town, our homes, despite all of the goodwill we've given him. We have earned the right to not live in fear, have we not?"

The man paused as a cheer rose from the onlookers. A few of them flung expletives at the man, bringing his mother's virtue into question. A rotten head of cabbage flew through the air, striking the prisoner in the side of the face, eliciting an uproar of laughter from the crowd.

Twilana turned to a white-haired man standing next to her. His style of dress was similar to the dapper man on the stage but his clothes were much older and more threadbare. He also smelled slightly of cheese. "What did he do?" she asked him.

"Stranger came to us a few days back." As the man spoke, the aroma of cheese intensified. Twilana leaned back in an effort to escape the wrath of his breath. "He stole a knife. Killed a young girl."

"What kind of knife was it?" she asked anxiously.

"Does it matter?" The man shot her a quick glance over his shoulder, recoiling at the sight of her light blue hair. Twilana placed her hand on her pocket, feeling the wild vibrations of the Blade through her pants. Ignoring the old, odd-smelling man, she turned to Michael.

"Could be he has the shard."

Michael shrugged. "Maybe. But I don't think we should be getting involved. Doesn't look like they take well to strangers."

Twilana turned back to the stage and started to push her way through the crowd. The dapper man resumed his speech.

"We don't have the time for insolence, theft, and murder!" Emotion crept into his voice. He spoke passionately and gestured wildly. "We have a right to live in peace, the way that we choose. This man destroyed our innocence when he took the life of that girl. In return, his life will be taken from him!" The crowd erupted in cheers and applause. The unconscious man on the stage began to stir, pushing himself up on his arms. Twilana reached the stage and placed her hands on the old wood, looking up as one of the big men punched the prisoner in the face. The prisoner grunted and a spray of bloody spit splattered to the floor.

"I want to talk to him," Twilana shouted, pointing to the prisoner.

Michael shook his head from behind her and leaned in close. "Don't do this," he whispered.

"Back off," she mumbled over her shoulder. "If he has the shard, we need to know." She turned back to the well-dressed man on the stage as he stepped closer to the edge and looked down at her.

"I'm sorry. And you are...?"

"Doesn't matter. Give me five minutes with him. Alone. I just want to talk to him."

The well-dressed man smiled with one side of his mouth. He looked out at the crowd, his eyes flicking from person to person. Those in front of the stage close enough to hear Twilana's words looked at her, trying to get a glimpse of the woman who dared to interrupt the execution. Murmurs rose from the back of the crowd as people wondered why the accused man wasn't swinging from his neck yet.

The man clasped his hands behind his back and turned his attention back to Twilana, staring deep into her purple eyes.

"Why should I allow you that favor?"

Twilana craned her neck to look up at him. She shook her head and, placing all of her weight onto her arms, pushed herself up onto the stage. The man took a step back as the two big men rushed toward her. The well-dressed man raised his hand and the guards stopped, watching as Twilana rose to her feet.

She stared at the man, holding her hands in front of her, showing that she posed no threat. "I don't want any trouble. I just want to talk to him."

The well-dressed man's eyes took her in, examining every

part of her. He scowled as he spotted the hilt of the Blade poking from her pocket.

"No trouble, huh? Is that why you come to us armed?"

Twilana looked down at the handle and slowly reached for it. She pulled it from her pocket and, crouching down, placed it on the floor of the stage. She rose to her feet, hands before her. "See? I'm making an effort of trust. I'd like you to do the same."

"Who are you to ask me for favors? You've still not answered my questions."

"My name is Twilana Salizar. I am a captain in the military of Janus."

"I've never heard of Janus before."

"It's…" she paused for a moment. "Far from here."

The man continued to stare at her, his hands clasped behind his back. He cocked his head slightly before giving the guards a nod. He watched as they turned and picked the prisoner up from the floor, dragging him down the stairs. The well-dressed man looked out to the crowd.

"Everyone, I've decided to grant this woman's request! Please be patient. I assure you that the villain will be punished for his crimes." A rage of *boos* and *hisses* rose from the crowd. The well-dressed man turned away from them. Twilana extended her hand and mouthed the words "thank you" as he approached her.

He looked at her hand as if she had offered him dog excrement. Locking his gaze on her, his eyes smoldered with irritation. "My name is Harlan Braddock and I hope you have a good reason for disappointing my townspeople."

CHAPTER 25

Belial shot through the nexus like a cannonball. With the Blade having gathered enough energy after being reunited with the shard Lucifer gave him, it transmitted images into Belial's brain, pulling him across the void to the location of another piece. Belial could feel the Limbotic presence rolling over his body as the mists swirled all around him. A feeling of anxiety welled up in him, having returned to the wretched place that acted as his prison for so long. But he buried the feelings; it would soon be over.

A massive pulse ripped through his arm and he stopped. The buzzing of the Blade tingled his arm. Rearing the sword back, he slashed the air, tearing a deep gash in the fabric of space and time. He swooped down and burst through the breech, his insides turning to jelly as he broke through the plane. Despite his infusion of power, Belial was still weak and the exertion was starting to take its toll. He landed on a stone pathway with a heavy *thud*. Belial knelt on the path, his body convulsing, to get his bearings. He looked down at the Blade in his hand, watching as the edges of the sword blurred with vibrations, and smiled. *It's close*, he thought.

Rising to his feet, he gazed out over an enormous hill that rose before him. He looked down at his feet, focusing on the path that led to a stone stairway carved into the hill. At the top of the steps sat an old castle, cold and grey. Like a stalwart protector of the countryside, the fortress stared down at him, mocking him.

Belial recognized the castle immediately.

Shortly after he came to power, the angels outsourced their

military, building outposts in many of the more populated worlds across the universe. Dubbing them "Houses of the Cosmic Protectors", these fortresses acted as monasteries, recruiting and training some of the fiercest fighters around. Their mission was to alert the Angelic High Military of any impending force that could threaten their world and hold it off until the angels arrived. They were basically the first wave of defense that called in the cavalry, outfitted with some of the AHM's impressive artillery.

Belial killed his fair share of Cosmic Protectors in his day, keeping a running tally with a few of his cohorts. If he recalled correctly, he was in the lead by the time he was imprisoned, even though Samael was slowly catching up. He gave a quick thought to where the figures were at before shrugging and glancing up at the late-afternoon sun. Slipping the Blade into the sheathe, he flapped his massive wings and lifted from the path, heading toward the castle.

As he drew closer, Belial watched as the sun played off the cracks in the stone, highlighting the weathered decay in the brickwork. There was an eerie stillness to the surrounding courtyard, lacking in any signs of life. He swung around the south side of the building, swooping down below the cliff before climbing back up to peer over the outer wall. It was the same over here; no one around and the place was completely quiet.

Circling down, Belial came to a rest on the hard, packed-dirt ground. He looked around the courtyard, at the barren emptiness. An overturned hay cart lay in front of the closed portcullis, blocking the pathway from the castle. To the left of the gateway, the stairway leading up to the watch tower crumbled and littered the entrance with jagged boulders and shattered stone. The parapet ringing the outer wall was in shambles, with half of the covering caving in on itself. The interior of the courtyard fared no better, the brick walls scorched and marred by flames with the remnants of hundreds of charred arrow shafts littering the ground.

Belial sniffed the air, detecting the faint traces of ether and ozone, two definite traits of Hellfire. He grinned, mentally adding to the tally for Samael. This victory definitely had to go to him. He felt the buzzing on his hip and placed his hand on the Blade. Using it as his guide, he followed the curtain wall, disappearing through the threshold of the flanking tower.

Two steps in and Belial was consumed by the darkness.

Lifting his hand, he ignited a ball of flame and the room burst into a bright orange light. Shadows flickered as the fireball sputtered. Belial crept along the stone walkway leading deeper into the castle, listening to the vibrating of the Blade at his waist.

Stopping at an intersection, Belial paused a moment and closed his eyes, placing his hand on the sheathe. He looked left, gauging the strength of the pulsing. Turning right, he felt the tremors rocket up his arm. His eyes snapped open and he hurried down the corridor.

Belial emerged in a massive room with vaulted ceilings towering high above him. The far wall was constructed of a large wooden frame with hundreds of small indents carved into it. Long spears hung vertically from the frame. To his left, Belial spotted a trio of barrels, empty and upended. Glancing at the few black granules around the spouts of the barrels, he figured this room was the armory. Ripped to shreds as it was, Belial's thoughts again drifted back to the battle that tore through the castle.

He strolled toward the barrels and kicked one of them to the side. It thundered throughout the cavernous room as it rolled across the cracked stone floor. It shattered against the far wall, littering the floor with splintered wood. As it impacted, Belial felt a blast surge through his leg. He crouched low, holding his hand near the floor, tiny explosions bursting as the flames ignited the gunpowder.

A glimmer of purple light caught Belial's attention. He reached over and he felt a sharp prick in the palm of his hand. Closing his fingers around the object, he pulled back and looked at the tiny shard he held.

As he smiled down at the shard, pain tore through his back, throwing him off-balance. He fell forward, the shard spilling from his hand and clinking in the darkness as it tumbled away from him. Pushing himself up on one arm, he rose to his feet and spun on his heels, coming face to face with an old man dressed in a tattered orange robe.

The man was less than half Belial's height, his waist as thin as the hair on his head. He stood with his hands clasped behind his back and his eyes locked on Belial.

"You do not belong here," the man said, his lips barely moving.

Belial shot him a grin, the glow in his bright, green eyes

intensifying. "You must be one of the Cosmic Protectors. Tell me, what happened to the rest of your buddies?" His roared with laughter, the bellow echoing through the room.

"You do not belong here," the man repeated.

"I have to say, you don't seem surprised to see me," Belial said as he lumbered toward the tiny man.

"That's because I am not," the man replied. His eyes were transfixed on the demon, completely unwavering. The tiny man was calm, poised, and, most oddly, relaxed. He watched as Belial flexed his arms and stretch his shoulders. "Evil like you cannot be destroyed. I have witnessed this many times over. At best it can be contained. But it always manages to find its way back, burrowing into the hearts of men like maggots into rotting meat."

The man moved his foot back slightly, widening his stance. He pulled a thin sword from its sheathe and held it before him, clutching the hilt in both hands. "You will not burrow into my heart, beast," he announced, leaning forward. "And I will contain you."

Belial chuckled. "You have spunk, old man. It's a shame I have to kill you." Pulling the Blade from his hip, the demon lunged and brought it crashing down into the floor. The old man spun out of the way, slashing Belial's forearm. The demon reared back in pain as blood oozed from the wound. "You think that little pig-sticker can stop me?" he asked as he circled the old man.

Movement twitched the side of the man's mouth. Belial placed his hand to his ear. "What was that? You're going to have to speak up."

"I said 'you talk too much'."

Belial chuckled. Drawing his arm back, he generated a second fireball and flung it. The old man crouched low, watching as the ball of flame sped closer to him. Shifting his weight, he kicked into the air, flipping out of the way as the fireball smashed into the floor. The stone erupted as the flames ignited a pile of gunpowder, creating a white hot flash, blinding Belial.

Belial stumbled backward as a foot collided with the side of his face. He thrust his sword, slashing wildly as the old man punched him in the small of his back. He tried to get a bead on the old man but his vision was flooded with twinkling dots, making it impossible to focus. A sharp pain pierced his side and he dropped to his knees. The demon swung his arm and felt a hard knock on the back of his hand. He listened as the old man slammed against the floor and tumbled a few times, his sword clattering across the stone. Belial blinked away the spots and turned to find the man pushing himself up on his arms.

"You have some moves, I'll give you that," Belial said, scowling down at the man. "But you haven't seen even half of what I can do." He leaped to his feet and rushed at the man, his figners flexing around the end of the Blade. The man rolled out of the way as Belial kicked out at him, his foot missing the man's face by inches. Spinning on his back like a breakdancer busking for change, the man pinwheeled to his feet and rabbit-punched Belial in the side. He flipped backward, grabbing his sword from the corner of the room and jumped at Belial. The demon turned in time to deflect the attack, pressing the flat of the Blade with his free hand to hold the old man back.

Belial pushed against the Blade, sending the man sliding backward on his heels. The demon narrowed his eyes on the him. "This isn't a fight you want to have."

"You are finally correct. I do not want to have this fight. But I will."

Belial thrust the Blade at the old man's belly. He stepped to the side, the tip of the Blade just barely poking the sash tied around his waist. The old man flicked his wrist, knocking the Blade to the side with his sword. He flicked his wrist again, slashing at Belial's chest. The tip glanced off of the thick armor, leaving a trail of sparks in its wake.

Shoving the old man back, Belial stalked forward, swinging the Blade angrily, slashing and hacking with each step. The old man parried and blocked each of the demon's blows, retreating as he staved off the attack. With a roar, Belial reared back and prepared a vicious downward swing, forcing the man to roll to the side. He swatted at the man, catching him in the temple. He sprawled backwards, blood trickling down his face as his eye swelled shut. Leaping to his feet, the old man held his sword before him, his body tight and ready for another attack. Belial's laughter echoed through the armory.

"You're like a fly at a window. No matter how many times it bashes its face, it will never get out."

The old man straightened his back and splayed his legs, placing the tip of the sword against the floor. Clutching the hilt with both hands, he closed his eyes. Belial watched as he stood still as a stone, completely motionless. The demon stepped forward but the old man didn't flinch. He stepped again, but the man stood his ground. Reaching his arm back, Belial swung at his neck. The man leaned away from the attack and leaped straight into the air. As the old man came down, he spun and slashed at Belial's face. The demon stumbled backward, roaring in pain.

"I'm done playing with you," Belial shouted, sliding the Blade back into its sheath. Balling his fists, he closed his eyes and focused his power inward. A faint humming filled the air as sparks of energy erupted from the demon's skin. The old man crouched low and watched as light emanated from Belial. The humming intensified and Belial's body started to change.

The spikes in his shoulders grew to twice their length. His horns extended, curling around both sides of his head. The plates that covered his arms and legs burst into flame, engulfing his limbs in fire and magma. The glow of his eyes intensified, two bright, green spotlights shining from the center of his helmet.

Belial's eyes slowly opened, a grin spreading across his face. His hand moved like lightning as he reached out and snatched the old man's sword from his grip. He clenched his fist, snapping the steel like balsa wood and dropped the two halves to the floor. The old man stepped backward, retreating from Belial's advances, backing himself against the wall. He watched as Belial punched at him, ducking just as the demon's fist crashed into the wall above him. Stone dust showered down on the man as he rolled clear. Leaping to his feet, the old man bolted across the room. As he neared the exit, his foot caught on half of his sword blade. His eyes went wide as he lost his balance and stumbled to the ground, smacking his head on the stone floor.

Belial grabbed the old man's forearm, yanking him from the ground and tearing the shoulder from its socket. The man's screams filled the chamber as the demon crushed the bones in his arm. Pain flooded his eyes and fear flashed across his face.

Belial stared at the old man as he swung helplessly from his grasp. Wrapping his fingers around the man's waist, Belial pulled him closer. "Nothing to say, little man? No words of wisdom to save yourself?"

The old man grimaced as he pushed the pain aside, focusing his attention on Belial. "The great evil can be defeated by the greater good. You are the greatest evil I've ever faced. But there is a force more powerful than you."

Belial smiled. "No, there isn't." He flexed his fingers and crushed the man's torso. His body went limp in the demon's giant hand, his head flopping lifelessly to the side. Belial dropped the old man's broken body on the stone and turned toward the corner. He ignited another fireball, lighting the room. Pulling the Blade from its sheathe, he tapped it to the shard lying on the floor and a flash of blue light engulfed them, spreading outward and covering Belial in its glow.

The light dissipated and the demon looked down at his sword, marveling at the size and weight of it. His fingers wrapped around the Blade as the power flooded his body. He cleaved the air before him, opening a portal into the Limbo and leaped into the void.

CHAPTER 26

Harlan Braddock descended the steps and walked around the back of the stage, followed closely by Twilana and Michael. He strolled across a small, barren courtyard that led to a squat building separated from the rest of the town. Pulling a large iron keyring from his belt, he unlocked the heavy wooden door and shoved it open. He stepped aside, allowing the pair to enter before him.

Twilana stepped through the threshold into a dark room. It took her eyes a moment to adjust to the little bit of light that filtered through the barred windows. Looking around the cramped, dusty room, she spotted the iron gate that cut off a third of the room from the rest.

"A jailhouse?"

Braddock turned to Twilana and nodded as he closed the door behind Michael. He walked toward the desk at the opposite end of the room. Fishing a dented Zippo lighter from his pocket, he lit the wick on an old oil lantern and hung it from a wall hook. He pulled a rickety rolling chair from beneath the desk and settled himself into it.

With the help of the lantern's flickering yellow light, Twilana examined the room. The jail was affixed to the room's longest wall, divided into three equally-sized cells. Each cell was large enough to house two people rather uncomfortably, holding two bunk beds and an old rusted pail. Most of the beds were stripped of their beddings; only one was dressed in a dingy sheet with dents and wrinkles in the fabric showing that someone had used it recently.

Twilana eyed Braddock as he sat in his chair, his legs propped up on the edge of the desk. He held a thick brown cigar between his teeth, puffing it as he used the Zippo to light it. Clouds of smoke erupted from the cigar as the tip burst into flames. He snapped the Zippo shut, pulled the cigar from his mouth and blew out a stream of smoke. His eyes fell on Twilana and he raised his hand, waving to a pair of seats across from the desk.

"So," he began, drawing out the vowel as Twilana and Michael sat, "what business do you have with my prisoner?"

"We need to speak with him," Twilana said. "We believe he may have information that is vital to our mission."

"Is he wanted by your military?"

Twilana shot a glance at Michael and tilted her head to her lap. She didn't want to lose Braddock's trust by lying to him but she also didn't feel that talking about a powerful sword that shattered across the cosmos and her mission to find and reassemble the weapon was the best track to take. "Yes. He is a soldier who abandoned his post. We've been searching for him for quite some time." She could feel Michael's eyes burrowing into her as she spoke but she held Braddock's gaze. His expression remained fixed, almost as if he failed to comprehend Twilana's words. A moment passed before he looked at Michael.

"And you are...?"

Michael's head snapped toward him and he blinked wildly, stammering over his words. "I...I...I'm Michael. I am her..."

"Second in command," Twilana interjected.

Michael exhaled sharply, his cheeks flushed. He relaxed slightly and forced a smile to his lips. "Right," he said flatly. "I'm her First Lieutenant."

Braddock pooched his lips and nodded, taking a few quick puffs from the cigar. Moving his feet back to the floor, he leaned on the desktop and flicked the cigar over the glass ashtray, rolling the burning embers in the pile of ashes it dropped. He looked up at Twilana and shifted his gaze to Michael, hovering on him a moment before looking back to her. The uncomfortable silence hung in the air along with Braddock's cigar smoke.

Twilana was the first to break the silence. "Mr. Braddock, if you don't mind. We've traveled far to get here and now..."

"Captain," he said curtly.

Twilana was taken aback by his interruption. "I'm sorry?"

"You called me 'Mr. Braddock'," he said, leaning back in the chair. He took another puff from the cigar. "I'm a captain, like you. In the British Royal Navy. Or, was, at least."

Twilana raised an eyebrow. She turned to Michael to find that he had a similar expression on his face. "I'm not really following you."

Braddock looked up at the ceiling and shook his head. "It really doesn't matter." He turned back to Twilana. "I'll be willing to let you speak with Trodoro but I can't allow you to take him from me."

"Why not?" Michael asked.

"The man committed a crime. In my city. He needs to be punished."

"Well, I can assure you, mis…Captain, that he will be punished," Twilana said. "We have every intention of bringing him to justice for the crimes he's committed."

Braddock placed the cigar in the ashtray and leaned back. The chair squealed as he steepled his fingers across his chest. He looked up at Twilana and stared at her, allowing his silence to permeate the room. "No," he said plainly.

Michael shook his head and shifted sideways in his seat. Leaning forward, he placed an elbow on his leg and looked at Braddock. "Sir, I don't think you understand the gravity of this situation."

Braddock shot forward in his chair and leveled a finger on Michael. "No, you don't understand the gravity of this situation!" His voice had turned harsh and he punctuated his words with a poke of his finger. "A girl has gone missing and my people demand action. We cannot allow you to take our prisoner with the promise that he will be punished. We have a right to deliver our own justice."

Twilana cocked her head to the side. "How do you know he had anything to do with the girl's disappearance? Has he confessed?"

"Quite the opposite." Braddock inhaled deeply and the redness drained from his face, his demeanor returning to its former stoicism. "He's denied the accusations profusely."

"Has a trial been held?"

Braddock scoffed at her words. "A trial. Miss, we've lived

here for decades without incident. Two days after he shows up, the girl goes missing. I'm sorry but a trial would just be a waste of time."

"Regardless of your beliefs," Michael began, "the man deserves a trial, wouldn't you say?" Twilana looked at him, the irony of his sentiment not escaping her. Less than a year ago, Michael ordered her to be assassinated on the chance that she was working against the Angelic High Military. Yet here he was two feet from her advocating for the fair trial of a man accused of kidnapping or worse. She wasn't sure if he was keeping up a charade or if he truly felt that way.

"No, I wouldn't say, actually," Braddock responded. The old man was obstinate and refused to relent.

Twilana sighed and wiped her hand down her face. "You said we can speak with him."

"Yes, ma'am, I did."

"When he...abandoned his post, he took something. An artifact. Very rare and very valuable. We'd like to get it back."

"What was it?"

"I'd rather not go into detail, Captain," Twilana said.

"If that's all you want, I may be able to save you the time. His effects were confiscated when he was arrested. Could be I already have your 'artifact'."

Could getting the shard be as easy as just asking for it? Twilana thought to herself. She shot Michael a glance and shrugged.

"Yes, OK. It's a gem. Like a dark stone. Black, with flecks of white."

Pushing up from the chair, Braddock grabbed the cigar from the ashtray and puffed on it. Gripping the cigar between his teeth, he turned from the desk to a row of filing cabinets that lined the wall behind him. He grabbed the handle of the top-most drawer and gave it a tug. It flew from its casing, shaking the cabinet as it reached the limits of its rollers. Braddock lifted himself on his tip-toes and peered into the drawer. He rifled around for a moment, pushing a stack of papers to the side. Pulling out a puffy, manila envelope, he slammed the drawer shut. He opened the flap of the envelope and squinted inside, shaking it to shift the contents around. Turning, he up-ending the envelope onto the desktop and the items fell with a clatter.

"Nope. No gem."

Twilana looked at the items as they scattered across Braddock's desk; a gold pocket watch, a dull, rusty knife, an embroidered pocket square. No shard.

"Then we need to speak with him," she said, looking up at Braddock. Her voice cracked, her patience waning. "We need to know what he did with the gem."

Braddock looked at her sideways. He hadn't trusted them since the moment he met them, but the woman's request seemed important. The gem might have been valuable to her but he couldn't imagine it would be anything Earth-shattering. He closed his eyes and nodded slowly. "Yes, ma'am. I told you you could have some time with him and I'll keep my word." He sauntered to the door and opened it wide. White moonlight flooded through the doorway and framed his massive body. The tails of his jacket flapped as a cool breeze brushed past him. He raised his arm and waved, taking a step back as the two large men pushed into the room, dragging Trodoro between them. They released his arms, dropping him callously. Trodoro's body shook as his jaw smacked against the hard, wooden floor. The big men pushed past Braddock and out of the room.

"There's your man," Braddock said, giving them a mocking salute. "You have ten minutes." He exited the room, closing the door behind him.

CHAPTER 27

Twilana jumped from her chair and rushed to Trodoro's side. Grabbing him by the shoulders, she rolled him onto his back. His face was mangled, covered in gashes and bruises. Long, dark hair was matted to his face. His skin was covered in a mix of dried sweat, dirt and blood. He was barely conscious, his eyelids fluttering as she moved him. When she grabbed his right arm he jumped, a small yelp escaping his mouth. He jerked back and cradled his arm with his left hand. Twilana could see that it was broken but no one had bothered to treat it.

"Trodoro," she whispered. "Trodoro, wake up." She grabbed his face and shook him gently, trying to rouse him. His eyes slowly opened and began to scan the room. They settled on her, staring at her for a moment, his face devoid of recognition. His brow furrowed as he spotted her hair. He dug his heels into the floor and tried to push himself away from her.

"Who are you?" Trodoro gurgled. She leaned forward, placing some of her weight on him to keep him steady. As he spoke, she could see that a few of his teeth were missing. *They really did a number on this guy*, she thought.

"We need your help," she said softly. "We're looking for a rock. A black rock with white dots all over it. Do you have it?"

Trodoro relaxed as he heard her voice. He shook his head and winced. "I had it. But it's gone."

"Where did it go?" Twilana asked. She wound her arm around his back and lifted him into a sitting position.

He gently lay his right arm across his legs. Placing his left hand on the floor, he held himself up and locked his gaze on Twilana. "Just gone," he said with a shrug. His speech was better, the gurgling subsided. Shifting his weight, Trodoro looked over and noticed Michael for the first time. He gave the man a curt smile and waved. Trodoro cocked his head back to Twilana. "I was in the pub. Drinking. Drunk. Passed out and when I woke up, it was gone."

Twilana could feel a faint buzzing on her hip. Reaching down, she pulled the Blade from her pocket and clutched it as it vibrated softly. She looked up at Michael and handed it to him.

"It's still reacting," she said. "Like there's a shard nearby."

Michael leaned forward and took the Blade from her. He wrapped his fingers around it, carefully avoiding the sharp, jagged edges, and felt the weak vibrations.

Trodoro reached out and grabbed Twilana's wrist. "Wait." His eyes had glazed over and he stared up at her. "There was a girl. Young. She was looking at it. Said it was pretty and asked to hold it. Maybe she…"

"Who was she, Trodoro?" Twilana's voice grew desperate.

Trodoro's breathing labored. He coughed, a spray of blood and spit splattered against the floor. He wiped his mouth with the back of his hand. "Gone, too. The girl… She's the one they say I…" His eyes grew wide as the realization hit him. He reached out for Twilana, grasping her wrist tighter. He pulled her closer, pushing his face into her shoulder. "You can't let them!" he sobbed. His voice was wracked with emotion, his words nearly incomprehensible. "I didn't do anything to her! I was asleep! I couldn't have!"

Twilana pulled her hand from his grasp and leaned back. She patted him on the back, his sudden outpouring of emotion making her physically uncomfortable. She rose to her feet and looked over at Michael. "Do you think she…?"

Michael shrugged. "It's possible. You discovered its powers completely by accident. There's no saying this little girl didn't."

Twilana's eyes dropped to the floor. If the girl *had* used the shard to open a portal, then they may be able to find her and clear Trodoro's name. She didn't see much of an option. They needed the shard back so if that meant going to some pocket dimension to rescue a little girl, then it had to be done. But something didn't feel right. "If she disappeared with it... If it's not even here anymore, why would the Blade react like this?"

"Residual energy," Michael said plainly. "Depending on how long he had the shard, his body stored some of the energy. That's what the blade itself is finding."

She crouched down in front of Trodoro and grabbed him by the shoulders. He was calmer now, his outburst passed, but his cheeks were streaked with tears. She looked him square in the eyes, her face a slate of seriousness.

"We're going to help you." Twilana spoke slowly and clearly, as if she was speaking to a child. "We'll find the girl and bring her back. We will prove that you're innocent. OK?"

Trodoro nodded and sniffed, a wad of snot dribbling down his lip. Twilana patted his shoulder and rose, turning to face Michael.

"So, where do we start?"

CHAPTER 28

The purple globe appeared in the middle of the street, halting traffic and further irritating the already aggravated commuters. Car horns blared and drivers tossed expletives as the sphere grew larger and larger. The bright light flashed through the roadway, forcing the pedestrians to shield their eyes. As the light subsided, Lucifer and Lauren stood in the center of the road, a matching pair of confused looks on their faces.

The blast of a horn caught Lucifer's attention. He spun on the balls of his feet and found the front grill of a semi-truck barreling straight toward him. Raising his arm, he pointed his fingertips at the truck and flicked his wrist. The truck careened to the right and ran up on the sidewalk, colliding with a street lamp.

Lauren reached over and grabbed Lucifer's wrist. Still clutching the shard, she lifted her hand and focused her Hellfire, slowly levitating from the ground, dragging Lucifer behind her. They floated over the street toward the sidewalk and Lauren gently settled them onto the concrete, surrounded by a crowd of confused and awed onlookers.

It only took a few moments for the excitement to die out, before the crowd ignored Lauren and Lucifer, pushing past each other to resume their rush toward their destinations. Car horns blared, victims of the daily late-afternoon rush hour traffic. The only casualty was the smoking box-truck up on the sidewalk, the driver shouting into a cell phone pressed to his ear.

Lauren craned her neck to look up at the tall glass and

steel buildings rising up all around them. Turning, she spotted the Haziel Convention Center a few blocks down the street and her eyes grew wide with recognition.

"How did we get back to New Eden?" she shouted over the din of the crowd.

"I have no idea but we need to get off the street," Lucifer replied, wrapping his arm around her waist. "The angels will be all over us if we don't move." He ushered her into the path of a nearing crowd, melding into the group of pedestrians. They walked for a couple dozen yards before Lucifer spotted a thin alley between two buildings. He quickly veered off from the crowd, pulling Lauren with him.

Lucifer leaned against the wall, to catch his breath, feeling his heart pound in his chest. He looked Lauren up and down, examining the ballgown she wore. Looking down at his own clothes, he realized they needed to be more inconspicuous. He placed his hand on his chest and focused his energy, turning the tuxedo into a salmon-colored polo shirt, a crisp pair of khaki pants and a tan windbreaker.

"You do the same," he told Lauren.

"But I like this dress."

He narrowed his eyes and looked at her sternly. She sighed and flicked her hand, a flash of purple light enveloping her. As the light faded, she reappeared wearing an orange knit sweater that ended at her knees accompanied by a pair of black leggings. A matching knitted beret sat on her head and a tiny black purse was slung over her shoulder. She unzipped the bag and slipped the shard inside, patting it as the bag slapped against her thigh.

Satisfied with their appearances, Lucifer ducked from the alleyway and hustled down the street with Lauren three steps behind him. He glanced up at the numbered signs above the building doors, noting each one as he passed. Stopping at an intersection, he shifted from foot to foot impatiently as cars whizzed past. Raising his hand, he flashed his Hellfire at the traffic light, changing it from red to green. The red-light camera attached to the pole clicked furiously as a half dozen cars sped through, unable to stop in time. Lucifer rushed out into the street, halfway through the crosswalk by the time Lauren reached the corner.

Stopping at a corrugated metal bay door, Lucifer read the stenciled lettering on the side of the building. "In here," he said, waving Lauren over. He ran up a small flight of stairs flanking the loading bay to a windowless door. He pounded on it three times and waited for someone to answer. Moments passed with no response so he pounded on the door again. The door swung open and Lucifer threw himself through it, brushing right past the big man that stood in the doorway. Lauren ran up the steps and through the threshold, grabbing the door handle and slamming it shut behind her.

The Demon turned his back to the door and eyed Lucifer suspiciously. Demons, by nature, aren't very intelligent but they had their uses. Big and strong, Demons make perfect soldiers, doing what they are told without question. They also make great bouncers and night security.

Lucifer leaned over the railing, breathing heavily. He wiped a few beads of sweat from his forehead with the back of his hand. Inhaling slowly, he composed himself, straightening his back and ensuring his shirt was neatly tucked into his pants. Satisfied, he faced the Demon, spotting the patch on his leather biker jacket that read "Lucifer's Loonies". The name gave Lucifer a chuckle even though it made no sense to him. Patting the Demon on the shoulder, Lucifer shuffled down a set of metal steps as Lauren cautiously squeezed past the large man's thick chest to follow her brother.

The stairs led them into a cavernous warehouse. Rows of conveyor belts ran the length of the room. Stacks of boxes lined the far wall, each stamped with the logo for "Satan's", Lucifer's chain of convenience stores he franchised across New Eden. A platoon of uniformed warehouse workers scurried across the floor, carrying boxes from the conveyor belts, sealing and taping the flaps, and distributing them among a line of waiting transport containers.

Lucifer paused a moment and watched the demons working, his mouth curling into a half smile. Turning, he spotted the door to the foreman's office on the other side of the warehouse. He waded his way through the activity of the workfloor, his eyes falling on a silhouette through the tinted office window.

The door rattled as it slammed against the opposite wall. A head snapped toward Lucifer and watched as he stormed into the office. A pair of dark brown eyes met his, stopping Lucifer in his tracks. Lucifer's hand froze on the door knob as he recognized Nathaniel leaning back in the high-backed office chair, boots propped up on the desk.

Nathaniel's eyes went wide at the sight of his boss. He swung his feet from the desktop to the floor. "Let me call you back," he said into the phone pressed to his ear before leaning forward and placing it on the cradle. He shot up from the chair and crossed the room in two long strides.

"Holy shit," Nathanial exclaimed as he wrapped his arms around Lucifer and lifted him in a giant bear hug. "I thought I'd never see *you* again."

"Easy there, guy," Lucifer said, slapping Nathaniel on the back. "We weren't gone that long." Nathaniel placed him on the floor and gave his shoulder a reassuring squeeze.

"No hug for me?" Lauren asked, leaning against the doorframe. She gave Nathaniel a big, flirtatious smile.

He looked up at her and smiled back sheepishly. He could feel his cheeks turning red, his face going hot. "It's good to see you, too, Lauren."

Lucifer brushed past Nathaniel and circled around the desk, plopping himself in the office chair. He opened the desk drawer and rifled through the file folders.

Nathaniel leaned against the corner of the desk, cringing as he watched his boss tear his well-organized system apart. "But no, really. Where have you been all this time?"

Lucifer slammed the drawer shut and pulled open a second. Reaching into the far back, he grabbed a dark grey Rolodex and placed it on the desktop. He removed the lid and flipped through the yellowing cards. "We were hiding off world for a while. Until the heat here died down."

"Then you were gone longer than you needed to be," Nathaniel said. "Ever since they excommunicated Michael, the AHM has been a mess."

Lucifer froze at Nathaniel's words, his face registering a look of shock. "Shut up. They kicked Michael out?"

Nathaniel nodded. He dragged the chair from the side wall to the desk and settled himself into it. "Yep. 'Crimes against angeldom'," he said, hooking his fingers in airquotes as he stated the charge. "Last I heard he was living in a little village in some Scottish moor."

Lucifer threw his head back and erupted into a burst of laughter, his chest convulsing with each peal. Wiping a tear from his eye, he looked back to the Rolodex and continued to flip through the cards. "Who's running things now?" he asked.

"Lamechial."

Lucifer pooched his lips and shrugged. Promoting Lamechial to the head of the AHM made a strange sort of sense. He always had an unnatural fascination with keeping the house in order. It figured they would drop him in charge after the way Michael spiraled out of control. "How are things going here?"

"Just trying to maintain business as usual," Nathaniel said. As he spoke, Lauren sashayed next to him, placing her hand on his shoulder. She leaned over him, her hip brushing against his arm and grabbed a letter opener from the pencil cup on the desk. Turning, she sat on the corner of the desk and cleaned under her fingernails, shooting the occasional glance at Nathaniel. He grew increasingly more uncomfortable as Lauren showered him with attention. Clearing his throat, he continued. "Making sure the shipments get out on time. That all the vices are in order."

Lucifer smiled and slammed his hand on the desktop as he pulled a card from the Rolodex. He dropped the lid on it and pushed it to the side. Grabbing the phone, he held the receiver between his ear and shoulder and dialed the number from the card.

"Who are you calling?" Nathaniel asked.

"The angels."

"What? Why?"

"Belial's back. And he's pissed."

CHAPTER 29

"All we need is a couple of days," Twilana told Braddock as he secured the door to the prison cell. Her eyes were trained on Trodoro lying curled up into the bottom bunk and snoring loudly. Braddock stared at her contemptuously and fastened the keys on his belt.

"Don't know why I should give you any time. This scum here confessed to you, didn't he?"

"He didn't confess a thing," Michael said as he stood in front of the desk. "He has no idea where the girl is but we do think she's alive."

"You shouldn't be entertaining his drunken lies." Braddock pushed past them, rounding the desk and pulling out the chair. "That boy is guilty as sin and will hang from the end of a noose."

"But what if we can find the girl?" Twilana pleaded. "Bring her back. Won't that prove that he's innocent?"

Braddock considered for a moment. "I suppose it would. But he ain't innocent."

Twilana dropped her face and shook her head. *He's as stubborn as an ox.*

"But you know what," Braddock said as he lowered himself into the chair. "I had to reschedule his execution until noon tomorrow. You do whatever you feel you need to do but if you don't have concrete evidence by noon, he'll meet his sentence."

"That only gives us less than day," Michael said, his face scrunched up in frustration. "How are we supposed to…"

Braddock raised his hand. "Noon tomorrow. Take it or leave it."

Twilana met Michael's gaze before turning back to Braddock. She nodded. "We'll take it."

"Good. Now get out of my office."

*   *   *   *   *

Twilana and Michael walked in silence through the town. They watched as a trio of dirty, raggedy children played Tag in the streets, shouting at each other. The children looked up at them as they passed, their eyes wide with wonder.

"How are we supposed to do anything in sixteen hours?" she asked, frustration dripping from her voice. "We don't even know where to begin!"

"It doesn't matter," Michael said. "We have no grounds to argue with him." His eyes swept the streets, examining the buildings as they shuffled along. He watched as a woman came through her front door and poured a bucket of dirty water into the ditch that ran the length of the road. She looked up and locked eyes with Michael, her face twisting in a nasty grimace. She thumbed her nose at him and turned back into her home, slamming the door behind her. Michael sighed and looked over at Twilana. "Besides, what difference does it make? We just need to find the shard. This Trodoro isn't really our concern."

Twilana stopped and faced him. "How can you…? He's being tried for murder because a girl disappeared after finding a piece of the Onyx Blade. If it weren't for us, the Blade never would have fractured, that piece never would have landed here and that girl would still be with her family. We are responsible for…"

"For saving the universe!" Michael's face turned red and his eyes narrowed. "Had we not done…had *you* not done what you did, everyone would have disappeared. Lucifer put us in this position. You had no other choice."

Twilana held his gaze. "That doesn't mean he deserves to die. He's innocent and we're both sure of that." She paused, blinked twice and turned away from him. "Besides, at least we have more than half a day. What harm does it do to try to find the shard before then?"

Michael dropped his head and sighed. He continued

walking, leaving her where she stood. "Fair point. Though I think it's a fool's errand."

Twilana jogged to catch up to him. "Maybe it wouldn't be if we could figure out where to start."

Michael gave her a smile. "Remember what I said about the Blade's residual energy? If we use that to trace it to its source, get a bead on it, we might be able to open a portal and follow it."

Twilana threw her hands up in frustration and released an exasperated sigh. "Again... Where. Do. We. Start?"

"Do you ever pay attention?" Michael asked with a smirk. "Trodoro said he was drinking, so..." He pointed up. Twilana tilted her head back and looked up at an old, moldy sign hanging above them. A frothy beer stein had once been painted on the wood in bright, vibrant colors but had long since faded through the years. "We start at the tavern."

The irritation on Twilana's face slowly faded, changing into a grin. She looked over at Michael, then back up to the sign, then back to Michael and shook her head. "OK, I'll give you that one," she said as she pushed her way into the tavern.

CHAPTER 30

The tavern was dark, as far as taverns go. A few oil lamps were bolted to the walls, their flickering light doing little to illuminate the room. A large chandelier hung from the center of the ceiling, the spokes holding the remains of candles that have long over-served their purpose.

Michael looked around at the few patrons sitting at the old, crumbling tables. Many of them looked like they'd been there for hours, taking their meals in the form of whiskey or ale. Turning to the bar, he spotted a heavy-set man rolling a large cask to the back of the room. His head was ringed with a horseshoe of gray hair and his face pock-marked with a large scar running down his left cheek. He wore a blue button-down shirt, the fabric just barely holding around his ample midsection. The sleeves of the shirt had worn so thin they'd become almost transparent.

Stepping up to the bar, Michael slid himself onto an empty stool as Twilana sidled beside him, leaning her elbows on the bartop. Feeling a cold wetness soak through her shirt, her lip curled and she reared back. She examined the sticky wet spot her sleeves had sopped up.

The bartender hefted the heavy barrel onto a shelf against the wall and turned, spotting Michael and Twilana. Wiping his hands on the front of his pants he shuffled over to them, grabbed two mugs from beneath the bar and placed one in front of each of them. "What can I get for you?" he asked, the rasp of his voice making the question sound like a belch.

"Two ales would be fine," Michael said. The bartender nodded and, grabbing the mugs, shuffled back to the barrel. He pulled the spigot and a stream of pale yellow liquid flowed into the mugs. Wiping his forehead with what remained of his shirt sleeve, he waited until the mugs were nearly full. Turning, he hobbled back to Michael and Twilana, a cascade of foam overflowing from the mugs and down his fingers. He placed the drinks on the bar and Michael fished a silver coin from his coat pocket, sliding it to him. The bartender picked it up and gave Michael a nod before limping off to the other end of the bar.

Twilana grabbed the mug and pulled it closer. "So, what now?" she asked, taking a sip. She grimaced at the taste of the warm, bitter brew. The ale reminded her of her time with Aaron, specifically of how they'd wound up in a place called "a bowling alley" where Aaron taught her the intricacies of the sport. Once that lost its appeal, they spent the rest of the time drinking. That is, up until Michael and the angels arrived and tried to kill them.

Twilana glanced over at Michael, recalling the incident vividly. A flash of apprehension flared within her, making her wonder if his newfound tranquility was real or if it was just an act. She shook her head and sipped the ale, scowling at the rancid taste and her own mistrust.

Michael looked up at her, a line of foam across his upper lip. He wiped it away with the back of his hand before reaching down to pull the Blade from her pocket. He placed it on the bar and listened to the faint buzzing it made as it vibrated against the beer-stained wood. "We're still picking something up."

Twilana placed her hand on the dagger. "But it's a lot weaker than it was earlier."

Michael shook his head. "We don't have much time. The energy is dissipating. We'll need to hurry while we can still track it."

Twilana grabbed the Blade and turned to face the tavern, leaning her back against the bar. She grasped the hilt of the dagger tightly, laying the flat of the blade against the palm of her free hand. The soft vibrations tickled her skin as she looked around the room. She noted the locations of the tables and benches, where each of the patrons were seated. She even took note of the puddle of beer in the center of the floor no one bothered to clean up.

Closing her eyes, she pushed herself away from the bar, cradling the dagger in her hands. She walked around the tavern, concentrating on the pulsing of the Blade. She turned left, feeling the vibrations grow weaker. As she turned right, she noticed them grow stronger.

Twilana ambled like this for minutes, blindly walking the length of the room, drawing the attention of the late evening barflies. She stopped just before stepping into the puddle of beer and opened her eyes. "Here," she announced, turning to Michael.

Shooting her a smile, Michael held up a finger and grabbed his mug from the bar. He drained the ale in one long gulp. Slamming the empty mug on the bartop, he released a soft burp from the side of his mouth and hopped from the stool.

Twilana twirled the Blade between her fingers. Grasping the hilt, she closed her eyes again and inhaled deeply. She focused her mind on a picture of the Blade, full and intact, as best she could remember it. Pooching her lips, she exhaled and slashed the Blade through the air. She felt the dagger catch into something. Her eyes snapped open, fearing that she'd stabbed a stumbling drunk but she was greeted by a flood of purple and blue light flowing over her hand. She turned to look at Michael, a pleasant grin spread across her face.

"Looks like we found it," she said. Turning back to the Blade, she wrapped her fingers around her hand and slowly dragged the dagger downwards. The hole in space lengthened, allowing more light to flow through, casting the tavern in a bright, eerie glow. The tables and floor twinkled as the light reflected off of the dried ale stains. Heads turned to her, the bar patrons shielding their eyes as the harsh light flooded the tavern.

Rising, Twilana slid the Blade into her pocket and thrust her hands into the gap before her. She spread the two halves of reality like a window curtain. She could smell the stench of burning motor oil and apple pie wafting from the abyss. A shiver ran through her as the cold air played across her fingers. Turning to Michael, she cocked her head to the side, surprised to find him astonished by the sight.

"You look like you've never seen this before," she said.

"I haven't. Not like this. Angels can transport through space but I've never seen what lies between everything. It's..."

"Pretty amazing," Twilana said, stepping back to look at the rift. She stared at it, a sea of emotions raging inside of her. She had grown tired of jumping between worlds, getting farther and farther away from her home and the people she cared for. The non-stop traveling and life-and-death situations drained the energy from her. But despite her fatigue, she couldn't help but be awed by the majesty of the nexus. Looking out at the swirling miasma, the mashing of colors and sickeningly sweet aromas, she had to admit it had been an amazing journey.

She turned back to Michael. "OK, let's get going."

Reaching down, Michael grabbed the axe handle that dangled from his pack. He untied the strap and clutched the axe at arm's length. Inhaling deeply, he looked over at Twilana and nodded. Michael closed his eyes and stepped forward, a cold tingling sensation rushing through his body as he disappeared into the purple light.

CHAPTER 31

Belial tore through the fabric of space and slammed into the ground, the rocky earth shattering from the weight of his impact. A wave of pain flowed through his body, incapacitating him for a moment. Pain was a new sensation to him; previously, his power made him impervious to pain but his time in Limbo and lack of the Blade made him a shadow of his former self. Struggling to regain the control that he sought and the prospect of never having to deal with pain again was enough motivation to find the rest of his sword. Reaching up, he grabbed a tall stalagmite and pulled himself to his feet, cradling his throbbing arm.

He sniffed the air. The odor of the room felt strange. Familiar, but he couldn't place it. The air around him was warmer, heavier, but the cavern completely dark. Holding the Blade above his head, he channeled his energy through it. The sword glowed, reflecting a bluish-purple light off of the walls, illuminating the cave just enough for him to see. It was devoid of anything save a few pebbles and cracks in the walls. Turning, he spotting a short tunnel that descended into even more darkness. He followed the tunnel using the glow of the Blade to light the way, crouching low to avoid the massive stalactites that hung from the ceiling.

The tunnel was short, ending at a wall of stone split by a long, jagged crack. Peering through, Belial saw another cavern on the other side. Red light flickered in the adjoining room. Standing as tall as the low passage would allow, the demon drew his sword back and brought it crashing into the wall, shattering it in an explosion of dust and gravel. He stepped down a steep incline and into the room, a devious smile spreading across his face.

The lingering smell was much stronger here. Belial licked his lips as he finally recognized the crisp aroma of fresh sulfur. Jets of steam shot up from holes in the floor, filling the cavern with the odor. A thin stream of magma flowed through the center of the room, super heating the cave. Belial closed his eyes and reveled in the intense heat of the room, feeling strengthened by it.

At the far end of the room, a set of rocky steps rose to a plateau, atop which sat an intricately carved granite throne. The jet-black chair sparkled in the glow of the magma, the tiny silver and white flecks twinkling. Symbols carved into the stone created an ornate pattern throughout the throne, giving it an ambiance of power and authority.

"My home," he bellowed, stretching his arms wide. He walked across the small bridge that rose over the stream of magma and lumbered up the steps to the throne. Belial settled himself into the seat and dragged his finger down the arm of the chair, feeling the familiar coldness. Placing the tip of the Blade against a boulder next to the throne, he channeled a wave of energy through the sword as he thrust it into the rock. The boulder shuddered and hummed as energy crackled all around it. Belial turned to look out at the cavern, inhaling deeply again.

"Time to rebuild my army." Closing his eyes, he lifted his arms and faced his palms toward the empty cavern. Energy shot up from his sword and raced across his body, dancing between his fingers. He flicked his wrists and the energy erupted from his hands, skipping across the floor. It struck the stream of magma and exploded, sending a spray of molten rock splashing across the cave. As the magma settled on the hard stone, Belial's energy jumped from smoldering spot to smoldering spot like lightning across rain puddles. The magma quivered and bubbled, inflating into balls of varying sizes. The balls swelled. Arms erupted from the magma spheres, scratching and clawing at the stone floor. Legs kicked out, taking purchase on the floor and standing upright. Faces formed. Eyes. Noses. The creatures growled from their new mouths, like newborns crying for the first time. The magma cooled, covering the creatures in a thick, rocky carapace.

As the final wave of energy dissipated from the room, Belial sat on his throne, looking down as his army of stone demons took shape. Fingering the jagged end of the Blade next to him, he smiled.

"And now to find the angels."

CHAPTER 32

Michael felt a bubbling of nausea as he tumbled end over end through the depths of the nexus. The swirling colored mists enveloped him, flowing over his skin and setting his nerve endings on fire before washing his entire body in ice water. His head felt like it was spinning, an intense vertigo overpowering his senses. The only thing worse than the spinning was the pounding in his head. The rhythmic drumbeat that shook his entire body. He felt his heart pounding along with the beat, turning his body into a symphony of thumping. Closing his eyes, he counted out loud, concentrating on the ascending numbers in an effort to take his mind off of the pain and the sickness. He tasted the rancid ale rising in the back of his throat and regretted his decision to finish the beer before jumping into the rift.

The back of his eyelids exploded in a barrage of stars and a flash of pain rattled his skull. He reached up and rubbed his head, massaging a fresh lump forming on his scalp. Opening his eyes, he stared up at a ceiling of dark, craggy stone and the thousands of tiny pock marks etched into the rock. He took deep breaths, steadying his heart rate and trying to calm himself. Twilana's face appeared above his, her blue hair hanging down, casting her face in shadows.

"You OK?" she asked, a concerned look on her face.

Her sudden appearance surprised him and he jumped, banging his elbow on a rock. The nausea rose up in the pit of his stomach. A sudden cramp grabbed his abdomen and he rolled over onto his side, retching up the warm ale.

Twilana covered her nose and mouth as she turned from him. She retched a few times before stepping away to avoid the stench of vomit and bile and waited for his sickness to pass.

Michael wiped his mouth and looked down at the warm puddle of puke next to him. He pushed himself up on his elbow and rose to his knees.

"Well," he said breathlessly. "That was different." He pulled the knapsack from his back and fished out the canteen. Taking a swig, he swished the water around his mouth and spit it out next to him. He recapped the canteen and climbed to his feet. The pounding in his head subsided and his heartbeat slowed to normal.

"You get used to it," Twilana replied. She placed her hand on the wall and felt the thin crevasses and tiny cracks that ran the length of it.

"Where do you think we are?" he asked, picking up his axe from the corner of the room.

Twilana shrugged. "No idea. Some kind of cave." She pulled the Blade from her pocket and held it in both hands. "But we're close. This thing is going crazy now."

Michael could hear the buzzing of the Blade from five feet away. Placing his hand on a stalagmite, he climbed the rocky spire to look out further into the cave. It was dark. He saw a few separate paths hollowed out in the walls but what lay beyond was shrouded in blackness.

"Can you pinpoint where we need to go?" His voice was hoarse and his throat hurt. He rubbed his neck to alleviate the pain.

Twilana stepped next to Michael, clutching the Blade. As she neared him, the vibrations intensified, causing the sharp edge to cut into her flesh. She ignored the drops of blood that dribbled down her finger. "Definitely this way," she said, sprinting across the cave.

Michael jumped down from the stalagmite. Raising the axe above his head, he brought it crashing down, cutting a groove in the stone floor. He made a second groove, creating a small "X" to mark their arrival spot before trotting off behind Twilana.

Twilana neared the far end of the cave and the sharp smell of sulfur burned her nostrils. She reared back, pinching her nose, her face on fire from the aroma. Tears welled up in her eyes as she crouched down, bracing herself against the smell.

"What?" Michael shouted, spotting her retreat. "What's going on?" As the words passed his lips, he caught a whiff of the stench, stopping him in his tracks. He shook it off. "You get used to it," he told her with a chuckle. Twilana looked up at him with a grimace, unappreciative of his humor.

Twilana pulled in short, shallow breaths, slowly acclimating herself to the heavy smell in the air. The pain in her nostrils faded and she stood up straight, nodding to Michael. She held the Blade in front of her and looked up at the myriad of tunnels that opened up before them.

Placing her foot into a tiny hole in the wall, she lifted herself up and peered into one of the larger openings. Looking down the shaft, she saw that it only extended three feet into the wall. She jumped down and shifted further down the line to investigate a second tunnel. Crouching low, she could see a tiny ball of light far in the distance.

"Hello!" she shouted, her voice echoing loudly in the cramped corridor. She hesitated a moment, waiting for a reply. The room was so quiet she could hear the crunching of the gravel under Michael's feet as he shifted his weight impatiently. His labored breathing. The buzzing of the Blade. She extended the Blade into the tunnel and felt the strength of the vibrations grow.

"She's down there," Twilana said, looking back at Michael. "I can feel it."

"That tunnel is way too dark. Even if it is down there, we'll never find it."

"'Her', Michael," Twilana said sternly. "We're looking for the girl."

"But it's the shard we need."

"I get that, but the life of an innocent girl is more important."

Not with how powerful this particular sword is, Michael thought to himself. He sighed loudly and unslung his knapsack, tossing it to the side. Stepping back, he hefted the axe handle in both hands and hammered the wall with the blade. Chunks of rock clattered to the floor. Michael placed the axe on the ground and gathered up a few of the chunks, carrying them to the knapsack.

Kneeling, he flipped the top of the knapsack and rummaged through it, pulling out an old sweater and a mason jar containing a viscous orange liquid. He placed them on the floor and looked over at Twilana, curling his fingers in a "gimme" gesture. She tossed the Blade to him and he caught it by the hilt.

Michael reached over and grabbed the axe, laying it across his knees. He used the dagger to saw through the handle just below the metal head. The head clattered to the ground and Michael tossed the Blade back to Twilana.

Grabbing the sweater, he laid it out flat before him. He placed the chunks of rock in the center of the fabric, laying the wooden axe handle on top. He wrapped the arms of the sweater around everything and tied them together, securing the bundle tightly.

Picking up the mason jar, he unscrewed the lid and flinched as the sharp odor hit his nose. He held his breath and drizzled the orange liquid over the sweater, allowing the wool to soak it up. He recapped the jar and stuffed it into the knapsack.

"Step back," Michael said to Twilana as he repositioned himself next to the bundle. He dug into his pocket and pulled out the book of matches. Tearing one off, he struck it, touching the tip of the flame to the sweater, igniting the liquid. The blaze *whooshed*, turning the bundle to a bright orange torch. Michael picked up the handle and passed it to Twilana.

"It's not a flashlight but it should do."

Twilana smiled, grabbing the torch from him. She crouched down and knelt on the edge of the tunnel, leaning in to light the passageway. She shifted the Blade in her pocket and lowered herself to the ground, shimmying across the rocky floor on her belly.

The light from the torch danced across the walls, casting shadows on the floor as it played along the jutting rocks. Twilana waddled further into the tunnel, the ceiling slowly rising, giving her more room to move. She rose to her knees and inched her feet under her body, duck-walking the rest of the way.

Back at the entrance, Michael knelt on the floor and watched the orange light as it bounced along the tunnel. Being alone in the dark unarmed made him feel vulnerable. As a general with the Angelic High Military, he was well trained in combat but always had a weapon on hand. Weapons relaxed him. He just hoped that nothing would creep up on him in the darkness.

"See anything yet?" he shouted, his voice echoing through

the cave. He waited a moment for a response. The flickering light in the tunnel grew fainter. Impatience getting the best of him, he grabbed his knapsack and dropped to his knees, crawling into the tunnel. He dragged his body along the rocks on his elbows, following the bobbing light far ahead of him.

He watched the ball of light turn left and disappear from sight. The ambient light slowly faded, leaving him in growing darkness. Michael's heart pounded as he doubled his pace and pulled himself through the tunnel as quickly as he could.

A bright flash filled his eyes. He flinched and bumped his head on the craggy ceiling. His eyes watering, he heard Twilana's voice.

"Hurry up. I think I found something."

Michael rubbed the back of his head, feeling the twin lumps he now wore. Cursing softly, he rounded the corner of the shaft and continued along the way. He could see the end of the tunnel a few feet ahead, the twinkling of the torch visible just below the rock. Spinning his body in the tight space, Michael kicked his feet out in front of himself and jumped down next to Twilana. The impact sent a stiff jolt up his spine.

This new cavern was smaller than the first but almost identical. The smell of sulfur also permeated the air and the walls were cluttered with an array of holes and chasms. Rays of light shined down from holes in the ceiling, provided by the sunlight winding its way through the tons of rock over their heads.

"I heard something from down this way," Twilana said, rushing off across the room.

Michael's eyes traced the walls, noticing a row of indentations in the rock. He placed his finger on the imprint, feeling his way along them. He realized there was too much of a pattern to them, their formation too angular to be naturally occurring.

Twilana turned to him, waving the torch. "Over here. There's another tunnel down here."

A grimace crossed Michael's face. "I don't like this. Maybe we should just..."

His words trailed off and he found himself unable to express his concerns. As he turned, he spotted Twilana stalking back toward him, her face stern, the Blade clutched tightly in her hand. Before he could move, she placed the flat of the blade against his forearm. The cold stone vibrated against his skin, making his arm tingle.

"Do you feel that?" she asked, her words harsh. "It hasn't vibrated this much since I found the first shard. We're so close. We just need to go a little further." She pulled the Blade away from his skin, letting her arm hang limply at her side. Her eyes bore into his, waiting for him to respond.

Michael took a deep breath and stared back at her. He wiped his hand down his face and rubbed his temples. He knew if he had any chance with the AHM, he needed the Blade. All of it.

"Fine," he said.

Tucking the Blade back into her belt, Twilana turned and rushed back toward the tunnel. Michael sighed and stepped slowly across the cavern.

Twilana thrust the torch into the passageway and the walls began to twinkle. The cavern was deathly quiet, the only sound coming from their footfalls, the vibrations of the Blade, and the sputtering of the torch. She steadied her breathing and moved as quietly as she could. Placing her fingers on the wall, she dragged them along as she walked, feeling the cold smoothness of the stone. She looked over and admired the beauty of the rocky wall, the tiny flecks of silver and white refracting the light and illuminating the tunnel in a rainbow of colors.

A cold feeling grabbed her by the chest and she stopped dead in her tracks. Leaning over, she looked closer at the stone. She pulled the Blade from her pocket and leveled it against the wall, her eyes flicking between them and noticed something strange.

The Blade was made from the same stone as the cavern.

CHAPTER 33

Gazing down upon his army of magma soldiers, Belial recollected the events of his last battle. How the AHM were able to overthrow him despite his power. He examined his strategy, trying to decipher where his plans went wrong and give the pathetic angels the upper hand. Even with the power of the Leviathan behind him, a creature composed of pure hunger and rage, a group of armed pigeons was able to best him and banish him to Limbo.

Then he remembered.

"Lucifer." He said the name with as much disdain as he could muster. His plan relied on Lucifer holding up his end of their bargain. When Belial restored Lucifer's power, the fallen angel swore fealty to the demon. Belial's mistake was that he believed him. But when the time came, Lucifer didn't hesitate to side with the angels to further his agenda.

Belial regretted not eviscerating Lucifer back at the museum.

"No matter," he said to himself. "There will be plenty of time for that." He now had the strength of fire and stone at his control. The elements were his to wield. First, he would take his army to the doorstep of the Angel High Military and make them pay for their arrogance. But their defeat wouldn't be enough. He had to do more than simply destroy the angels; he needed to wipe them from existence. After that, he would find Lucifer again and redefine the word "pain" for him.

Belial glanced down at the sword tucked snuggly in the

boulder. He pulled the fractured Blade from its sheathe. Pointing its tip at the ambling creatures below, he focused his power through the stone, sending a wave of purple energy washing over them. They froze as the energy engulfed them, immobilized by his power. The purple light changed them, strengthening their rocky exteriors. Sharp protrusions of stone erupted from their carapaces. Their limbs glowed orange as flame-kissed blood flowed through their veins. The purple energy dissipated and Belial dropped his arm to his side. Looking out over his newly enhanced army, he smiled to himself.

Rising from his throne, Belial stalked toward the edge of the plateau. He looked down at his soldiers and felt a strange sensation jolt up his arm. He lifted his sword and held it before his face, watching as the edges of the Blade vibrated wildly. He closed his eyes and focused his energy into the weapon, reading its essence. Images flooded his mind, pictures of a purple-eyed woman clutching a small yet powerful dagger.

The dagger called to Belial, reached out to him. He concentrated on it, feeling its energy lick at his mind. He could taste the familiar feeling on his tongue. Opening his eyes, he knew that his sword was pulling itself back together. Soon he would regain his full power, and would become invincible.

Belial tilted his head back and released a loud roar, his bellow echoing across the cavernous room. The shambling minions stopped and looked up at him. Tightening his grip on the sword, he raised his arms above his head.

"Go out among the caves!" he shouted to his army. "Whatever you find, destroy it! Whoever brings me what remains of my sword shall take the place as my right hand!"

A cacophony of roars rose among the creatures as they turned and rushed from the cavern. They flooded every available exit, spreading out through the labyrinth of tunnels. They pushed to get through the narrow corridors, punching and shoving each other, each eager to be the first to please their master. Belial had imbued them with obedience and they aimed to bring him that which he sought.

Belial turned back to his throne, slipping the sword into the boulder. He settled into the seat and wrapped his fingers around the arms of the chair. Leaning back, he smiled to himself.

"Soon."

CHAPTER 34

Twilana held the torch close to the dagger, the yellow flames licking at the cavern wall. She poured over the details of the stone, examining the way the white flecks reflected the light exactly like the Blade. Rubbing her knuckles against the wall, she felt the chill of the rock, the same cold numbness the Blade always exuded no matter how long she held it.

Looking over her shoulder, she cocked an eyebrow at Michael. "Do you see this? The Blade... It's the same as this rock."

Michael leaned closer to her, his eyes snapping between the Blade and the wall. He nodded. "I suppose the myths about the Blade being made from the universe were a little embellished." He turned and continued along the passage.

Twilana grimaced at his back as he walked away. She tucked the Blade into her pocket and jogged after him. "But...but how? I mean, if the Blade is just stone..."

"It's more than just stone," Michael said, turning to face her. "It's infused with energy. Belial's energy. Haven't you seen enough to realize how much that makes a difference? Given everything you've experienced: the rending of space, a blood-thirsty mass of tentacles, men with wings. Do you really think that everything in existence can be pigeonholed by set rules of physics?"

Twilana stared at him silently. His words hung between them as she tried to grasp their meaning. She had a hard time contemplating magic. Accepting its existence. Her home city of Janus was very much steeped in scientific understanding. They made long strides in technological development, using it as a way to survive the harsh surroundings of the planet. Her people needed to explain the world around them but magic contradicted that. She had dealt with people that seemed to be more than human, and many that were seemingly less, but at the end, they were still just people. Not cosmic entities bent on controlling the universe. But ever since the day Aaron and Matt appeared in her life, she had seen plenty of things that her science couldn't explain. Could these things be explained by any kind of science, or did she just need to shrug her shoulders and accept the idea of "magic" blindly? The latter made her feel very uncomfortable but given her circumstances, she didn't have the luxury of caring.

She shook her head and chased the confusion from her mind. Despite her beliefs, she'd seen what the sword can do. It didn't matter if it was magic or science; all that mattered was that they find the girl and bring her back to Braddock, and hopefully the shard as well.

Twilana rushed down the passageway, pushing past Michael, holding the torch high above her head. Squinting through the darkness, a large opening came into view. She could feel the Blade vibrating against her hip stronger than ever.

As she turned to Michael to tell him they were getting closer, a twitch of movement caught her attention. Cocking her head, she noticed something jutting out from the wall, close to the floor. She crept over to it, lowering the torch so she could see it better. It was much lighter than the cave, almost white, a stark contrast to the dark blackness of the stony wall.

Fabric crinkled in her hand as she reached down to touch it. Pushing the torch closer, Twilana saw a white dress, made of cotton and crinoline and a rush of blonde hair spilling over the top of it.

"She's here," Twilana shouted, her voice cracking with excitement.

"What?" Michael's voice was incredulous. Gravel crunched under his feet as her drew closer to Twilana.

"The girl. I found her." Twilana reached under the girl's hair and placed her fingers on her neck, searching for a pulse. Her heart jumped as she found one. "She's alive!"

"Does she have the shard?" Michael asked.

Twilana looked at him, her eyes narrowed. She shoved the

torch at him and turned back to the girl. Carefully winding her arms under the tiny body, she lifted her from the floor. Twilana brushed the hair back on her head and examined the girl's young face. Her skin was smooth, free of blemishes and a tiny nose peeked out from between her cheeks. Twilana could hear her short, shallow breathing. The dress she wore was threadbare, most likely a hand-me-down from older sisters. It had been patched in multiple places in a fruitless attempt to prolong its life.

She placed the girl's head on the ground. As she pulled her hand away, she saw that her fingers were covered in blood. "She's bleeding." Looking at Michael, she tilted her chin at his knapsack. "Do you have anything in there to help her?"

Michael laid the torch on the ground, the light dimming as the flame struggled against the stone floor. He unslung the knapsack and rummaged through it, the soft *tink* of glass bottles echoed in the tunnel. Pulling out a squat, blue bottle, he held it close to his face, squinting through the glass at what it held. Shaking his head, he placed it on the floor next to him and returned to the knapsack. He produced a jar containing a thick, white jelly and handed it to Twilana.

"Put that on her head. It'll stop the bleeding."

Twilana grabbed the jar and unscrewed the cap, letting it clatter to the floor. She stuck two fingers into the jar and pulled out a glob of the jelly. Her nose scrunched as the rancid smell wafted up to her face, like rotting cardboard and old bananas. Ignoring the odor, she lifted the girl's head with her clean hand and spread the jelly on the wound.

Gently laying the girl's head on the ground, Twilana wiped the remaining jelly on her pants and looked over at Michael, watching as he uncorked a second bottle. It was tall and thinner than the rest, partially filled with a clear liquid. He inched closer to them and waved the bottle under the girl's nose. Her eyelids shot open, revealing two clear, deep blue eyes. She looked up at Twilana, then to Michael, her face a mask of frightened confusion. Her body shook as she sat up and pushed herself away, her bare feet scrabbling against the hard stone floor.

"It's OK, sweetie," Twilana said soothingly. "Don't be afraid. We're here to help you." She reached out to caress the girl's shoulder, to assuage her fears.

The girl stared at the blue hair dangling in Twilana's face, her mouth agape. Her head moved back and forth and tiny wrinkles crinkled her forehead.

Twilana placed her hand on her chest. "My name is Twilana. This is Michael." Her voice was flat and even. She rose to her knees and extended an arm to the girl, her palm faced upward. The girl's eyes flicked to Twilana's hand. "What's your name?"

The girl relaxed at the sound of Twilana's voice, her small body unclenching slightly. Her mouth opened but all that escaped was a tiny squeak. She coughed, and spoke again. "Tabitha." It came out in a soft whisper.

"Tabitha," Twilana repeated. "That's a pretty name." She reached out and rubbed the girl's arm, feeling her cold, dry skin. "We're not going to hurt you. We just want to take you home." Twilana's hand moved down to the girl's. Tabitha slowly wrapped her fingers around Twilana's hand and rose to her feet. Turning, they found Michael rising as he slung the knapsack over his shoulder.

"What about the shard?" he asked from the corner of his mouth. "That's the reason we're here."

Twilana nodded, and crouched down in front of Tabitha, leveling her eyes on the girl's face. "We know you're scared, and you're not in trouble, but you took something. Something that wasn't yours."

Tabitha's eyes widened and her lip started to quiver. Her back stiffened and she stepped away from Twilana.

Twilana reached out and took the girl's other hand. "No, no, no. We just want to know where it is. Do you still have it? The rock you took?"

Tears welled up in Tabitha's eyes. She wiped them with the back of her hand.

"But… Papa's going to punish me."

"No, honey," Twilana said. "Papa's worried about you. He misses you and can't wait to see you again. He doesn't care if you took that man's gem."

"Really?" Tabitha sniffled as a single teardrop ran down her cheek. Twilana nodded exuberantly, a giant grin plastered across her face.

"We do need to bring the gem back, though, Tabitha," Michael said softly. "Do you still have it?"

Tabitha pulled her hand away from Twilana and shook her

head. "I dropped it," she said, pointing to the far end of the passageway. "It fell someplace over there."

Michael reached down and picked up the torch from the floor. Turning in the direction Tabitha pointed, he waved the torch but the dimming flames did little to light the tunnel. He shook the handle gently, twirling it between his palms. The fire spit and rose, giving off a little more light. Michael shot a glance at Twilana.

"Stay with her. I'll check it out."

Twilana nodded, placing her hands on Tabitha's shoulders. The girl looked up at her as Twilana stroked her hair comfortingly.

Michael toed down the tunnel, holding the torch low to light the ground. The flames sputtered and spit, sending flaming pieces of fabric fluttering to the floor. The floor sparkled as brightly as the walls, tiny white spots shimmering in the light. Moving slowly, Michael inched his way down the path, his eyes scanning the ground carefully for the chunk of the Blade.

He felt something bounce off of his boot. Crouching low, he swept his hand over the ground. Something hard grazed his finger and Michael heard it skitter across the floor away from him. He brought the torch closer and saw the shard a few feet away. Reaching out, he grabbed it and bolted to his feet.

"Found it," he shouted, rushing back to Twilana. As he approached, he noticed Twilana's eyes had gone wide and she was staring over his shoulder. He turned and spotted a trio of lights flickering at the other end of the corridor. They fluttered and swayed, reflecting off of the shining walls.

"What is that?" Twilana whispered to Michael.

Michael reached around and tucked the shard into the side pocket of his knapsack. Grabbing Twilana's arm, he gently pulled her back the way they arrived.

"I don't know, but I don't think I want to find out."

CHAPTER 35

Lucifer sat at the small white table at one of his favorite French cafés in New Eden, *Le Petit Ange*. A large red umbrella shaded him from the early afternoon sun. He chose this place figuring it would be perfect to arrange a meet with Lamechial. A public venue would prevent the angel from doing anything rash, like attacking him in the crowd of brunchers. But even if Lamechial was willing to take a few civilians as collateral damage, the café allowed Lucifer to place Lauren and Nathaniel nearby to provide some back up, should he need it.

Lifting the tiny cup from the table, he placed it to his lips and sipped the espresso, shooting Lauren and Nathaniel a glance through his dark sunglasses. Nathaniel sat back in his chair and folded his hands in his lap, looking restless as Lauren blathered on about something. She leaned forward with her elbows on the table and accentuated her story with animated hand gestures. Every now and then, Nathaniel would look over at Lucifer, painfully uncomfortable with the situation.

Lucifer smiled. He was well aware of Lauren's affections for Nathaniel. After all, it's not like she kept it a secret or anything; she would shamelessly flirt with him at any time. For a while, Lucifer had written it off as a school-girl crush. As something that would pass. He trusted Nathaniel to not make a move on his little sister. If he did, Lucifer would have to kill him. But as time went on, Lucifer's feelings about the situation changed. He wanted Lauren to be happy and he at least believed Nathaniel would not hurt her. Which wouldn't have made any difference because if he did, *she* would kill him. Painfully. He didn't bother to tell either of them about his change of heart, of course, which is why Nathaniel was so uncomfortable in her presence. Despite how much Lucifer liked and respected Nathaniel, seeing him squirm was so much fun.

Glancing over his shoulder, Lucifer spotted Lamechial at the corner of the street. He was surrounded by three soldiers dressed in combat fatigues. Angelic bodyguards. Each AHM general is assigned a guard when on Angelic duty. Usually it's only one, however. Two almost never happens. But three? Either Lamechial is in constant danger or the guy was paranoid as hell.

The soldiers had the hilts of their flaming swords tucked into their belts and they each wore heavy Carthedrial tunics, designed to repel most types of magical attacks. Magic like Hellfire especially. Lucifer smiled to himself, relishing the way Lamechial tailored his protection for him.

Lucifer watched as Lamechial scanned the crowd, the angel's eyes finally spotting him. He gave Lamechial a brisk wave and a smile. Lamechial responded with a frown and pointed to his troops, giving each of them specific orders. They scurried off, surrounding the café, and Lamechial crossed the street toward Lucifer.

Lucifer raised his foot and pushed the adjacent chair out as Lamechial approached. "Please, have a seat," he said.

Lamechial shook his head and grabbed the back of the chair, pulling it further from the table. His dark gray beard fluttered in the wind. He squinted in the bright sunlight, crinkling the wrinkles around his temples. Brushing the hair back on his head, he settled into the chair and folded his legs, leveling his eyes on Lucifer.

Leaning forward, Lucifer placed his hands on the table and shot Lauren and Nathaniel a quick glance. They both straightened their backs and fixed their eyes on him. *Good*, he thought to himself. *At least they're paying attention.*

"So what was the big emergency, Lucifer?" Lamechial asked. As he spoke, a black-vested waiter floated past the table and placed a tiny cup and saucer in front of Lamechial. The angel looked down at the cup, then back up to the waiter, who nodded and floated back into the restaurant.

"I hope you don't mind," Lucifer said. "I ordered for

you."

Lamechial reached down and grabbed the handle of the tiny cup. He took a sip, giving the espresso a curt smile before placing it back on the saucer.

"Good, huh?" Lucifer asked.

Lamechial shook his head. "Yes, it is good. But I doubt culinary delicacies are the reason you called me down here."

"Too true," Lucifer said, repositioning himself in the hard, wooden chair. Pushing his cup to the side, he leaned in closer to Lamechial. "What do you know about the Onyx Blade of Belial?"

"You mean besides how you stole it and hid it away after we imprisoned Belial in Limbo?"

"Yeah, besides that," Lucifer said with a wave of his hand.

Lamechial rolled his eyes. "Look. If you're trying to get back in the good graces of the AHM with talk of the Blade, too, then I have to say that it's entirely too late."

Lucifer leaned back and placed a hand on his chest, releasing a raucous laugh. He wiped a tear from the corner of his eye with a knuckle as Lamechial stared at him, the angel's face stoic and unamused. Lucifer's laughter continued for a moment before he realized what Lamechial said. The humor draining from his face, he leaned forward and fixed his eyes on Lamechial.

"Wait... What do you mean 'too'?"

Lamechial shot Lucifer a smirk, pleased that it was his turn to mock. "I don't see how that's any of your concern."

"See, I think it is. I just had a conversation with Belial, oh," Lucifer looked at his naked wrist, "not too long ago and let me tell you, he is not a happy puppy right now. I suppose being stripped of power and locked away for thousands of years is enough to tick a guy off."

Lamechial cocked his head. "What do you mean you spoke with Belial?"

"Ah, now you want to talk." Lucifer looked over his shoulder, spotting the waiter. He waved to him and pointed to the cups on the table, then held up two fingers. He turned back to Lamechial and folded his hands in front of him.

"Yes, I met Belial. You know about the Leviathan. How the human woman defeated it with the Onyx Blade, which was destroyed in the process. What you may not be aware of, however, is that the sword was not 'destroyed'. Only shattered. Now Belial is free from his Limbotic prison and he's looking to pick up the pieces. Literally. From what I've seen, he's got at least two shards of the Blade."

"Well, how many shards are there?"

"I have no idea. But each one he gathers, he gets stronger. I've seen it for myself. We need to do something or he'll be coming back with a vengeance."

Lamechial's eyes dropped to the table and he nodded absently as he contemplated Lucifer's warning. He reached up and stroked his long, white beard. He knew most of this from his conversation with Michael. Lucifer merely filled in a few of the missing pieces.

The waiter appeared beside them, placing two cups in front of the men, whisking the empty cups away. Lamechial pushed his saucer to the side and folded his arms on the table. "What do you propose?"

Lucifer shook his head. "Last time, it took the full force of the Angelic Military to stop Belial. But the AHM has been broken for years. You know that as well as I do. You will need my help if you have any hope of stopping him when he comes. And I am willing to offer my help. But it won't be free."

"Figures someone like you would use a situation like this as a bargaining chip," Lamechial said, disgustedly. "What is it you want?"

Lucifer flashed him a smile, showing two rows of pearly white teeth. "I want the Blade back."

CHAPTER 36

Michael held the torch low as he led Twilana and Tabitha through the tunnel. Even in the darkness he knew something was following them. He could feel them drawing closer. What that something was, however, he had no idea. He considered extinguishing the torch and finding their way back in the dark. That way the...whatever it was couldn't follow the flaming ball of light like a homing beacon. But since that would leave them effectively blind and would make moving through the caverns impossible, he decided to keep the light low and, hopefully, inconspicuous. This was a bad idea, he knew, but they had no other choice.

Looking back, he watched as two glowing figures appeared at the far end of the corridor. They were large, very tall and bulky. Their heads were oddly shaped. Boxy like, and in the center of their faces sat two glowing, red orbs. It took Michael a moment to realize those orbs were eyes and they were looking right at him. A chill ran down his spine as they began to stalk through the passageway.

"Hurry," Michael said, grabbing Twilana's wrist. He pulled her closer and handed her the torch. Placing his hand on her back, he urged her down the hallway. "Get the girl out of here."

"What about you?" she asked, her voice hushed. She watched as he slid the knapsack from his back. "I'm going to buy you some time," he said, handing her the bag.

Grabbing it, she slung it over her shoulder. She pulled the Blade from her pocket and offered the handle to him.

140

Michael took it and nodded, a hint of a smile on his face. His eyes lingered on Twilana for a moment before turning toward the creatures. Raising the Blade, he watched them as he listened to the girls' footsteps receding down the tunnel.

Michael's eyes widened as a pair of monsters lumbered toward him. Massive black things, their eyes burned brightly, as red as the magma flowing through their veins. With each step they took, the air in the tunnel warmed, wrapping Michael in a stifling blanket of humidity. Sweat dripped down his back as he tightened his grip on the hilt of the Blade, preparing himself for an attack.

One of the creatures lunged for him. He dodged left, the colossal fist missing his face by inches. He slashed at the creature, slicing it just below its armpit. Glowing red magma oozed from the wound and it released a howl of pain. Michael kicked at the creature's leg and it dropped to its knees.

He turned to find the second creature rushing toward him. Its shoulder collided with his chest, knocking him backward into the wall. Michael wheezed in pain, watching as the creature's fist came toward him. He ducked out of the way and the fist crashed into the stone above him.

Rolling to the side, Michael sprung upward. The creature pivoted and grabbed his wrist as he rose. He shrieked as the heat seared and blistered the flesh of his arm. The pain forced Michael's hand to flex and he dropped the Blade. He heard it clatter to the floor as the creature lifted his body into the air. Michael struggled in the monster's grip, twisting himself and bashing his knee into the beast's neck. It reared back, dropping to the floor. Michael reached out with his free hand and snatched the Blade, burying it into the creature's eye. Magma poured down its face as it roared in pain, clutching at its eyes.

Pain exploded in Michael's back as he fell to his knees. Looking over his shoulder, he found the first creature standing behind him, fist rearing back, preparing for a second punch. Michael leaned on his hands and kicked both feet out, catching the creature in the chest. He spun on his knees to face the beast. Grabbing the hilt of the Blade in both hands, he jumped, stabbing the creature through the chin. It froze, its arms flopping to its sides. Michael pulled the Blade from the creature's head and it fell backward, crashing on the hard stone floor.

Michael panted heavily and the muscles in his arm and

back throbbed. He heard the thrashing of the second creature behind him, listened as it punched blindly with its giant fists. Sliding around the monster, Michael buried the Blade between its shoulder blades. The creature dropped to its knees and fell on its face.

Michael stood over the lifeless bodies of the creatures, feeling a sense of familiarity as he examined the corpse. He'd seen them. A long time ago.

In a battle against Belial.

Turning, he ran down the passageway.

* * * * *

Twilana rushed through the tunnel, the light of the torch flickering dimly as the flames slowly died. Tabitha's wrist turned white in Twilana's fingers but the little girl didn't complain; she was so scared that she barely felt the pain. She struggled to keep up with Twilana but her short legs and flared skirt made running difficult.

They burst through the exit of the corridor and lunged to the side. Twilana placed her back flat against the wall and wrapped her arm around Tabitha, holding her close. She craned her head around the corner, sticking the torch back into the tunnel and held her breath, hoping to see Michael's face rushing toward them. Waiting to hear him say everything was fine. A rush of noise erupted from the tunnel, a deafening roar ringing in her ears. Twilana ducked back inside, hugging Tabitha closer to herself and counted to ten under her breath.

Moments passed and the noises waned. Twilana looked down at Tabitha, staring as the girl huddled against her hip, shivering in the darkness. She stroked the girl's hair, calming her.

Twilana stepped away from the wall and led Tabitha across the dark cavern. She heard the girl sob softly as the fear became too much to handle. Twilana crouched, bringing Tabitha's tiny face next to hers. The torch light cast dancing shadows across her cheeks, changing her platinum blonde hair to a bright orange. "It'll be OK," Twilana said sweetly. "We're going to get you home."

Tabitha stared at Twilana and sniffled. Tears streamed from her eyes and her face was ruddy and pensive. She wiped her cheek with the back of her tiny hand and gave Twilana a nod. Twilana smiled and rose to her feet, taking the girl's wet hand in hers.

Twilana waved the torch across the wall, examining each hole, searching for the one they arrived through. She thought back to when they arrived, trying to remember the height she had to jump from. Her head snapped left to right and back again, recalling the distance to each wall. Her eyes settled on the far side of the cavern, seeing a hole in the wall about the right size. She rushed across the room, unslinging the knapsack as she moved. A deafening roar echoed through the cavern and Twilana's head angled toward the noise. She stared at the darkness for a moment. Looking down at Tabitha, she watched as the little girl inhaled deeply, her trembling body going stiff.

Dropping the torch and the knapsack in the opening of the tunnel, Twilana grasped Tabitha beneath the arms and lifted her into the hole.

"Look at me," she said, picking the torch up from the passageway. Tabitha's eyes quivered as they focused on Twilana's face. "Stay here. I need to check on my friend. It's going to be dark while I'm gone but if you stay in there and keep quiet, you'll be fine."

The fear inched across Tabitha's face. "Don't leave me here!" she shouted, her body trembling.

"I won't, sweetie," Twilana said, shaking her head. She grabbed the girl's hand and gave it a reassuring squeeze. "I'll be back. I just need to make sure Michael is OK."

"Promise?" Tabitha squeaked.

Twilana nodded. "I promise."

Wordlessly, Tabitha spun herself around and crawled on her hands and knees into the tunnel. Twilana watched as the girl disappeared into the darkness, the light of the torch just barely permeating a foot into the passage. Twilana rushed back through the cavern, gripping the torch with both hands. She ran through the tunnel, her eyes ignoring the shadows on the wall.

A face materialized out of thin air, making Twilana's heart jump into her throat. She leaped back, swinging the torch like a club. A pair of hands shot up, one holding a familiar black dagger.

"Easy there!" Michael shouted. "It's me."

Twilana stared at him for a moment, her eyes falling on the red and purple welt on the side of his face.

"We need to move," he continued. He placed his hand on the small of her back and ushered her back the way she came.

They erupted from the tunnel into the cavern. Stopping for a moment, she looked around the room and noticed a barrage of flickering orange lights peeking out from the holes that lined the walls.

"What is it?" Twilana asked.

Michael looked up at the far wall and spotted the orange spots. "Trouble."

CHAPTER 37

"There's no way I'm letting you keep the sword," Lamechial said, crossing his arms over his chest.

"Then I guess there's no way you're going to win this thing," Lucifer responded, mocking Lamechial by crossing his arms and making a disdainful look. Glancing over at Lauren and Nathaniel, he rolled his eyes. He knew Lamechial wouldn't go for the idea of giving him the Onyx Blade but negotiations had to start somewhere. He also knew that he couldn't let Lamechial know that he knew Lamechial wouldn't go for it.

Lamechial looked up at the sky and expelled a loud sigh. He considered Lucifer's warnings, remembered the last battle with Belial. It *had* taken all of the resources of the Angelic High Military, and them some, to take the demon down. And as much as he hated to admit it, Lucifer had a point. The AHM wasn't at the same level as it was back then. Hell, despite Lucifer's interaction, Michael himself had been the turning point in the original battle, but he had been excommunicated. *Though if I had to*, Lamechial thought to himself, *I could always pull him back into the fold.*

"What if…" he said, stroking his long white beard. "We had something else to offer you?"

Lucifer raised an eyebrow and slowly turned back to Lamechial. "I'm listening."

The angel leaned forward and placed his elbows on the table. "The Blade. It's a powerful weapon. Too powerful, in my opinion. Since this experience showed us that the Blade can be dismantled, what if once we find it, we divide it in half? You keep one half and the AHM keeps the other."

Lucifer pooched his lips and pondered the offer. He looked down, grabbing the handle of the tiny cup and sipped the espresso. He scrunched up his face and replaced the cup on the saucer. Reaching over, he pulled a small white packet of sugar from the little holder on the table and shook it. He tore off the top and sprinkled half of the packet into the coffee, swirling it for a moment. Lifting the cup, he looked up and watched Lamechial, a swell of pride rising as he spotted the beads of sweat forming on the angel's forehead. Lucifer downed what remained of the espresso and placed the cup on the table.

"I can do that," he said. Rising from his seat, Lucifer straightened his jacket and waved to Lauren and Nathaniel. They pushed up from their chairs and wound their way through the crowd of tables and diners toward him.

"I trust you remember my associate Nathaniel and my sister, Lauren," he said to Lamechial. "They are going to assist me as I help with your little 'problem'."

CHAPTER 38

Twilana quickly surveyed the room, watching as the floating orange orbs drew closer and closer. The cavern became brighter as the creatures lumbered through the tunnel toward them. She grabbed Michael's wrist and pulled him backward, heading to the far wall. To Tabitha.

Looking down, she spotted the Blade in Michael's hand, his fingertips growing white as he clutched it tightly. "Should I be worried?" she asked, half-jokingly. Michael's eyes glanced down, the corner of his mouth curling up slightly. He flipped the dagger in the air, caught it by the blade and handed it to her. She grabbed the hilt and nodded, holding the knife closely against her forearm.

Handing Michael the torch, Twilana looked out at the far wall, scanning the holes for any sign of Tabitha. She felt a shove against her back and tottered forward, finding her footing just before she fell to the ground. She looked back at Michael, his hand against her back, moving her away from the wall. Just past him, she spotted two square heads come into view, their beady orange eyes fixed on her.

"What the heck are those things?" she asked, the fear creeping into her voice.

"Probably the same as those," he said. Twilana turned to the wall as a dozen heads popped out from the different tunnels. Pairs of glowing eyes stared down at them. Twilana's breath caught in her throat. She felt Michael's body clench as he pressed his back to hers.

One of the creatures leaped from the wall, his body landing with a *thud*. Twilana stepped to the side, raising the Blade behind her, the other arm stretched across her chest. She crouched, preparing for the creature to attack.

"Come get me, big guy," she growled. The creature sprung at her, its arm pulled back, ready to deliver a solid punch. Twilana pressed her shoulder backward, leaning into Michael as she ducked low, the blow passing over their heads. She shot up, slashing the Blade under the creature's arm. It roared as she wrapped her free arm around its face, covering its eyes. The heat from its skin singed Twilana's flesh but she ignored the pain, stabbing the creature in the base of the skull once, twice, three times. The beast fell to its knees as Twilana jumped from its back.

Michael rolled to the side of the tunnel opening as two more creatures emerged from the passageway. He reached out and grabbed one of their arms, dropping his weight and dragging it down with him. The creature tumbled to its side, falling over Michael and smashing its head on the floor. The second creature flung itself at him, snagging his shoulder. It yanked him back, shoving him against the wall. The torch clattered to the floor as Michael's head slammed into the rock, stars erupting behind his eyes. The creature held his body against the wall, his head buzzing as his feet dangled uselessly.

A blade ripped out through the darkness, tearing across the creature's throat. Steaming hot magma spilled from its neck. Its grip weakened and Michael dropped to the floor. Willing his eyes to focus, he watched as the creature's lifeless body flopped backward and Twilana's face came into view.

"Are you OK?" she asked, wrapping her arm under his.

Michael looked up and spotted another creature rushing toward Twilana. He opened his mouth to shout, to warn her, but the words failed. The creature slammed its shoulder into her back, sending her headlong to the floor. Her face smashed against the rocky ground and the dagger flew from her grip, tumbling end over end across the cavern.

Twilana pushed herself up onto her elbows, a trickle of blood flowing down her cheek. She searched the floor, trying to find the dagger but the swelling of her eye made it difficult to see. Turning, she looked back at Michael, watching as he struggled against the creature picking him up from the ground.

"A little help here," he shouted as the beast shook him. He grunted when the creature pulled him back and slammed his body against the wall.

Twilana scrabbled to her knees, crawling across the ground, frantic to find the Blade. She heard Michael's breath become labored, heard him yelp as the creature pounded its enormous fist into his body.

Crawling closer to the wall, Twilana's hands patted the floor, searching for the Blade. The torch light had all but vanished, the glowing skin of the creatures the only illumination in the cave. The light shifted, changing the way the shadows landed across the floor, making it impossible for her to focus.

Twilana's fingers brushed against something cold. Almost frigid. Reaching out, she felt a sharp prick cut her finger, causing her to jerk her arm back. She slowly extended her hand again, placing it on a long, jagged object. The familiar cold rush spread through her palm.

The Blade! Her mind cheered and her heart pounded. Wrapping her fingers around the hilt, she shot to her feet. Looking toward Michael, she watched as the creature slammed him against the wall one final time before tossing him to the side.

Michael landed on the ground with a grunt and struggled to crawl away as a second creature joined the first, slowly stalking toward him. Rolling onto his back, he lifted his hands and faked a sheepish smile.

"Maybe we can talk about this..."

The first creature roared, its head snapping back as it raised its fists high in the air. Twilana lunged, emerging from the darkness. Wordlessly, she buried the Blade into the creature's chin, its shout fading as the glowing red magma flowed down its chest. She pulled the Blade from the beast and stepped backward as its limp body fell to the floor. The second creature turned to her, bellowing as it rushed her. Twilana stepped sideways, slashing at its belly. A gash opened in its side, fiery blood gushing from the wound. She stepped behind it and stabbed it through the back. The creature fell to the floor as Twilana pulled the Blade free, molten magma dripping from the tip.

"Let's go," she said, watching Michael struggle to his feet. She ran to the far wall as more creatures emerged from the tunnel.

Sliding the Blade into her pocket, she grabbed Michael's

arm and pulled him closer. He reached up and clutched the end of the hole in the wall, lifting himself into it. Twilana bent down and grabbed his legs, pushing him higher. She watched as his feet disappeared into the tunnel before climbing the wall to follow him.

Michael raced through the passageway on his hands and knees. His vision was blurry and blood poured from his lip. His body burned like hell but he ignored the pain. He needed to move, to get out, to try and find a way home. Looking back, he hoped to catch a glimpse of Twilana but the raging darkness prevented him from seeing anything. As he crawled farther, a few details came into view.

"We're almost there," he whispered. He heard no response but the scuttling of the gravel that covered the floor let him know Twilana was still close. Michael spotted the end of the tunnel and spun himself on his butt, inching closer to the edge. He pushed off the wall and landed on the hard, rocky floor. Turning, he spotted Twilana's face emerge from the tunnel. He reached up, offering her a hand. She threw her legs over the edge of the shaft and grabbed him, jumping down.

"Where's Tabitha?" she asked, looking up at Michael.

A voice rose from the blackness. "Is that the little whelp's name?"

Twilana's and Michael's heads snapped toward the voice as a rush of orange light flooded the room. Before them stood Belial, surrounded by a cadre of fire demons. His massive arm was wrapped around Tabitha's body, his hand covering her face. She looked tiny as he clutched her close to his chest, her feet kicking against his hip. Her hands pulled at his fingers as she struggled to free herself, her muffled screams echoing in the cavern.

Belial looked at Twilana, spotting the Blade in her hand. His lips curled into a devious smile. "Thank you so much for bringing back my sword," he said. He turned to Michael. "And it's especially nice to see you again, General."

CHAPTER 39

Belial leveled his finger at Twilana and Michael. Three of the creatures leaped toward them, their arms outstretched. Twilana spun in front of Michael, slashing the Blade across the belly of the nearest creature. Its stomach split open and it tumbled to the ground, twitching. The other creatures stepped over their fallen comrade, their hands grasping for Twilana. She slashed and hacked as they reached out for her, slicing their arms and faces. Michael backed away from the melee, pressing his body against the wall as Twilana's attack came precariously close to him.

Michael felt a tug on his arm, pulling him to the side. A creature wrenched his arm up, twisting him around and slamming his face into the wall. It leaned against him, forcing its weight down on top of him. Michael struggled to free himself from the beast but the weight was too much and he dropped to his knees.

The creatures stalked toward Twilana, backing her against the wall. One of them swung at her, its massive fist barely missing her face. She ducked to the side and stabbed the Blade upward, catching the creature just below its ribcage. It roared in pain and retreated a few steps.

"Oh, don't be such a baby," Belial said, his tremendous voice splitting the silence in the room. "Just get in there and get her."

The creature looked up at Belial and nodded. Turning back to Twilana, it swung at her again, grazing her cheek. She stumbled to the side and the second creature caught her in its grip. It

151

wrapped its arms around her and squeezed, crushing her chest, forcing the air from her lungs. She raised her feet and kicked the first creature in the head, slamming it against the wall. Her momentum sent the creature holding her falling backwards, her weight crushing it as it smashed against the ground. Its arms opened and she rolled to the side, springing to her feet. She stared up at Belial as a creepy smile spread across his face.

"I see the Blade has been affecting you," he said, taking a step toward her.

"What are you talking about?" She spun the Blade in her hand, holding the flat of it against her forearm. She spread her legs, digging her heels into the floor. Her heart pounded and she was out of breath but she ignored the fatigue.

"You can't expect me to believe a human like you has the talent to do something like that. To take down my soldiers so easily." He grabbed Tabitha by the back of the neck and handed her to one of the creatures. Reaching down, he pulled his half of the sword from its sheath and held it in front of Twilana. "See that? Look familiar? The little knife you have there," he flicked his wrist toward the Blade in her hand," is a smaller part of a magnificent weapon. A *powerful* weapon."

"Yeah, I've heard the fairy tales already."

Belial's eyes went wide. "Fairy tales? I assure you, my dear, that there are no tales here. What you hold in your hands is pure, unadulterated evil, condensed down into a handy sword."

From the corner of her eye, Twilana spotted Michael tapping against the floor. The creature held his right arm firmly behind his back but his left stretched out in front of him, reaching for his knapsack. She could see his fingers drawing closer to the bag, his fingertips playing against the nylon strap. He nodded to her.

Belial lumbered toward Twilana, swinging the sword in wide circles alongside him. Twilana crouched low, her legs splayed, and placed one hand on the floor. She twirled the knife in the palm of her hand, grasping it by the blade. The sharp stone dug into her fingers causing trickles of blood to run through her fingers. Belial watched her curiously as she allowed the knife to cut into her flesh.

"An interesting way to wield a weapon, I must say. Allow me to show you how I wield mine." Clutching the sword in both hands, he raised it over his head. His shoulders tensed and he brought the blade down on Twilana. She spun to the side and windmilled her arm. The hilt of the Blade cracked against Belial's sword. The attack knocked him off balance and he lurched backward.

Michael's fingers wrapped around the nylon strap of the knapsack. He dropped to his side and swung the bag back against the creature, slapping it in the face and knocking it against the wall. Michael heard a *pop* as he pulled his arm free from its grip and rolled away. Rising to his feet, he lowered his head and ran toward Belial, grabbing the demon around the waist. Belial slammed against the floor as Michael's weight landed on top of him.

"Go!" Michael shouted. "Grab the girl and get out of here."

Twilana pivoted to face the creature holding Tabitha. She grabbed the hilt of the Blade with her left hand and balled her right to staunch the bleeding. She leaped, burying the Blade between the creature's eyes. Tabitha dropped from its grasp, whimpering as she landed on the stone floor. Twilana kicked off the creature and dropped to the ground. Reaching down, she scooped the girl up into her arms.

"Are you OK, honey?" she asked softly. Tabitha nodded and smiled, a small bruise already forming on the side of her face.

Twilana closed her eyes and spun on her heels, slashing the Blade in a large arc. The air split and a gust of wind blew across the cavern. A bright light emanated from the vortex, the swirling miasma casting the room in its purple haze. Twilana looked over at Tabitha and found the girl wide-eyed in astonishment as she stared into the vortex.

Belial grabbed Michael's face and tossed him across the room. He slammed against the wall, his right arm hanging uselessly by his side. He looked sideways and spotted Twilana standing in front of the portal. Summoning what remained of his strength, he flung the knapsack at her. It landed at her feet in a slump.

"Get out of here," he said. He words were weak, his breath failing him.

"Stop them!" Belial shouted, leveling a finger on Twilana.

The shrill voice snapped her from her trance. Turning, she spotted a trio of creatures running toward her. She reached down, hooked the Blade around the strap of the knapsack and ducked into the rift. As she disappeared into the nexus, the vortex sealed behind her, closing her off from the creatures.

Belial watched as Twilana vanished into the ether. His face contorted into a vicious sneer and he raised his arms above his head and bellowed, a scream of rage so intense that it shook the walls of the cavern. As the last vibrations of his shout died away, he looked around at his soldiers standing silently, their heads hanging in shame. He hobbled over to Michael, looking down on the angel's limp body, his grimace replaced with a cold, evil smile.

"I may not have gotten the Blade," Belial said, reaching down and grabbing Michael by the throat, "but at least I got myself a consolation prize."

CHAPTER 40

A hole tore through the ceiling of the tavern, pouring swirling purple smoke down into the room. Twilana appeared in the center of the smoke, spat out like a mouthful of rancid milk. She fell, slamming into the corner of a bar table. As she landed, she wrapped her arms around Tabitha, shielding the girl as the heavy oak table flipped over and landed on her leg. Twilana groaned, placing her foot on the edge of the table and pushed it to the side.

"Are you OK?" she asked Tabitha. The girl nodded and crawled from her arms. Climbing up to her feet, she turned around and bent over Twilana, offering her help. Twilana smiled and reached up, taking the tiny hands into her own and rising to her knees. Tabitha looked up at her with big blue eyes.

"We made a mess here, didn't we?"

A sharp laugh erupted from Twilana's chest. As she looked down at the girl, emotion welled in her. Tears flooded her eyes as she was struck by Tabitha's innocence. Twilana knelt down and grabbed the girl in a warm hug.

Twilana's eyes flicked to the hole in the ceiling. She watched as the miasma swirled overhead, the flickering blue and purple lights flashing like strobes hitting a disco ball. Holding her breath, she waited for Michael to appear, hoping to see his prone body slam into the floor as hers had. She watched nervously as the hole slowly stitched itself up, extinguishing the lights and leaving them in near darkness. Twilana's eyes remained glued to the black ceiling, the happiness she'd just felt being replaced with an

155

overwhelming sense of loss.

"Don't you dare move," a voice shouted from the darkness. Twilana placed her hands on Tabitha's shoulders and moved the girl back slowly. Craning her neck, she looked up over Tabitha's head and across the bar. Her eyes widened as she found the flared barrel of a flintlock rifle pointed at them.

"I told you not to move," the man said. "I will shoot you."

The room was nearly dark, the only light a few strays of early morning sun that permeated the windows. Twilana's eyes followed the barrel of the rifle toward the man holding it, recognizing the shiny bald head and thin patchy beard. His nightshirt flapped open, revealing his round belly.

A woman rushed into the room, her hair tucked up into a hairnet, her dingy sleeping gown flowing behind her. She carried a brass oil lantern, the light spilling out over the man. Twilana's eyes fell upon the dumbfounded gaze of the bartender.

The little girl turned, her eyes widening as she spotted her father. Her mouth curled up into a huge smile. "Daddy!" She ran across the tavern, her arms wide.

"Tabby?" The man's voice cracked as he watched his daughter run toward him. The gun clattered to the ground and he dropped to his knees. Tabitha jumped into his outstretched arms, hugging him around the neck. He held her tightly, picking her up off the floor and buried his face in her long blonde hair. Tabitha's mother placed the lantern on the edge of the bar and wrapped her arms around her family, tears streaming down her cheeks.

Pushing herself up from the floor, Twilana dusted off her clothes. She looked at her hand, at the gash that covered her palm. Squatting down, she grabbed the knapsack and rummaged through it, pulling out an old cotton shirt. She tore a strip of fabric and tied it around her hand. Stuffing the rest of the shirt back into the bag she spotted the small shard Michael found in the cave.

The thought of Michael made her heart flutter. She felt guilty about leaving him behind after he sacrificed himself to save her and Tabitha. Belial would surely kill him. But what if he managed to get away? Could Michael escape that place?

Twilana removed the shard from the bag and shoved it into her pocket. Grabbing the Blade from the floor, she rose to her feet and faced the bartender.

"I'm sorry for what I did to your bar," Twilana said, sliding the Blade into her pocket. She stepped toward them and felt her ankle give way. Stumbling forward, she grabbed the edge of a nearby table to break her fall. She inhaled deeply, pushing her foot against the floor to test the strength of her ankle. It felt like a sprain, which was better than a break, but still caused her considerable pain. She straightened her back and hobbled toward the bar.

The man's eyes opened and floated toward Twilana's face. He handed Tabitha to his wife and turned to face Twilana. His eyes were wet and puffy and he eked out a smile through breathy sobs. Stepping forward, he grabbed Twilana's hand, his massive paw engulfing hers and pumped her arm up and down, his smile turning into a goofy grin.

"You saved my daughter," he continued. "My little girl. Everyone had given up. Hell, even I had given up, but you risked yourself to bring her back. If it wasn't for you, I don't even..." His words broke away as he struggled to hold back the tears. He took a moment to compose himself and continued. "Whatever I can do for you, just ask. There is no favor too big."

"You don't need to thank me," Twilana said, wheedling her hand from his grip. She rubbed her fingers with her other hand, reviving the nerves that had fallen asleep from his handshake. "But right now, I need to speak with Braddock."

CHAPTER 41

Lucifer pushed his way through the revolving door of the Angelic High Military building. The lobby had changed extensively since the last time he visited, which wasn't all that long ago. Of course, his last visit did involve some widespread mayhem and the attempted destruction of the entire known universe so he wasn't in any rush to come back. Despite that, they did a great job revamping the place.

The hand-woven tapestries had been removed or, more likely, burned to ashes. The walls now sported a fresh coat of winter green paint and decorated with framed artworks from famous artists throughout the universe. Van Gogh's *The Starry Night* hung a few feet away from Carzitsian's *Portrait of Mercury as Seen from Phobos.* Lucifer noted the irony of Van Gogh's Impressionism being so close to the expressionistic style of Carzitsian and pondered if maybe a more suitable work would help to compliment both pieces. He shrugged and wondered whom he'd have to talk to about that.

As he walked toward the rear of the lobby, he found himself drawn to the fountain that sprung from the floor in the center of the room. Standing over ten feet tall, the marble construction was a memorial to the events that occurred in the building eight months prior. Twilana's stoic face, meticulously carved in the smooth, white marble, looked down at Lucifer. She held the Onyx Blade of Belial high above the defeated corpse of the Leviathan, the creature Lucifer sought to control. He felt a pang of guilt for the death of the Leviathan. Then he realized it was a blood-thirsty creature and would have happily devoured him the moment he lost control of it and the moment quickly passed.

"I can't believe they memorialized her like that," Lauren said as she stepped beside Lucifer, her voice dripping with contempt. "I mean, angels building a statue of a *human*? It makes no sense."

"Well, not to take sides or anything, but she did save the universe. That has to count for something."

"I guess, but still. What a bitch."

Lucifer nodded as he stared at the sword in the statue's hand. The black granite they choose for the blade added a beautiful stark contrast to the white marble and implied the realism of the weapon. As Lucifer stared at it, he couldn't shake the feeling that there was something off. He rubbed his thigh, feeling a sudden twitch in his leg.

"If you would please join me over here," Lamechial announced. He and Nathaniel stood in front of a row of elevators, watching the lighted numbers on the wall descend. Lucifer shook himself out of his reverie and strolled across the lobby. The elevator dinged and Lamechial stepped inside the car, holding the door for Lucifer, Lauren and Nathaniel.

An awkward silence permeated the elevator ride. Lamechial's eyes remained focused on the ascending numbers over the door while Lucifer stood next to him, his hands clasped behind his back. He looked over and studied Lamechial's face. A few white hairs strayed away from the rest of his beard and were curling up toward his ear. Lucifer lifted his hand.

"Please don't," Lamechial said, his eyes glued to the wall.

Lucifer heard Nathaniel stifle a laugh, which made him smile. A moment passed and the elevator dinged. Lamechial led the others through the doors and into a vast hallway, its lack of decoration a shock compared to the lobby they just left. There was no warm, inviting feel here. The walls were painted a dark brown and barren of any artwork. Half-moon sconces hung on the walls but their dim light did little to illuminate the long room. The floor was lined with black tiles, giving the strange illusion of falling into nothingness. Lucifer marveled at the bleak choice of decorating and wondered how he could incorporate the style into his own home.

Lamechial stood in front of a tall wooden door. A detailed carving of creeping ivy decorated the border of the wood, curling inward into the shape of serpents' heads. The heads pointed to a large, golden doorknocker placed in the center of the door. Lamechial reached up and rapped the knocker, the clapping noise echoing off the walls of the tight hallway. A moment passed and the door swung inward, allowing the group to enter.

The room was split by a long crinoline curtain hanging from the ceiling. A large fire roared on the other side of the curtain, the flames sputtering and spitting from a golden bowl. The light from the fire cast three tall shadows, silhouetting a trio of figures against the curtain.

"The Tribunal," Lamechial said, swinging his arm in a wide arc.

Lucifer looked at the shadows, his expression showing his boredom and disinterest. He'd known of the existence of the Tribunal for years; after all, they were the ones that voted for his expulsion. And despite that, he never once cared to meet them.

"Why did you bring us here?" Lucifer asked curtly.

"You know that all Angelic movements must be first approved by the Tribunal. If you're to get involved with the fight against Belial, we must have their blessing."

Lucifer chuckled softly and rubbed his chin. *Typical*, he thought to himself. "So, let me get this straight… You have a big, bad evil knocking at your front door, ready to tear the house down, and when someone offers their help, instead of just saying 'thank you', you run to Mommy and Daddy for permission?"

"It is Angelic law that the Tribunal must be prescient over each decision that includes the Angelic High Military."

Lucifer shook his head. "No wonder most of the universe are atheists."

Lamechial closed his eyes. He looked up at the shadows of the Tribunal and frowned. "You know, I can just say 'no'," he said turning back to Lucifer. "The only reason you're even here is because I'm allowing you to be."

Lucifer threw his arms up in defeat and sighed. "Fine. OK. Let's get this over with."

Lamechial faced the Tribunal and bowed low. The shadows remained motionless as he rose and clasped his hands in front of himself. "My lords. You are aware of the evil that the

Angelic High Military now faces."

"We are." The curtain fluttered as the trio of voices boomed in unison.

"With a threat as severe as this, we are in need to seek outside help. That help has come to us in the form of Lucifer and his ilk."

"Lucifer?" said one of the voices.

"What does Lucifer have to offer us?" asked a second.

"He claims to have intimate knowledge of the threat," Lamechial responded.

"Yes, most likely because he is in collusion with the enemy," the third voice said.

"Hey!" Lucifer shouted from the back of the room. Eyebrows curled in irritation, he looked over at Nathaniel. "They can't just assume that."

Nathaniel shrugged. "They have good reason to."

"But still," Lucifer said, turning back to Lamechial. "They *shouldn't* assume it." He crossed his arms petulantly and frowned.

Lamechial glared at Lucifer as he waited for the outburst to pass. Satisfied that the interruption was over, he turned back to the Tribunal. "He brings a great deal to the table: Combat experience, trained soldiers, and knowledge of the threat. But his assistance comes with a price."

"Naturally," said the second voice. "And what is this price?"

"His initial request was that we bequeath the Onyx Blade to his custody."

The shadows of the Tribunal went quiet. They looked out through the curtain, their invisible eyes focused on Lamechial. A moment passed, then two, before the Tribunal made any acknowledgement of the request.

"This is not satisfactory," the first voice said.

Lamechial nodded his head. "I am of the same opinion, my lords. However, we seem to have come to a compromise and seek your approval. Should the demon Belial be defeated and his sword commandeered, I feel that it prudent to divide the Blade in half, to keep its power from falling into the wrong hands. The halves should be separated, kept far apart from each other. Of course, the Angelic High Military will retain one half and Lucifer has agreed to take the second half as…payment for his services."

Lucifer tugged on his suit jacket, straightening the collar. He looked up at the shadows, watching as they turned to each other in silent conference. Lucifer looked over at Nathaniel and Lauren as he waited for their response.

The shadows straightened themselves and turned back to the quartet, the light from the flames making them appear larger than they had before. The first voice cleared its throat.

"We feel that there is danger in this agreement."

"But my lords," Lamechial interrupted, stepping forward. "The battle ahead of us is great and..."

"Allow me to finish," the voice admonished. Lamechial could hear the annoyance and bowed his head, taking a step back. "As I was saying, this agreement is dangerous. But we are willing to accept that danger to avoid a catastrophe with Belial. We sanction this arrangement."

Lucifer clapped his hands, congratulating their decision. Stepping forward, he looked up at the shadows. "Thank you, 'my lords'," he said mockingly. "You've made a wise decision on this. I suppose it was bound to happen eventually." Turning to Lamechial, he slapped the angel on the shoulder. "So, bossman. Where do we begin?"

CHAPTER 42

The stars twinkled down from the night sky, winking at Twilana as she followed the bartender through the streets. He led her to the village jailhouse and rapped on the old, wooden door, his meaty paw shaking with each pound. Twilana peeked through the dingy glass of the window and spotted a tiny, flickering light within. As the bartender knocked on the door a second time, she noticed a black mass move inside the room.

The door swung open, revealing Braddock standing in the threshold. He was dressed in a ratty old nightgown, his eyes bleary with sleep. He looked at the bartender through squinting eyes.

"What do you want?"

The bartender stepped to the side and Twilana took his place. She pushed her way past Braddock and into the room. He watched as she stormed over to the jail cell, peering through the bars. Her face contorted when she discovered a row of empty cages.

"Where is he?"

"Who?"

"Trodoro," she said, pointing to his cell. "The prisoner. I found the girl and brought her back. Where is he?"

Braddock furrowed his brow. He turned to the bartender standing sheepishly just outside the door. "She found your daughter?"

The bartender nodded his head vigorously, a big smile stretched across his lips. Braddock rubbed his hand down his face,

163

clearing away the cobwebs of sleep. He looked up at Twilana with a mask of astonishment.

"How?"

"That's not important." Twilana's face grew long and grim. She looked at Braddock from below her brow, staring him down like she was questioning a criminal. She took two deliberate steps toward him, placing her hand on the hilt of the Blade. "Where. Is. He?"

Braddock looked over to the jail cell. Turning, he walked toward the desk and pulled out the chair, settling himself in the seat. He picked a thick brown cigar from a humidor and snapped open the old Zippo lighter, flicking it to life. Holding the flame to the end of the cigar, he puffed three times, blowing out a heavy cloud of gray smoke. "We executed him a few hours ago."

Twilana's eyes grew wide at his words and she took a step back. "What? You told me I have until tomorrow."

Braddock shrugged. "It doesn't matter," he responded. "I never expected you to find the girl and my people demanded answers. No one will miss him. And you finding the girl? Well, at least this story has a happy ending."

The bartender walked into the room, his mouth agape. He could barely believe what he was hearing from the Captain. For years, he and the other townspeople followed Braddock because they thought he was an honest and honorable person. But to hear that he broke his vow to the woman that saved his daughter's life astounded him.

Twilana's face grew flush, her anger bubbling up inside of her. Her eyes narrowed as she pulled the blade from her pocket. She lunged at Braddock, her fury overtaking her. The bartender reached out and wrapped his arm around her waist, pulling her back. He wound his other arm under her shoulder and held her as she struggled to break away from his grip.

"You gave me your word!" she shouted, anger frothing her mouth. "I followed through with my promise and brought the girl back. I told him he would be safe."

"Looks like you broke a promise as well," Braddock chuckled. He puffed on the cigar and rose from the chair. "But what's done is done. No sense crying now. If you'll excuse me, I am returning to bed." Braddock walked to the back of the office and climbed the stairs to his quarters.

Twilana watched as his feet disappeared around a corner. With one final shove, she pulled herself free from the bartender's grasp and stalked through the door, out into the early pre-dawn darkness. The bartender rushed out behind her.

"Where are you going?" he shouted as she rounded the building. He had to jog to keep up with her, making his words come out in breathy puffs.

"Away from here," she said over her shoulder. Reaching into her pocket, she pulled the out the shard and, closing her eyes, tapped it against the tip of the Blade. A flash of purple light erupted from the stone, engulfing her. The bartender raised his hand, shielding his eyes from the flash.

As the light dissipated, Twilana looked down at the Blade, marveling at its size. She gripped the hilt tightly, feeling the power flow through her arm. Images played through her mind, terrible images of the things she would do to Braddock for lying to her. For making her break a promise to Trodoro. Closing her eyes, she inhaled deeply and pushed the thoughts away. She pictured a face that calmed her, the face of a person she cared for. A small smile crept across her face.

Her hand slashed across her chest, leaving a gash in the air. Slashing downward, she bisected the cut, revealing the void beyond. Twilana ducked low and dove into the nexus, disappearing into the miasma.

The bartender watched as the blue-haired woman vanished before his eyes. He blinked twice, staring at the hole in space, dumbfounded. After a moment, the 'split slowly stitched itself, covering the strange opening the knife made and separating Twilana from this reality.

CHAPTER 43

Belial stood next to his throne and focused his energy through the sword sheathed in the boulder. Purple lightning flashed around him. The floor bubbled as arms flailed up from the molten rock, grasping and grabbing at each other. A horde of creatures pulled themselves out of the ground. They pushed and shoved their way through the crowded cave, lining themselves along the far wall, making room as more soldiers rose up from the rock. Belial stared out at his army, his face contorted in a wicked grin.

Releasing the sword, the energy surge retreated into the Blade, sapping the lightning from the room. Belial stepped toward the edge of the plateau and stood at the top of the stairway, looking down at his army of demons. He closed his eyes and listened to their vicious growling. He could feel their anxiety, their eagerness to wreak destruction. Their hunger for the flesh of the angels and for the chance to prove themselves to their master. The wait was nearly over.

He walked toward his throne and lay his hand on the Blade, yanking it from the boulder. Crackles of energy wrapped around his hand as he admired the deep blackness of the weapon. Looking up, he raised his arms above his head, drawing a cacophony of roars that shook the walls of the cave.

"My legion!" he shouted above the din of the creatures. "The time has come. *Our* time has come. We go into New Eden to find and destroy those that opposed me. To those that locked me away. And those that betrayed me. They will know the folly of their actions. They will pay for what they've done. In blood."

Turning, he thrust the sword outward and the tip of the Blade disappeared. He walked the length of the stairway, slicing the air. Pulling back, he turned and slashed the Blade downward, slitting the horizontal gash through the middle. The folds of reality fell apart and opened a portal to the abyss of Limbo. Belial stared at the swirling purple light, recalling his long years of imprisonment. The memory fueled his anger.

Belial stepped to the side and the horde of creatures marched toward the rift. One by one, the army crossed through the nexus, disappearing into the ether. Belial smiled and turned to the throne. He walked across the plateau toward the far wall and looked up at Michael.

The angel's arms were bound to the wall by a pair of heavy iron shackles, his hands and fingers turning white as the blood drained from his limbs. He dangled above the ground, his feet a few inches from the floor. His head hung limp, his face a shattered mess of blood and bruises. He strained to see, his left eye swollen completely shut. His right ear was half-severed, hanging from a few strands of remaining flesh.

Belial drew closer to Michael and leaned in to his left ear. Grabbing a tuft of his dirty, matted hair, he pulled Michael's head back, focusing the one good eye on his face. Belial watched as the pupil danced from side to side as he tried not to look directly at the demon.

"Your friends are going to die tonight," he whispered. "Because of what *you* did to me. I think that it will be fun for you to be there." Lifting the sword, Belial hacked at the chains binding Michael. His limp body dropped to the floor and he released an audible grunt as he landed. Belial bent down and grabbed the back of his neck, dragging him across the plateau and leaped into the nexus.

CHAPTER 44

Twilana's feet smacked against the concrete sending a jarring shock up her spine. She paused for a moment, allowing her nerves to settle before rising from the ground. Looking up, she spotted a group of pedestrians gathered in the middle of the sidewalk, watching her with confusion. Her gaze passed from person to person before she gave them a quick salute and rushed off down the street. Shaking off the oddness of her sudden appearance, the crowd turned back to their lives, bookmarking the event to tell their friends over cocktails on the weekend.

Rounding a corner, Twilana studied the huge buildings that flanked the street. Monuments to man's ability, formed of steel and brick blotted out the view of the sky, reaching high up into the clouds. Sunlight reflected off of the glass windows, casting the street in a blinding yellow tint. Twilana shielded her eyes from the glare as she hurried down the sidewalk, dodging an oncoming group of fast-food coffee swilling yuppies.

A strange sense of familiarity nagged at the back of her head. She watched as cars and buses zoomed along the road, their car horns blaring at the few people that dared dart out into the crosswalk. A man leaned out of his window, shouting to a car in front of him that shot into an empty parking space he had been eyeing. Even the smell of the city seemed to elicit a memory but she couldn't place her finger on how.

Coming upon a bus stop, her attention was drawn to the plexiglass bus shelter. Like most big city bus shelters, this one was decorated with an over-sized advertisement for the latest in men's fashions, featuring a man with a chiseled angular face wearing an attractive scowl but not much else. But unlike those other men's fashions advertisement, this model had a chiseled angular face, an attractive scowl and a pair of long, white wings.

Twilana stopped dead in her tracks. *I'm in New Eden*, she thought.

Her heart raced and a smile played at her lips. *If this is New Eden, I can go to the angels for help. After all, they had the resources to stop Belial the first time.*

Turning, she watched a man in a dark blue uniform exited a McSeraph's, the gold star on his chest and nightstick hanging from his belt indicating him as law enforcement. Twilana rushed over to him, his body visibly rigid as he watched her approach. She slowed down, holding her palms in front of her.

"Didn't mean to startle you, sir," she said calmly. "I just have a question."

He placed his translucent food bag on the hood of his black-and-white and relaxed slightly. "How can I help you, miss?"

"I'm looking for the Angelic High Military building. I'm...uh...meeting my brother for lunch."

The officer looked her up and down, his gaze stopping at her hair more than once. He raised his arm and pointed behind him. "You're not far. Go down two blocks this way, catch a right on 12th, go another three blocks and it'll be on your left. Big building with 'AHM' over the door. Can't miss it." He took a sip from his styrofoam cup. "But I do have to say, you don't look much like the sister of an angel."

Twilana scratched her head and gave him a toothy grin. "Well, half-sister, actually. My mother was a throne. Anyway, thanks so much for your help."

The officer opened his mouth to respond but Twilana brushed past him and hurried down the street. She pushed through the throngs of people meandering along the sidewalk, gabbing into their cell phone and getting lost in the music blaring from their earbuds. A few shouted after her as she ran by, saying rude things and making even ruder gestures but Twilana ignored them, knowing they'd be appreciative once she saved the universe for a second time.

CHAPTER 45

Lamechial pressed the button on the wall and the thick metal door rose into the ceiling with an ear-piercing shriek. He stepped into the room, his hand searching the wall next to him for the light switch. Finding it, he flicked it and rows of fluorescent overheads sprung to life, illuminating the stacks of shelves that lined the room from floor to ceiling.

"The Angelic Armory," Lamechial stated, turning to Lucifer and his crew.

Lucifer's jaw dropped as he crossed the threshold. His eyes danced from shelf to shelf, admiring the vast array of weaponry the room held. Swords, firearms, explosives. Even blunted weapons were readily available. He started to not regret pairing with the angels for a change.

The Angelic artillery had come a long way since his expulsion from New Eden. In his day, they had to choose between a sword and a flaming sword. If an angel was lucky, he may have been able to bring a morning star or an axe into battle but for the most part, bladed weapons (flaming or not) were the standard.

Running his fingers down the cold steel of a Black Hole Generator, Lucifer tucked his hands under the gun and lifted it from the shelf.

"Not that one," Lamechial said as he sauntered past him, his hands clasped behind his back.

Lucifer dropped the weapon and craned his neck toward the angel. "Why not?" His voice had the dejected whine of a five-year-old being denied an ice cream cone.

"Quite a few reasons, actually." Lamechial faced Lucifer and looked up at the weapon. "First, the AHM only has one of those. With good reason. Secondly, special permission needs to be obtained for anyone to use the BHG. The last time resulted in the loss of two and a half solar systems. You can imagine the paperwork that was involved to explain away that little situation. And lastly, if you think there's any way in Heaven that we'll allow *you* to wield that weapon, then you truly are out of your mind." He flashed Lucifer a wide grin. "I'm sure you can find yourself something a little less destructive."

Lucifer stared at Lamechial with a frown, his brow furrowed. He huffed and turned back to the shelf, browsing the rest of the weapons. Passing a display of medieval blades, he rounded the corner to find himself among a collection of long-range energy weapons. Looking up, he spotted Lauren quietly toeing toward him. "Are you going to tell them that you have a piece of the sword?"

Lucifer ignored her question. He picked up a small black handgun and inspected it. "I don't really think it's pertinent, do you?" he said finally, his eyes focused on the gun. "After all, they do plan on giving me half of the sword anyway. What's one little, tiny extra piece?" Cocking his head, he shot her a grin as he placed the gun back on the shelf and shuffled further down the aisle. His gaze fell on a shiny, metallic cannon.

Lucifer flipped the cannon over in his hands and examined it. It had a long, round barrel, about twice the diameter of a standard shotgun. The rectangular stock featured an array of dials and buttons and no less than three lighted gauges. Lucifer turned the dials on the side playfully, pushing one of the buttons. A string of lights danced the length of the barrel and the weapon started to hum. The gun was bulky but surprisingly not heavy. He slid the strap over his head. Curling his lip in a mock snarl, he leaped around the corner and aimed the gun at Lamechial.

"Say 'ello to my little fren!"

Lamechial closed his eyes and shook his head, pinching the bridge of his nose. "Very clever," he said, his voice sarcastically flat. "I've never heard that one before. Really." Stepping next to Lucifer, he reached over and pressed the large, red button on the butt of the stock. The lights flickered and went out, the humming faded away. "And can we please not play with the destructive weapons in here?"

"So what does this thing do?" Lucifer asked, lifting the strap from his neck and handing the cannon to Lauren.

"That is a Cosmic Ray Thrower. It harnesses the power of a small sun, directing it at the enemy and tearing them apart on a molecular level. It is very dangerous."

Lauren's eyes went wide. "Dibs!" she shouted, snatching the gun from Lucifer and slinging the strap over her shoulder. She stared down at the weapon, her eyes taking in every the detail and walked off toward Nathaniel.

Lamechial placed his hand on Lucifer's shoulder and leaned closer to him. His face leveled with Lucifer's, his eyes grew serious. "Make no mistake, Lightbringer," he said with hushed tones, enunciating his words carefully to emphasize the importance of his message, "that despite our arrangement, I do not trust you. I don't trust you being in control of these weapons and once this is over, my full attention will be on you."

Lucifer stared at him, his black eyes boring into the angel's face and smiled. "Makes no difference to me. I need to protect my investments."

Lamechial's gaze burrowed into Lucifer for a moment. The room's fluorescents flickered, replaced by the pulsing flash of red lights. Klaxons blared throughout the room, starling Lamechial and making him jump. His eyes tore away from Lucifer's and he ran toward the door. A platoon of soldiers rushed down the hallway and turned toward the armory, coming face to face with their commander. The angels drew back as they spotted Lamechial emerging from the room.

"What's happening?" Lamechial asked, his voice more curt than he intended.

"It's started, sir," the angel in the lead responded, the one Lamechial recognized as Nuriel. Nuriel pushed past the general and grabbed a weapon from the shelf before rushing out. "Belial has invaded New Eden!"

CHAPTER 46

The asphalt buckled from the weight of the falling magma demons, creating spider-web cracks in the New Eden streets. The driver of an old, gray sedan cut the steering wheel, swerving to avoid running into the crack only to drive up onto the sidewalk and through the front window display of a department store. Another car careened off of the curb and spun out of control, finally stopping after slamming into one of the demons. The driver looked up into its burning red eyes, the sight filling him with terror. The creature clamped its fingers around the hood of the car and lifted it above its head, tossing it into a nearby bus shelter. The plexiglass enclosure shattered and the car crumbled like paper, trapping the driver inside.

The demons spread through the city, wrecking havoc. They shuffled down main roads and flanked off onto the side streets, destroying whatever they found. A cacophony of screams echoed through the air as a pair of demons caught up to a crowd. One of the creatures grabbed a nearby fire hydrant, tossing it into a group of pedestrians, knocking them over like bowling pins. He turned to the geyser of water spraying into the air and placed his hand on the stream, pointing it at the rest of the crowd. Steam billowed from the creature's arm as the water hit them like a truck and they tumbled over each other, slamming into the window of a fast food joint across the street. The creatures head arced back and it laughed, releasing a bone-chilling shriek of amusement.

Another creature walked out into the center of the road,

smacking abandoned cars out of its way. Kneeling, it placed its hand on the tarmac and sent an intense wave of heat flowing through it. The tar began to bubble and wisps of steam flowed from the superheated asphalt. Car tires melted and the vehicles fell into the ground, getting mired in the depths of the molten tar. Doors flew open, revealing the scared faces of a few stranded drivers. They emerged from their cars, struggling to climb up onto the hoods of their vehicles as they slowly sunk into the street. The heat from the road permeated the metal chassis. One driver, unable to stand the heat any longer, stepped down onto the ground, his ghastly shout reverberating among the chaos as the flesh burned from his leg.

A trio of demons circled around a building, tearing away at the concrete structure. Smashing the walls, they reached into the foundation and pulled the steel girders that created the building's frame. They ran out into the streets, chasing a group of unfortunate pedestrians as they fled from the chaos. The creatures laughed manically as bodies flew through the air.

Belial emerged from the nexus into the heart of the bedlam, dragging Michael's body behind him. The sight of the smoldering city made him smile, his heart racing at the fearful shouting of the panicked citizens. He lifted Michael up by the neck, holding him out and faced him toward the aftermath of the invasion.

"See what you've wrought? You are to blame for this."

Michael's eye flicked from side to side, struggling to see as the destruction unfolded all around him. The color drained from his face and his jaw dropped as he watched the chaos. The sound of screaming from every direction curdled his blood and he felt the pity rise in his chest. He had seen the results of battle, witnessed the deaths of fellow soldiers. But to watch helplessly as this carnage was inflicted on the innocent... A tear rolled down his cheek.

Belial spun him around so that their faces met, his smile turning into a deep grimace. "This is only a fraction of what I plan to do to your 'brotherhood'. And once I'm finished here, I intend to spread this pain to every known world." His smile returned and he reared his head back, releasing a deep, malicious laugh.

Gasping for air, Michael's throat quivered. His chest burned with rage. With hatred. With guilt. He pushed the pain to the side and summoned the strength to speak.

"They'll stop you." The words were choppy and raspy. But even as he said it, Michael realized that it was more of a wish than a threat.

Belial's laughter cut short, the last few chuckles mingling with the chaos. He looked down at Michael and frowned.

"You'd like to think that, wouldn't you?" He squeezed Michael's neck, causing his face to curl up in pain. Belial's frown widened and he squeezed harder. "Now, let's go find your friends," he said, dragging Michael down the street as he walked farther into the pandemonium.

CHAPTER 47

Twilana burst through the revolving door of the Angelic High Military building and froze as she looked at the lobby, barely recognizing the place. It was as cavernous as she remembered; all of the upper floors had a view down into the center of the lobby and the skylight that topped the building flooded the room with natural sunlight. But other than that, everything was completely different. Including the fountain that stood before her.

She looked up at the statue in the center of the fountain, recalling the day it memorialized. The memory was as vivid in her mind as if it had just happened, the minutest detail coming back to her clearly. She remembered the chaos that ensued after Michael and his angels crashed through the wall of the Ocularium. The stench of the Leviathan as it wriggled free from the Nexus. The fear she felt watching Aaron and Matt disappear, knowing she'd never see them again. Her heart felt heavy as she recollected that day, remembering all that she lost. All that was taken from her. It was hard to believe that the angels decided to commemorate that day with a statue in the center of the lobby. A statue of her, nonetheless. Although, she had to admit to herself that the marble was exquisitely carved and captured her likeness perfectly. She reached up and placed her hand on it, feeling the cold realism of the stone

A sudden trembling on her hip broke her reverie. She pulled the Blade from her pocket and felt it throb in her hand. Looking up at the statue, her eyes fell on the black granite blade in the figure's clutches. The white spots in the stone twinkled as the sun shining through the skylight reflected off of it. But there was something different about this stone. Something that didn't quite feel right about it.

Using her free hand, she grabbed one of the Leviathan's stone tentacles and climbed up onto its back, an eerie feeling of déjà vu flooding her hippocampus. She wrapped her arm around the statue and pulled herself to her feet. Reaching up, she tried to touch the granite with the tip of the Blade.

"What do you think you're doing?" the voice rang through the quiet lobby, startling her. She jumped back, her foot slipping on the slick marble of the statue. Twilana's hand shot out and she grabbed one of the tentacles, the Blade dropping from her grasp and clattering to the floor. Turning, she found a stout man with a thick, white beard, his stern eyes staring at her. His hands were placed firmly on his hips and his mouth curled into a frown. Long, white wings twitched gently behind him.

"I...I'm sorry," she stuttered as she scrambled down the side of the statue. Bending down, she grabbed the Blade from the floor and tucked it into her pocket. She strode around the fountain to face the angel and extended her hand courteously. "My name is Twilana and I need to speak with the general of the AHM."

Lamechial's eyes widened and his mouth dropped as he recognized the woman before him. He'd seen her face almost every day as he walked into the building but never had the honor of meeting her in person. Realizing his demeanor, he closed his eyes and shook his head. He stepped forward and reached out, wrapping both of his hands around hers. "Oh, I know who you are. It's a pleasure to meet you, my lady. A pleasure and an honor. My sincerest apologies for frightening you like that."

"No, it's my fault," she said, gently pulling her hand from his grasp. "I shouldn't have been climbing up on the statue."

"Well, without you, that statue wouldn't be here, would it?" He reached up and stroked his beard, his eyes boring holes through Twilana's face. "None of us would, in fact. So I suppose a modicum of leniency is allowed in this case." Lamechial gave her a goofy grin.

Twilana's eyebrows arched and she cocked her head. "Right. Anyway... Who can I speak to?"

Lamechial clapped his hands, suddenly remembering her

request. "Yes. The general. Well, you are speaking with him. My name is Lamechial, Fourth Degree Archangel and appointed Commander General of the Angelic High Military." He extended his arm for a handshake. Looking down at his hand, he remembered that they'd already gone through those pleasantries. Clearly his throat, he lowered his arm and clasped his hands behind his back.

Twilana rubbed the back of her head, her face feeling flush. This angel didn't look like much of a Commander General. In fact, he looked like he hadn't seen combat in quite some time, if at all. He seemed more like a politician instead of a field leader, like the top brass that she had to deal with on Janus. Despite his flaws, Michael had the tactical skills to put together a proper military strike. It was clear that after the incident with Michael, whoever was in charge at the AHM decided to place a leader that wouldn't question their authority. Someone they can dictate their orders to. Someone they felt would be easily controlled. That's when it occurred to her that this man was *exactly* like the top brass that she had to deal with on Janus.

"OK. Well, then, I suppose you're the one that I need to talk to. Anyway, there's the huge demon and he's coming. Here. I think. I don't really know for sure, but he's big and powerful. He's got Michael. I hope. He could be dead but I don't know. What I do know is that he's got an army and he's really pissed off and…"

Lamechial watched Twilana's mouth as it moved but couldn't keep up with her rambling. Closing his eyes once more, he raised his hands. She stopped talking. "Let's start from the beginning," he said.

"We don't have time," she said, panic entering her voice. She pulled the Blade from her pocket. "Belial. The guy who owns this sword is coming. Here." She pointed the tip of the Blade at the floor to punctuate the last word.

Lamechial looked down at her hand. He reached out to touch the Blade but she pulled her arm back. "What are you doing?" she asked brusquely.

Lamechial gave her a gentle smile. "I must request that you surrender that weapon to me. It belongs to the Angelic High Military."

"I don't think so, pal," she said, tucking it behind her back. "I got this from Lucifer when he tried to summon the Leviathan, who got it from Belial. At some point, I think. Anyway, nowhere in that chain of custody was the AHM so I have no intentions of giving it up right now. It saved my life a few times already and I suspect that it's got a few more to go before it's done."

Lamechial sighed. He stroked his beard, his eyes lingering on her face. "Very well. But I must ask you to come with me. We know about the arrival of Belial and have begun our counter attack."

Twilana's brow furrowed in confusion. "How could you possibly know about Belial? The Ocularium was destroyed months ago."

Lucifer's voice wafted through the air. "I told them."

CHAPTER 48

Twilana lunged at Lucifer, her knuckles turning white as she tightened her grip on the hilt of the Blade. Seeing him grinning at her caused the anger to well up in her chest, bringing forth a flood of emotions she'd worked hard to suppress. Memories of the destruction of the Ocularium and the loss of her friends. Of the exile she'd had to endure and being cut off from the whole of civilization. Her suffering grabbed hold of her mind and she lost control of herself.

As her feet left the floor, Lamechial swooped in and looped his arm around her waist. He lifted her and spun her body around, putting himself between her and Lucifer. He grabbed her Blade-wielding arm and held it in place, his eyes boring into hers. She struggled to free herself from his grasp but each time she moved, he tightened his grip. Twilana felt his fingers digging into her wrist, placing pressure on her radial nerve, causing her hand to go numb.

"I need you to calm down," Lamechial said to her soothingly. He nodded in rhythm to her breathing, regulating her anger and relaxing her. "Believe it or not, Lucifer has brought us vital information and he and his team will be helping us stop Belial."

"You can't possibly believe that," she said, gritting her teeth. She lifted her free arm and leveled a finger on Lucifer. "*This* is the guy responsible for nearly destroying the entire universe less than a year ago. He destroyed the Occularium because of his petty gripe with Michael. And you're just letting him walk in here and have free reign of the place?"

Lauren stepped next to Lucifer, her face turned up into a scowl. Lifting the Cosmic Ray Thrower, she flicked the switch near the trigger-guard and the weapon hummed to life. "Want me to take care of her?" she asked, her mouth twisting into a smile.

Lucifer chuckled and waved his hand to her. "No, dear sister," he said, "but I thank you for being concerned for me." He stepped toward Twilana, his hands raised, palms facing her. "I don't blame you for not trusting me. I know I've done a lot of questionable things in the past. But this time is different."

"How's that? Because you're embarrassed that a big, pissed off demon may succeed where you failed?"

Lucifer smiled, cocking his head to the side. He tugged his earlobe and looked over at Lamechial, his face pleading with him to help her see reason. The angel nodded and turned back to Twilana.

"Belial is possibly the most dangerous threat the universe has ever known," Lamechial said. "He was barely defeated the last time he tried to take power. And we need all the help we can get, which is why we've let Lucifer and his ilk into the fold, despite his past transgressions. Belial threatens the ways of life of all of creation. We could really use your help as well, considering you have part of the Blade."

"Wait a minute," Lucifer said, locking his eyes on Twilana. "You have part of the sword?"

Twilana glared at him. She lifted the Blade and held it up, tightening her grip on the hilt. Lucifer tilted his head and whistled. Pooching his bottom lip, he nodded. "Not bad for a human. That must be how you wound up here."

Twilana nodded. "Here, and a few other places. I found Michael as well."

"Ah, Michael," Lucifer said. "How is the old man?"

"Not well considering Belial beat him and took him captive. He may even be dead by now for all I know." She allowed her words to trail off, her chest growing heavy once more with grief. Her eyes burned into Lucifer as the silence hung between them. Shaking her head, she looked over at Lamechial. "Fine. I'll help, even if it means working with him. But this doesn't change things between us."

"No, I wouldn't imagine it does," Lamechial replied. "But

we're glad that you've made a decision because there's one little flaw in your warning. Belial isn't coming. He's already here."

A set of double doors swung open at the far end of the lobby, slamming into the wall and echoing through the cavernous space. A platoon of angels flooded the room, each well-armed and well-armored. Diverging into groups of four, the soldiers spread out across the lobby, barricading and securing the entrances of the building. One of the angels headed straight for the electrical closet. Tearing the panel from the wall, he pulled the levers that controlled the building's power. The overhead lights died and a row of red emergency lighting sprung to life.

Twilana watched as the angels hunkered down, holding their positions. Her stomach churned, the fingers of fear spreading through her chest. If Belial was in New Eden, did she arrive too late? Could the angels stop him? If not, would her part of the Blade be enough to allow her to?

She inhaled deeply and counted to three, calming her nerves. Looking out through the front doors of the lobby, she watched as the sun slowly settled over the city. She turned back to Lamechial and forced a smile.

"So, what's the plan?"

CHAPTER 49

Belial looked up the side of the building and stared at the letters over the entrance. At the three gilded letters that mocked him, reminded him of what the Angelic High Military did to him. Squinting through the tinted plate glass that lined the front of the building, he tried to peer inside. The room behind the glass was dark, punctuated by flashing red lights, making it impossible for him to see what lie beyond. He released Michael's neck, letting the angel slam into the sidewalk before pulling his sword from its sheathe.

Michael tasted the blood as it pooled in his mouth, felt a broken tooth scrape the inside of his cheek. He turned onto his back, the movement sending a wave of pain throughout his body. Leaning his head on the curb, he looked up and watched as Belial grasped his sword in both hands, heaving it over his head. A purple glow emanated from the weapon, slowly slinking down his arms, washing over the demon's body. As the energy touched him, it changed him. His armor expanded, creating thick plates that sprung out of the joints, enhancing its strength. A dark brown helmet grew from his shoulders and engulfed his head, a black visor, exposing only his glowing green eyes. Two massive horns curled from the helmet, protecting the sides of his face. The purple light dissipated and Belial looked down at Michael.

"Like the armor?" he asked with a chuckle. "I had plenty of time to think of the new design while I was locked in Limbo." Stepping back, Belial walked toward the edge of the building and faced the street. He raised the sword in the air, the Blade creating flaming trails of energy behind it as it moved. The creatures all looked to Belial and lumbered toward him. He waited as they approached, holding out his arms and halting them.

He pointed to a group of creatures and motioned to the far end of the building. They released a massive roar and shambled down the street, disappearing around a corner. Belial faced another group and pointed to a nearby alley. They roared and shuffled away into the darkness. He looked at his remaining army. Nodding, he turned and walked toward the revolving door at the front of the building, the creatures following closely behind. He glared down at Michael, the glow of his eyes intensifying.

"Are you ready for the show to begin?"

Belial placed the tip of the Blade to the ground. Red sparks erupted from the concrete as tendrils of energy reached out across the sidewalk, winding their way under the front windows of the building. He dragged the Blade across the ground, slicing the concrete. Stopping, he looked down at the fissure and walked back toward the center of the line. He grasped the sword in both hands and thrust it deep into the crack. The ground shook and cracked before breaking away in large chunks, dropping into a massive chasm between the AHM building and the rest of the city.

He rested the Blade on his shoulder and reached down, grabbing Michael by the throat. The angel's hands shot up and clutched Belial's wrist as the demon lifted him from the ground. He held Michael up to his face, the green eyes boring into the angel's.

"Now comes the fun part." Pulling Michael back, he launched him across the sidewalk. Michael's body went limp as he flew through the air, pain exploding throughout his body as he crashed through the front window of the lobby.

CHAPTER 50

The window exploded, sending a shower of shattered glass across the lobby. Twilana lunged at Lamechial, wrapping her arms around his waist and pulling him to the ground. She lifted her arm to shield her face from the falling glass as it covered their bodies.

An eerie calm settled over the room as the final shards tinkled to the floor. Twilana pushed herself up on her elbow, wincing as tiny slivers of glass dug into her forearm. She shook out her hair and looked over at the front windows, spotting Belial standing in the street. His body glowed orange in the setting sun and his head was drawn back, his chest convulsing. She listened to his sadistic laughter and a chill ran down her spine.

She lifted herself up onto her knees and slung her arms around Lamechial, urging him up to his feet. Glancing over her shoulder, she watched as Belial raised his sword and pointed it at her. She saw that he looked different than he had before. Larger and more imposing. She felt the cold fingers of fear in her chest again.

A wave of Belial's soldiers launched themselves through the window, flooding the lobby. Their arms flailed as they rushed into the building, spreading out and surrounding her and Lamechial. Pillars of light flared all around her as the angels ignited their flaming swords. They attacked, clashing with the creatures, fists against flame.

One of the creatures rammed the statue of Twilana, shattering it with its broad shoulders. It lifted the base of the

185

sculpture from the floor and tossed it across the room. The heavy stone slammed against an angel as he flew into battle, knocking him down and pinning him to the ground. The creature growled and laughed as it watched the angel's body twitch against the stone, the life draining from him.

A door leading to the stairwell opened and a trio of angels burst into the room. They raised their energy rifles and opened fire, unleashing a barrage of green blasts across the lobby. One of the creatures took a blast to the face and flopped backwards.

"We need to get out of here!" Twilana shouted as the crackling energy winged over her head. She ducked, pushing Lamechial low to avoid the crossfire. Grabbing his wrist, she pulled him behind a tall stone column.

"I didn't expect the attack so soon!" he shouted. His body shook and his eyes darted from side to side. He examined the chaos, watching each of his soldiers being knocked back by the onslaught of demons. "We weren't prepared for this." He leaned his back against the column, slowly sliding down until he sat on the floor.

What a leader, Twilana thought to herself as Lamechial broke down next to her. Peeking around the column, she spotted a demon racing toward her. She grabbed Lamechial and prepared to jump from the creature's path when a bolt of energy struck its chest. It roared in pain and flew backward, cracking the marble tile as it crashed to the floor.

"What kind of firepower do you have here?" she asked, looking down at Lamechial

"Lots," he replied, his pathetic eyes looking up at her. "Some of the most powerful guns in the universe."

"I need something. I can help here."

"We need to get to the armory, then," he said. His eyes flittered across the lobby, settling on the bay of elevators. Placing his hand on the column, he pulled himself up. A giant fist smashed into the column and the white marble exploded, knocking Lamechial from his feet. He collapsed to the floor, his chin smacking against the tile.

Twilana spun on her heels to find one of Belial's creatures bearing down on her. It towered over her, its beady red eyes focusing on her face. Its stone cheeks twitched into what she imagined was a smile. The creature raised its fist and brought it smashing down. Twilana leaped to the side, tucking into a roll as she hit the floor, barely avoiding the attack. Raising the Blade, she grabbed the creature's arm and stabbed it just below the shoulder. The creature roared in pain and bucked backward, swinging its arm wildly. Twilana clutched tighter and climbed further up its forearm, shoving the Blade into the monster's chin. It went silent and stumbled forward. Twilana jumped from its arm as it collapsed to the floor. Leaning down, she grabbed the hilt of the Blade and struggled to free it from the creature's skull, carefully avoiding the fiery hot magma that dripped from the wound.

A pair of hands grabbed her shoulders, pulling her body back as a fist came crashing down in front of her. Looking up, she spotted Lamechial standing over her. His body shook and his lip quivered but he settled his gaze on her. She gave him a nod and rolled to her feet as a second creature charged her. Twilana kicked the beast in the stomach and it reeled backward, grabbing the crumbling pillar as it fell. She spun to her feet and kicked again, knocking it in the back of the head. Its face slammed into the remains of the column as Twilana rolled onto its back. Reaching over, she pulled the Blade from the dead soldier's skull and plunged it between the shoulder blades of the second creature.

Twilana looked up and spotted Lamechial backed against the wall, his eyes and mouth wide. She rushed to his side and grabbed his arm.

"The armory," she shouted, pulling him from his stupor. "Now!"

He nodded and led her across the lobby toward the bay of elevators. He slapped the button on the wall and listened as the machinery sprung to life. A long moment passed before the doors parted. Lamechial threw himself into the elevator car, followed closely by Twilana. Pressing the button marked "A", he flattened his back against the side wall and pinched his eyes shut, waiting for the doors to close.

The elevator car jolted as it climbed the building. Twilana looked over at Lamechial staring at the lighted numbers on the wall. "So, what do we do now?"

He stroked his beard absent-mindedly as his body trembled, not acknowledging her presence.

"Hey!" she shouted. The angel jumped, his eyes widening. He turned to her, giving her a confused stare. "I need to know what you plan to do here."

Lamechial nodded furiously. His eyes were glassy and his hands fidgeted with his tunic. "Right, right. A plan. We need a plan." He looked up at the numbers over the door, his attention completely gone from Twilana.

She rolled her eyes as the elevator dinged. The doors opened, revealing the barrel of a large weapon aimed right at her. Twilana jumped to the side and held the Blade before her. The barrel tilted back, revealing Nathaniel's surprised face.

"What the hell are you doing here?" His long black wings fluttered as he lowered the gun and stepped back.

"Big, bad demon threatening the universe," she said, brushing past Lamechial as she walked out of the elevator. She slipped the Blade into her pocket and stood face to face with Nathaniel. "The angels need me because I have part of his sword. Now that you're caught up, where's the armory?"

Nathaniel hooked a thumb toward the far end of the hallway. She sprinted past him, her long strides closing the distance in seconds. As she reached the door, she jammed the button on the wall with her fist and waited for it to open. Tense moments passed and she looked down at the control pad, pounding the butt of her hand on it repeatedly, growing increasingly annoyed with the door's stubborn insistence to remain closed. She raised the Blade and pointed it at the control panel, giving it an angry look.

A soft hand landed on her arm, pushing it down. She glanced up at Lamechial standing next to her. He smiled and shook his head. Placing his thumb on the control pad, a thin green light scanned his fingerprint and the panel beeped, raising the door up into the ceiling. Lamechial stepped to the side to allow Twilana to enter.

Twilana bound through the threshold and the lights sprung to life. Her eyes went wide as she looked out into the vast room lined with shelf after shelf full of weapons. She walked the aisles, her eyes scanning the different guns, swords, and artillery at her disposal.

"You weren't kidding when you said you had lots," she said, running her finger along the black barrel of an energy rifle.

Lamechial simply nodded as he stood at the front of the room, his hands clasped behind his back, watching Twilana stroll the armory.

"I need power," she said, picking up a gun and weighing it in her hand. It had a single barrel and pump action, like a Remington shotgun, but the barrel was about half a foot shorter than a Remington. It was made from a light plastic alloy and weighed less than a pound. Twilana held the gun to her shoulder and looked through the sight affixed to it. Shaking her head, she placed it back on the shelf and moved toward the next rack. "And accuracy, too. I'm good, but I want to make each shot count."

Lamechial opened his mouth but Nathaniel's words cut him off. "Why are you bothering with any of these?" He leaned against the doorframe, the barrel of his gun resting on his shoulder.

Twilana lifted an armored vest from a hook on the wall. She pulled the sweater from her body and tied it around her waist. Slipping into the vest, she zipped it up to her neck and flipped open the pockets on the breasts. "Are you not aware of what's going on downstairs?" She grabbed a handful of explosives from the shelves and tucked them into the pockets, hanging a few from the straps along the bottom of the vest. "Big, angry monsters looking to bring this place down around our ears. So instead of asking stupid questions, you'd be better off finding some more ordinance to help stop him."

Nathaniel rolled his eyes and pushed away from the doorframe. He walked softly down the aisle, watching as Twilana slipped her hands into a pair of padded gloves. She looked up as he approached, staring into his dark brown eyes.

"That's not what I mean. What I'm asking is why *these* weapons? These are nothing compared to the power you already have."

Twilana's head cocked to the side, her brow furrowing. Nathaniel continued. "That Blade on your hip. It's one of the strongest weapons in the universe. Even broken like it is, that piece contains more firepower than anything else in this room. You say that you need a powerful weapon. You've already got one."

Her eyes lingered on his mouth as he spoke, watching the way his soft lips moved with each word. She placed her hand on the Blade and felt the cool stone reverberating against her fingers. Pulling it from her pocket, she held the hilt tightly, tracing the broken corners of the stone blade. She thought back to her time in the foreign jungle, remembering the sharp stone she tied to it, how she used it to hunt. The sword had grown quite a bit since then, the length of the Blade about the size of her forearm. But Nathaniel had a point; it did have power. More than just being able to open portals in space. Every time she held the Blade, each time she clutched the handle, she could feel its energy surging through her body.

Looking up at Nathaniel, she clutched the Blade in both hands and held it close to her chest. She closed her eyes, pushing all of the thoughts from her mind, allowing her consciousness to be enveloped in deep blackness. A rush of warm air brushed over her body, blowing her hair back.

Nathaniel stepped backward as Twilana's body was lifted off the floor by a gust of wind. He and Lamechial watched as a bright purple light radiated from the Blade. She hovered motionlessly in the air and the glow engulfed her, covering her from head to toe. The light grew more intense, forcing Lamechial and Nathaniel to turn away and shield their eyes.

The light hardened, forming a thick, pulsing shell around Twilana. Her eyes snapped open, her face frozen. Her head flopped backward and her mouth opened wide. She looked like she was screaming but no sound escaped the bubble. The shell flashed violently, pushing Lamechial and Nathaniel against the wall.

Twilana's feet dropped to the ground, the boots making a resounding *thud* against the metal floor. Her eyes were wide, and her arms hung limply at her sides. She clutched the hilt of the Blade tightly, turning her fingertips white. Looking up at Lamechial and Nathaniel, her eyes floated between their shocked faces. They watched the swirling irises of her eyes change color, the purple slowly becoming a vibrant violet, reflecting the power that flooded her body.

Looking down at the Blade, she felt her hand tingle, a surge flowing up her arm and into her chest, spreading out across her body. She smiled at Nathaniel.

"Let's go."

CHAPTER 51

Lauren stood next to Lucifer as he crouched behind a pillar at the far end of the lobby, the Cosmic Ray Thrower tight in her grip. She flipped the red switch next to the trigger guard and the weapon hummed. The lighted gauges flashed from red to yellow to green, showing the power level was fully charged. Lauren turned the dial and the humming intensified. She pivoted on her heels, aiming the weapon toward the entrance and pulled the trigger.

A wave of green energy erupted from the barrel and rocketed through the lobby, colliding harmlessly with the front doors. The recoil from the weapon sent Lauren backwards, squealing as she landed ass-first on the tiles.

"Weren't expecting that, were you?" Lucifer asked with a chuckle.

Lauren gave him a dirty look as she pushed herself to her feet. "At least I'm trying," she said, aiming the gun into the lobby again. Leveling the weapon at a group of advancing creatures, she braced herself and pulled the trigger a second time. The green energy shot from the Cosmic Ray Thrower and rippled through the demons. They froze in their tracks, their heads thrown back and arms hanging at their sides. Screams of pain tore from their throats as the cosmic energy ripped their insides to shreds. Their skin erupted into flames half a moment before they exploded in a geyser of fiery blood and body parts. Lauren smiled and looked down at Lucifer.

"Can I keep this?" She giggled and fired into the lobby again.

Lucifer glared up at her. "I'm glad you're having a good time," he said. He peeked out around the pillar and watched as an Angelic soldier faced off against two creatures. The soldier fought deftly, attacking quickly and blocking their blows with his flaming sword. He pivoted to face one of them and drove the sword into the center of its chest. It roared and fell backward as the second creature swung at him. The angel ducked beneath the punch, rolling away from the attack. Springing to his feet, he slashed at the creature's stomach. The skin parted and magma flowed from the wound. It fell to its knees as the angel dropped his arms to his sides, panting heavily. The first creature clambered to its feet and lunged at the angel. He leaped back to escape but the creature grabbed his wrist and yanked, tearing his arm from the socket. The angel screamed in pain as the creature wrapped its fingers around his face. It lifted him from the ground and slammed his skull against the floor. The angel's body went limp and his sword clattered across the tiles, landing a few feet from Lucifer. The creature released a horrible, guttural noise before turning to find more angels to kill.

Lucifer dropped to his knee and reached for the sword. His fingertips fell on the pommel of the hilt, the sword just out of his reach. He wiggled his fingers, working the blade closer to him. It moved a few inches, allowing Lucifer to wrap his fingers around it and pull it closer. He tucked his body safely behind the pillar and grasped the sword in both hands.

"What do you intend to do with that?" Lauren asked, shooting him a quizzical look. "Give Belial a mani/pedi?" One of the creatures sprung toward her. She turned and fired a blast of cosmic rays into its face, ducking as a puddle of goo splashed to the floor next to her.

Rolling his eyes, he extended his arm and flicked his wrist. A column of flame sprung from the hilt. He could feel the heat on his face as he stared at the fiery blade. Flicking his wrist again, the flames receded. Though a flaming sword wasn't as powerful as a Black Hole Generator (he *really* wanted a Black Hole Generator), it was better than having no weapon at all. Dropping the hilt to his lap, he heard a soft *clink* rise from his pants. Puzzled, he reached into his pocket and placed his fingers on a cold, round object. He pulled it from his pants and held it in front of his face.

The Sphere of Ancaarta.

With everything that was happening, Lucifer had forgotten about it. Grabbing the handle of the sword, he placed the Sphere against the pommel. He closed his eyes and concentrated, sending a thick stream of Hellfire through the Sphere. It began to glow, absorbing the hilt of the sword into itself. As the glow receded, Lucifer looked down at the Sphere that replaced the sword's pommel. He smiled as he rose to his feet and rounded the pillar.

Lauren watched in confusion as Lucifer sauntered toward the center of the lobby. "What the hell are you doing?" she shouted.

Ignoring her, Lucifer focused his attention on a trio of creatures running toward him. Their hands balled into fists, they growled and snarled as they approached. He smiled and flicked his wrist. The flaming sword sprung to life, the Sphere intensifying its power. The blade was longer, the fire burning hotter than before. The white light rolling off the sword nearly blinded Lucifer. He held the weapon before him, his eyes fixed on the creatures.

Spotting the flaming blade, the group of demons stopped in their tracks. Their feet scrabbled backward, looking for purchase on the slick, cold marble. Lucifer crouched low and leaped into the air, flipping over them like the hero in a kung-fu movie. As his feet hit the ground, he pivoted on his heels and swung at one of the creatures. The blade sliced clean through its neck, melting its skin.

The other demons watched as the head bounced along floor, the two red eyes dimming to black as the life drained from them. One of the creatures looked up at Lucifer as he brought the fiery blade crashing down onto its head, cleaving its skull in two. The flames roared as its flesh caught fire, crackling and spitting in the heat. Lucifer tugged at the blade but the heat fused it to the creature's bones. He placed his foot on its chest, pushing the carcass from the sword.

The last demon reached out and grabbed Lucifer's arm. With a massive tug, it pulled him off the floor and punched him in the stomach. Lucifer gasped for air as his lungs deflated. He reached up and struggled to pry the creature's fingers from his arm but the beast swung again. Lucifer lifted his feet and kicked off its chest, lurching free from the attack. Reaching out for the creature's face, he dug his fingers into its eye sockets. It shrieked as Lucifer's fingers liquefied its beady red eyes. Tossing him to the side, the creature clutched its face.

Lucifer skidded across the hard floor, his chest burning as he struggled to breathe. Turning onto his stomach, he scrambled across the tile toward the sword still lodged in the monster's face. Climbing on top of the creature, he pulled at the blade, cursing as it refused to budge. His hands grew raw from the engraved metal digging into his flesh. Inhaling deeply, Lucifer wrapped his fingers around the hilt and twitched his wrist. The flames retracted into the handle, freeing the sword from the creature's corpse. Lucifer laughed to himself and sprung to his feet.

Spinning, he found the third creature barreling down on him, its arms flailing wildly, ocular fluids dripping down its face. Lucifer lifted the handle of the sword and flicked his wrist again. The flames burst to life, impaling the creature through the stomach. Its arms flopped to its side and it fell to its knees as the point cleaved its abdomen. Lucifer flicked his wrist again, recalling the flame.

"Lucifer!"

The voice echoed against the high walls of the lobby. He looked around, trying to find its location but the lobby was engulfed in darkness, his vision impaired by the bright light of the sword. He squinted, spotting a dark silhouette near the front windows. Though he couldn't see the speaker, he recognized the rasp.

He took two steps toward the windows. The ruckus had quieted, the floor littered with the bodies of angelic soldiers and Belial's beasts, shards of concrete and plaster dust. Lucifer kicked a chunk of black granite that lie near his foot, watching as it skipped across the tiles. Lauren padded her way toward him and looked up, her eyes falling on Belial.

"I hope this was worth it, monster," Lucifer said. "A lot of good people died here."

Belial's head reared back and he broke into a laugh. He placed his hand on his stomach and his chest shook. Wiping a tear from his eye, he straightened his back. "Are you going soft on me, Lou? There was a day when you and I would have competitions to see who could rack up the higher body count."

Lucifer nodded and looked over at Lauren. Her face was red, her eyes filled with tears of laughter. Lucifer chuckled. "Yeah, I know. But since I'm playing for the good guys today, I figured I needed to sound like a hero."

"Don't. It doesn't become you." Belial held his gaze on Lucifer, tilting his head to the side. "My offer still stands, Lou. Join me and you can be my right hand man."

Lucifer's face scrunched, mockingly musing Belial's offer. He shook his head fiercely. "Nah."

"Good. Because I was really looking forward to killing you."

"I don't think so," Lucifer said, placing a hand on his hip. "After all, there's no way you'll have that much power."

A curt laugh erupted from the demon's throat. "Oh, you're on a roll today." He raised his hand, the Onyx Blade glittering in the fading sunlight. "I have the sword. I have the power."

"You have *part* of the sword. A big part, I'll grant you…"

Lauren leaned closer to him. "That's what she said," she whispered. Lucifer brushed her away, trying to stifle the smile on his face.

"…But it's far from complete. And I have a feeling that you'll never finish assembling it."

Belial's green eyes narrowed. "Oh, yeah? What makes you say that?"

Lucifer reached into his pocket and pulled out a shard of black rock, holding it between two fingers.

"Because you'll need this piece first."

CHAPTER 52

Lucifer raced across the slick marble floor with Lauren trailing just a few steps behind. Looking over his shoulder, he spotted Belial's army, their long, heavy strides quickly closing his marginal lead. He turned a corner and rocketed down the hallway toward the heavy metal door of the stairwell. Lucifer threw his body against the crash bar and the door swung open, slamming into the concrete wall. Lauren ran past him, launching up the stairs two at a time as Lucifer grabbed the door and slammed it shut. Flicking his wrist, he ignited the sword and held the flame close to the hinges. The soft aluminum melted, fusing the door to the frame. Turning, he rushed up the stairs after Lauren.

* * * * *

Belial watched as his army rounded the corner at the far end of the lobby, his guttural growl reverberating off the walls. He roared and punched a nearby column, pulverizing the marble. The stone crashed to the ground as a twitch of movement caught his attention. Turning, he stepped closer to a crumpled bundle lying on the floor and smacked the heap to the side with the back of his hand.

"Oh, good. You're still alive."

Michael's clear eye stared up at the demon, his chest quivering as he breathed heavily. He pushed his palms against the stone floor, slowly inching away from Belial. Belial placed his hand on Michael's head, the sharp fingers of his gauntlet digging into the angel's skull.

"I have a need of you," Belial said as he closed his eyes and squeezed his fingertips into Michael's forehead. He flexed his hand around the sword, concentrating his power through his body and funneling it directly into the angel's mind. Using the power of the Blade, Belial rifled through Michael's parietal lobe, tapping into his memory center. He rummaged through the mental pictures floating through Michael's brain, absorbing the memories of the building's layout from the angel's time as leader of the Angelic High Military.

Michael opened his mouth to scream as a thousand hot knives pierced his skull but the sound caught in his throat. He could feel his synapses firing rapidly, his thought processes and memories being violently torn apart. His body tingled and went numb, his arms and legs seizing as Belial turned sections of his brain to mush. He closed his eyes and tried to ignore the pain, putting up mental barricades to keep Belial out of his secrets but he was too weak. Belial kicked his way through Michael's thoughts like a burglar scrounging around a house for priceless jewels.

The pain overloaded his brain and Michael's body went limp. Belial's eyes snapped open, a grim smile spreading across his lips. He dropped Michael to the floor and turned, spotting a group of creatures huddled in the corner. He walked over to them and watched as they knelt over a fallen angelic soldier, teeth ripping the flesh from his bones. One of the creatures tore the angel's wing from his back and threw it over his shoulder.

"You three!" Belial shouted, leveling the Blade at them. The creatures shot to their feet and stared at him. "Search the upstairs. I want Lucifer brought to me now."

The creatures roared, slapping their chests before fanning out across the lobby. One of them sped toward the bay of elevators and punched the wall. The button lit and the elevator doors spread. The creature jumped into the empty car and slapped the buttons on the panel, watching them light up as the doors closed.

The other two creatures ran toward the far end of the lobby, heading down the hallway to the stairwell. Belial watched as they disappeared from view. He stepped to the center of the lobby and looked up at the atrium far above him. The sun had set, casting the building in darkness, save for the red emergency lights that blinked steadily. Belial stared up at the moons hanging in the sky, watching as the stars twinkled through the skylight. His eyes flitted down, landing on the railing of the top most floor. Sifting through the memories he gleaned from Michael's brain, he knew that this floor housed the Tribunal. He also knew that if he wanted to bring the AHM down around itself, this was the place to start.

Raising the Blade over his head, Belial closed his eyes as energy crackled through his body. His backplate began to bubble and burst into flames, the fire tearing through his armor. A pair of jet black wings emerged from his back, unfolding to twice his height. He slowly flapped the wings and globs of fluid splattered across the floor. Beating his wings harder, faster, Belial's feet lifted from the floor. Lowering his arms, he rocketed up the height of the building, his thoughts set on taking out the Tribunal.

CHAPTER 53

Twilana rushed from the armory, the Blade clutched tightly in her hand. Her body bristled with the cosmic energy and she felt stronger. Gone were the fatigue and hunger that plagued her for months. She felt invigorated.

Her brain throbbed with a thousand voices; she could hear the thoughts of everyone around her. Angels, seraph, the disjointed ramblings of the creatures in the lobby. Closing her eyes, she leaned against the railing and focused her strength, pushing the voices to the side. She sifted through them, searching for one voice. One particular mind.

Images flashed on the back of her eyelids. A pane of glass came rushing toward her, a pair of shining moons surrounded by a thousand stars. She felt her back muscles stretch and contract, the pain weaving its way across her chest. A vision of herself came into view, her matted blue hair covering her face. Twilana's eyes shot open and she looked down over the railing, spotting the dark figure of Belial rushing toward her.

"He's coming!" she shouted over her shoulder to Lamechial and Nathaniel. Pivoting on her heels, she sprinted down the hallway toward the elevator.

Lamechial turned to Nathaniel. "What just happened back there?"

Nathaniel cocked his head to the side, squinting his eyes. "Really? They put *you* in charge of the AHM?" He watched as Lamechial nodded. "Then shouldn't you know about the Onyx

199

Blade?" Shaking his head, he raced after Twilana, leaving Lamechial alone in the armory.

Twilana reached the end of the hallway and leaned over the railing. Looking down onto the lobby, she watched as Belial rose through the air. The sword in his hand crackled with purple energy, his eyes glowing green with hate. Twilana stepped back from the railing and crouched low. She bit the edge of the Blade, holding it between her teeth. Kicking off her front foot, she launched herself in the air and grabbed the railing. Her body weight settled into her arms as she pushed off the bar. Flipping, she turned her body to face Belial as he flew toward her.

Gliding through the air, she untied the sweater from her waist and held the arms in each hand. Her eyes bore into Belial as she fell, glaring at him intently as she bit into the cold stone of the Blade.

Belial's eyes went wide as Twilana draw nearer, marveling at the energy crackling all around her. His wings stopped beating and he hovered in the air, watching as she plummeted toward him. He slashed the sword, the point of the blade passing harmlessly beneath her.

Twilana swung the sweater in an arc, wrapping it around Belial's head. She snatched at the free arm and pulled them both, tightening the sweater around his neck. He choked, his air cut off as the fabric crushed his windpipe, grabbing at the sweater with his free hand. He lost his balance when she slammed into him, her body weight dragging them down. Flapping his wings, he was able to keep them from dropping to the lobby floor. She wrapped her legs around his waist and snatched the Blade from her mouth, plunging it into his back just beneath his collarbone. Belial roared as the knife tore through his flesh, black blood oozing from the wound. His wings went slack as his concentration slipped and they began to fall through the building.

Nathaniel leaned over the railing, watching Belial's wings wrap around their bodies as they plummeted. Hearing a loud crash from behind him, he spun, spotting Lucifer and Lauren emerging from the stairwell. Lauren ran over to him as Lucifer lit the flaming sword, melting the hinges to the frame of the door. Satisfied, he turned and sauntered toward the railing, leaning over to gaze down at Belial.

"Is that...?" Lucifer asked.

"Yup." Nathaniel replied.

"Is she...?"

"Yup."

"What the hell happened?"

"She figured out how to use the Blade," Nathaniel said. "She's harnessed the power and thinks she can take him down."

"Can she?" Lauren asked.

Lucifer watched as Twilana gave Belial a right cross to the chin, a flash of purple light erupting from her fist as it smashed into the demon's face. He shrugged. "Sure looks like she can."

*   *   *   *   *

Belial reached down and grabbed Twilana by the hair, pulling her away from his body. He felt the Blade slide from his back and his blood gushing between his shoulders. Twilana pivoted and the sharp stone bit into his wrist, severing the tendons in his hand. It went limp and she jerked her head free, grabbing the horn on the side of his helmet as she fell. She pulled her body up, driving her knee into his face. He heard the *crunch* of his nose shattering.

Twilana looked down and watched as the floor raced up to meet them. She grabbed the horn on the other side of his helmet and placed her feet on Belial's chest. Locking her eyes on his, she blew him a kiss and kicked off his body, flipping gracefully through the air.

She landed softly as Belial slammed into the floor, opening an enormous crater beneath him. The Blade tumbled from his hand and clattered across the tile. His wings twitched, fluttering weakly, the impact of the fall paralyzing them. His chest convulsed as he gasped for air.

Reaching out, Belial placed his hand on the floor and pulled himself from the crater. He rolled to his side and his head lolled toward Twilana, his eyes struggling to focus. His lips curled into a smile.

"Did you," he began, his words short and ragged, "think that would stop me?" His eyes scanned the room for his Blade. Twilana lunged at him, sliding across the tile and kicked his arm. He dropped, cracking his chin against the floor. Balling his fist, he rolled onto his back and slapped Twilana on the hip, knocking her away. Dazed, she watched as he launched himself to his feet and swooped down to grab the Blade. He pivoted on his heels to face her.

"I won't stop, you know," she said, lifting herself to her knees. She placed a foot on the ground and drew the blade behind her back. "I'm going to take you down."

Belial smiled, clutching the sword in both hands. "You can try." He leaped forward, swinging the sword down on top of her. Twilana juked to the side, the tip of his Blade slicing the tile beside her. She rabbit-punched him in the knees and his leg buckled. Pushing up on her foot, she jumped into the air and punched him in the side of the neck. His head snapped sideways. He slashed at her legs, forcing her to jump back and narrowly avoid the tip of the Blade.

"You are an impressive fighter, I'll give you that," Belial said as he rose to his feet. "It's been quite some time since I faced an opponent that could keep me on my toes. But, like everything else, this will end with my victory." He pounced, swiping for her head. She stepped to the side and slashed at him, the cut careening off of his gauntlet. Spinning, he punched her in the stomach, just below her ribs, forcing the air from her lungs. She dropped to her knees, wheezing. Belial backhanded her across the face, sending her sprawling to the ground.

Belial looked down on Twilana as she lie on the floor, struggling to breathe. Stepping closer, he sneered as he kicked her in the side. Her body trembled and he kicked her again. Then again. He laughed as he heard her chest crunch, her ribs crumbling from each blow.

He crouched down and grabbed a handful of Twilana's hair, pulling her head up. Placing the tip of the sword to her neck, he dug the cold stone into her flesh. A trickle of blood rolled down her throat as he stared into her bruised and puffy face.

"You got in way over your head, little girl. But if it's any consolation, I am sorry that I have to kill you."

Rising to his feet, he lifted Twilana's battered body off the ground by her hair and threw her like a ragdoll. She slammed into the far wall, pain flooding her chest as she struggled to breathe. Her shoulder burned as she pushed herself up from the floor. A sharp buzzing rang through her skull. She rubbed her ear and shook her head but the buzzing continued to rattle her.

Looking to her right, she spotted her dagger lying a few feet away. Next to it lie a chunk of black granite, the stone she spotted in the hand of the statue of her. Squinting, Twilana watched as both the Blade and the granite vibrated in sync. It finally dawned on her why she was drawn to it earlier. The sculptor didn't use granite to emulate the Onyx Blade; he used an actual shard of the Onyx Blade.

Digging her fingers into the tile, she dragged herself across the floor. She could hear Belial's chuckling as he placed the sword on his shoulder. His footsteps crunched as he neared her, his massive feet crushing the shattered marble that littered the floor. She peered back at him, watching as his glowing green eyes stared down at her.

"Had enough?" he cackled, sauntering closer.

Turning back to the Blade, she reached out, her fingertips glancing off of its pommel. It spun on the cold tile, settling inches from her grasp. She looked back at Belial, watched as his face turned from delight to terror. He raced toward her, his arms pumping at his sides, his hand tightening around his half of the Blade.

Mustering the last of her strength, Twilana lunged for the Blade as Belial kicked at her. His foot landed on her hand as her fingers wrapped around the hilt, sending a wave of pain through her arm. She winced at the blow but held tightly to the dagger. He lifted his foot and stomped but she rolled clear, his foot crashing down onto the tile. She rose to her knees and looked over the floor, searching for the chunk of granite. Her heart pounded in her chest, her anxiety growing heavy as she realized she'd lost sight of it. She glanced up and watched as Belial turned to her, his face twisted in anger.

Belial clutched his Blade in both hands and heaved it over his head. Twilana dropped backward, crab-walking across the floor as the demon drew closer to her. Her hand came down on something sharp and a cold pain spread through her palm. Wrapping her fingers around it, she picked it up and slapped it against the Blade. She closed her eyes as an explosion of purple light flashed through the room.

Belial flew backwards, the flare knocking him into one of the remaining pillars. He bellowed in pain as an intense wave of heat engulfed his body. The pain dissipated and he rolled to his side, pushing himself up on his elbow. He stared up at Twilana skulking toward him holding the Blade tightly in both hands.

A bright purple glow surrounded her, healing her wounds. It slowly transformed into purple armor; a translucent chest plate, gauntlets and helm covered her entire body. She stood over Belial, legs splayed and placed the tip of the Blade against the floor. She looked down at the demon.

"What were you saying about killing me?"

CHAPTER 54

The flash of light erupted through the building, forcing Lucifer to turn his head from the railing and shielded his eyes. He felt a warmth envelop his body and his skin started to tingle. His eyes burned as the light bled through his hand and penetrated his corneas. As the flash dissipated, Lucifer blinked wildly, stars dancing in the middle of his vision. He shook his head and looked over at Lauren, hunched over the railing, her attention turned back to the lobby. He chuckled to himself as he spotted the pair of dark Ray-Ban sunglasses covering her face.

Lucifer leaned over the banister and watched as Belial lie on the floor. Twilana stood over him, her fingers wrapped around the hilt of the Blade. She moved slowly. Precisely. Lucifer watched Twilana's lips move, straining himself to hear the words, but was too far away.

"It may be time for us to go," he whispered, glancing over at Lauren.

"Huh?" she said, pulling the Ray-Bans from her face. Her brow furrowed in confusion.

"We need to leave," he repeated. "Now."

Lamechial sidled next to him and leaned his elbows on the railing. He clasped his hands together, staring down at Twilana. "I don't think so, Bringer of Light. You promised your assistance. You'll see this through. If she fails…"

Lucifer felt the heat rise in his face. He turned to Lamechial, pointing toward the lobby. "Look at what's happening!

That woman *singlehandedly* got closer to beating Belial than the entirety of the AHM ever did. If *she* fails, what am I supposed to do?"

Lamechial's eyebrows rose, mocking him. "Is the great Lucifer admitting that he has less power than a human?"

Lucifer chuckled. "Not at all. If I had the sword, I'm sure I could take Belial down."

"Well, what about the shard you've been hiding from me?"

Lucifer cocked his head to the side, giving Lamechial a look of ignorance. "I have no idea what you're talking about."

A door at the far end of the hallway burst open revealing a row of Angelic soldiers, swords ablaze. Lucifer looked over his shoulder, watching as the platoon surrounded him.

Lauren lifted the Cosmic Ray Thrower and squeezed the trigger. The angels ducked the blast, swooping up on her. A sword came crashing down on the barrel of the cannon, severing it. The seared metal crashed to the floor as two guards grabbed her shoulders and subdued her.

Lucifer raised his arm, lifting his sword. Fingers grabbed his wrist and squeezed, forcing his hand to go numb. He dropped the weapon and his arm was wrenched behind his back. A hand grabbed the back of his head, pushing him toward the railing. Lucifer struggled to turn his head, to look behind him but each time he moved, the hand pushed him down harder.

Lamechial reached into the front pocket of Lucifer's pants.

"Not gonna even buy me dinner first, Lamechial?"

The angel rolled his eyes as his fingers landed on the stone. He pulled it from Lucifer's pocket and held it up to the light.

"A beautiful thing," he said, staring at the spotted stone. "But so, so powerful. Too powerful, some would say."

Tears filled Lucifer's eyes as his arm was jerked upward. He spun on his heels, his back slamming into the railing. A face leaned in closely to his, the dark brown eyes boring into him. Nathaniel smiled as he twisted Lucifer's wrist, holding him in place.

"Nathaniel?" Lucifer asked. He shook his head, his eyebrows arched questioningly. "What are you doing?"

"What I should have done a long time ago," he said. Nathaniel wrenched Lucifer's elbow back, making him grimace. "My life has been a mess since joining you guys. You pretended to trust me but only kept me under your thumb. Lamechial offered me the chance to come back. Clemency for my time spent with you. And after thinking about it, I think it's a choice I should take."

Lucifer's face turned red, his eyes narrowed. He leaned closer to Nathaniel, as close as he could without his wrist breaking. "I gave you everything!" he spat. "I gave you your life back after the angels abandoned you. Did you forget that already? They left you to rot. I found you and put you back together!"

"No, *I* found *you*. You gave me wings and then you kept me around to do your dirty work. Not anymore." He twisted Lucifer's arm behind his back and grabbed the back of his head. Swinging him around, Nathaniel pushed him toward a pair of soldiers. They each grabbed an arm and dragged him down the hallway. Nathaniel stepped closer to Lauren, her eyes wide as he approached.

Lauren struggled against the angels holding her back. As Nathaniel drew closer, she relaxed, her hazel eyes watching him intently. He leaned in, giving her a knowing smirk. Lauren returned his smile and spit in his face. A giggle rose from the back of her throat as she watched the spittle dribble down his nose.

Nathaniel stared at her. Wiping his face, he looked at the soldiers holding her. "Take her away."

"We'll get you for this," she said softly. "You know that, too. We will find a way out of here, and make you pay for this." Lauren's eyes bored into Nathaniel's as the soldiers dragged her down the hall, disappearing through the doorway.

Lamechial watched as Nathaniel turned toward him, his face a mask of uncertainty. He held his arm out over the railing, the shard pinched between his fingers.

"Twilana!" he shouted. "Maybe you could use this." He dropped the shard, his eyes following it as it descended into the lobby.

CHAPTER 55

Twilana stood over Belial, her mind buzzing with thousands of voices, each fighting for space in her head. Wrapping her fingers tighter around the hilt of the Blade, she closed her eyes and pushed the commotion aside, allowing her thoughts to come to the forefront. Her name rose among the noise, but not from her mind. She heard someone calling out for her. Looking up, she spotted the outline of an angel leaning over a railing high above her. His words were drowned out through the distance but she spotted a tiny object racing toward her. She tracked it, reaching out as it grew closer. It landed in the center of her palm, the sharp edge pinching her flesh.

Staring down at the shard, she smiled. She lifted the Blade and placed the tip of it against the stone. A bright, purple flash erupted from Twilana's hand and the sword absorbed the piece of itself. Twilana clutched the Blade in both hands and looked down at Belial.

"I'm going to give you one chance to surrender," she said as she stepped toward him.

The demon lifted himself up on his knees. Leaning down, he grabbed his sword from the floor and sneered at her. He struggled to his feet, the weight of his body causing him pain. Raising the Blade in front of him, Belial's muscles tightened and his body grew taut. "That will not happen."

"Suit yourself." Twilana leaped from the floor and slashed at Belial. The dagger had grown considerably, both in size and

208

strength. She could feel the power coursing through her, giving her otherworldly energy. Making her bold. Her hands throbbed as her fingertips dug into the handle of the weapon. She had been a skilled fighter in the Janian military, proven herself stronger than many of her contemporaries. But the Blade offered power on a completely different level. Something that she'd never experienced before.

And she liked it.

Belial raised his sword to deflect her attack. Purple sparks exploded as the blades collided. Twirling on her heels, Twilana spun and slashed at his legs. He jumped over the charge and brought his fist down on her face. His heavy gauntlet clanged as the punch knocked against her helmet. She pivoted on her back foot, raised her leg and kicked him in the chin. Belial stumbled backward and Twilana slashed again, slicing his chest. He clutched the wound as thick, black blood trickling over his fingers. Shaking his head, he grabbed the sword with both hands and lunged for her. Twilana lifted her arms as Belial brought his Blade down on her, holding his attack at bay with the sword. Purple sparks bounced off of her armor as the swords crackled with energy. Belial pressed his attack, stepping closer to her, forcing her back.

"You've had the Blade for five minutes," Belial said. "I've had it for five millennia. You can't win." He kicked her in the chest. As she faltered, he sliced through the armor engulfing her body. The energy field quickly stitched itself together, sealing the breech as she found her footing and parried his attacks, pushing him back. Belial tripped over a chunk of granite and stumbled. Twilana knocked the pommel of her Blade into his stomach, sending him reeling. She grabbed the horn on the side of his helmet, pulling his head down into her knee. She slammed her knee into his face two, three more times before shoving him backwards. Belial tumbled over his feet, the facemask of his helmet crushed, blood dripping from his mouth. Twilana spun the Blade and brought the pommel down on the base of his skull. He dropped to his hands, his sword clattering to the floor.

Looking up, he struggled to focus. A ringing in his ears distracted him and he could barely hold his head up.

Twilana rested the point of the Blade against his throat, pushing his head up to face her. The glow of his eyes dimmed but she could feel them boring through her.

Belial gritted his teeth and swallowed hard. "You can't win," he said, his hand patting the floor beside him, searching for his sword. His fingers brushed over a large stone, laying his hand on it as he struggled to catch his breath.

"Yeah, you said that already," Twilana responded. She leaned down, pushing the point of the Blade further into his neck.

Belial clutched the stone and tossed his body to the side. He brought his arm up and threw the heavy granite at Twilana. She raised the sword to block it, allowing Belial to roll free. Lunging for his sword, he snatched it up and shot to his feet. He pivoted to face Twilana and brought the Blade down on her. She recovered her balance and blocked the attack, her face awash in a hail of purple and blue sparks.

Twilana's body ached. Her muscles quivered. She could feel Belial shift his weight, pressing down against her. She looked up into his face and saw him smile behind his crushed mask. Every nerve in her body screamed at her, told her to just give up and get some rest, even if it meant death. But her willpower refused. Closing her eyes, she pushed the pain and fatigue from her mind, focusing on the power that flowed from the sword.

A clear warmth spread over her arms and throughout her body. The pain in her muscles slowly disappeared and soon her entire body went numb. Opening her eyes, Twilana watched as a tiny spark erupted between the two Blades. It grew slowly. Steadily. Purple flames licked at the Blades, spreading out over her hands. She watched as the stone weapons melted into each other, fusing in a way that didn't seem physically possible. Twilana's eyes glanced up to the shocked look on Belial's face.

"No," he said, his eyes wide. "This can't be." His voice quivered with fear.

White light spewed from the spark and a massive explosion ripped through the room. It launched Belial from his feet and he slammed into a marble pillar, crumpling to the floor.

The white light washed over Twilana, warming her, bringing the feeling back to her nerves. She looked down at the sword in her hand, the Onyx Blade fully formed. She remembered the length. The weight. It looked as it did the day she slew the Leviathan. Though she hadn't held it in months, somehow the Blade felt right. Wrapping her fingers around the hilt, she looked down at Belial as he pushed himself up on his elbows.

He pulled his body across the tile as Twilana stalked to him. Her face was emotionless, her eyes empty. He could feel the fear bubble up inside him as she drew closer.

Reaching down, Twilana grabbed Belial by the horn on his helmet and lifted him from the floor. He dangled from her grasp like a Christmas ornament, his body swinging around so that his face met hers. She looked into his eyes.

"You're finished, Belial. You've hurt enough people. Done enough damage. You're going back where you came from."

Her arm shot out beside her and the Blade sliced the air. A gust of wind *whooshed* past his face, chilling his bones. He craned his neck to look to the side and spotted a long gash in reality, the floating miasma of Limbo beyond it. Looking back to Twilana, his eyes grew wide.

Twilana swiveled her waist, dragging Belial toward the rift. She thrust her arm outward, tossing him like he weighed little more than a wadded ball of paper. He shouted as his body passed through the rift and fell into the nexus. Twilana reached out and placed her hand on the gap, pinching the sides together. They melded together, drowning out the sounds of Belial's screams.

Her eyes glazed over as she stared at the spot where the tear had been. The purple glow surrounding her slowly faded and the rush of adrenaline wore off. Her teeth chattered as the warmth drained from her body. Her muscles ached and her legs screamed in pain. Placing the tip of the Blade on the floor, she lowered herself to the ground, crossing her legs on the cold, hard tile.

CHAPTER 56

The elevator *dinged* and the doors parted. Lamechial stepped from the car uneasily, his eyes darting around the lobby. He quickly surveyed the damage, relieved that the construction crews were still on a fairly regular schedule with the current remodel. He was hoping that everything would have been completed by Christmas but the extension seemed like a small price to pay for stopping Belial.

As he rounded the corner, he spotted the fallen angels scattered across the floor and mouthed a silent prayer for them. Though regrettable that so many soldiers had to die at Belial's hands, they fought bravely and their sacrifice would be remembered. Perhaps he would speak with the Tribunal about approving a Memorial Placard for the lobby wall. *That would be a nice touch*, he thought to himself.

He looked over at Twilana seated in the center of the lobby. The Blade lay on the floor beside her and her face was buried in her hands. He watched her silently for a moment as the bubble of light encasing her body vanished. Lamechial noticed that she seemed much smaller than before. Even serene, somehow. Clasping his hands behind his back, he slowly ambled his way toward her.

As he approached, he heard her ragged breathing. Her body shook with every breath and he could hear the soft sobs escaping her throat. Hiking up his slacks, he lowered himself to the floor and placed a hand on her shoulder. Her head snapped up, her hand hovering over the hilt of the sword as her eyes fell on his face. Recognizing him, she relaxed, placing her hand in her lap. Her eyes were red and puffy and her cheeks streamed with tears. She dragged the back of her hand across her face and cupped her chin.

"Are you OK?" he asked.

She nodded, sniffling.

"What happened to Belial?"

She shrugged. "I sent him away. Not really sure where. Toward the end it felt like the Blade was in control. I just held it."

"No, my dear. That was you." Twilana turned her head and locked her eyes on his. Her bottom lip quivered and she inhaled deeply, steadying her emotions. Lamechial gave her shoulder a reassuring squeeze. "The Onyx Blade may have great power, but it itself is not enough. The Blade found the strongest qualities of you and enhanced them. It found the strength, the goodness, the willpower that was necessary to defeat the demon. You were in full control of the power though you may not have realized it."

"Strength, huh?" she said with a chuckle. "Then why am I crying like a baby?"

Lamechial smiled gently. "It intensifies your emotions as well as your abilities. You seem to be a very stoic person, Twilana. You don't always show your true feelings. Just as the Blade brought your strength to the surface, it now brings all of that raw emotion."

Grabbing the Blade, she pushed herself to her feet and sauntered across the lobby. She walked around the debris strewn around the room. Around the lifeless creatures lying in puddles of steaming magma. Around the platoon of dead angels. Her eyes fell on one body in particular. She shuffled toward the unmoving form.

Michael.

Twilana stared down at his face into the cold, glassy eyes. Crouching, she gently waved her hand over his face, slowly closing his eyelids. She and Michael had a tenuous relationship, what with his trying to kill her when they first met. But the time they recently spent together showed her a different side of the ex-angel. And she was proud to call him a friend.

She felt a resurgence of emotion bubble up in her and her chest heaved. She inhaled deeply, steadying herself. Looking down at the sword, she slid a finger along the length of the Blade. The stone was cold to the touch and it tingled her skin. "What should we do with this? It's too much power for anyone to have."

"I agree," Lamechial said, rising to his feet. "We will lock it up here to keep it safe." He extended his hand to her.

Twilana gripped the hilt of the Blade tighter, feeling the thick, ribbed grip dig into her palm. "No," she said, waving her arm at the destruction of the lobby. "To be frank, I don't trust you. Or the High Military. Or the Tribunal. I've seen this place destroyed twice in one year and I think that the AHM is the worst place to house this kind of weapon. I'll be taking the sword. I will see that it's kept safe."

Lamechial stared at her, his mouth agape. He placed his hand on his chest, taken aback by her words.

"You can't do that. This…this is an Angelic relic. It deserves to be kept here. Where we can keep an eye on it. It is not for humans to deal with."

"Oh, you're right, there," she said. "This isn't for humans. I know just the place to hide it."

"Where?"

Twilana stared at him with a smirk. Raising the Blade, she slashed the air, slicing a hole in space. A swirling purple nexus opened before her. She wiggled her fingers at Lamechial and jumped into the void.

CHAPTER 57

A stiff breeze blew across the courtyard, chilling the old man. He had retired to his front porch to do a little early evening reading but found himself fighting the elements instead. Pulling the gray woolen blanket higher up on his chest, he watched the flame on the candle flicker in the wind. A moment passed and the breeze settled, the flame proving the victor in the battle.

Satisfied, he picked up the book from the table and turned his eyes to the dreary darkness rolling in. Winter was quickly approaching. A shiver ran down his body as he leafed through the pages to the old cash register receipt marking his spot, the dim candlelight just strong enough for him to see the words.

Placing the book in his lap, he leaned back and yawned. His mind raced and a headache settled into his skull, making reading difficult. He rubbed his eyes and massaged the sides of his temples. Sighing loudly, he snapped the book shut and placed it on the table. The wind intensified, extinguishing the candle, claiming the final victory. He shrugged and ignored it.

The old man pushed himself up from the chair. Placing his hands on his hips, he pivoted his back, a cacophony of cracks and pops erupting from his spine. He rubbed his cheek, feeling the stubble that he'd neglected in the past few of days. Being retired meant never having to look presentable unless by choice. He had to admit, though, that it was strangely liberating being lazy and unaccountable for anything.

A flash in his peripheral vision caught his attention. He

turned and watched something drop from the sky far off in the distance. It popped up out of the grass, twirling, looking around the open field. He could see the outline of a person framed against the rising moon but the light danced around it, obliterating all detail.

"Hello there!" he shouted, waving his hand above his head.

The man smiled as the figure waved back. It broke into a run, traipsing across the tall grass, rushing toward him. The man could hear the crunching of the dried leaves and the snapping of twigs as it drew closer. The figure's features sharpened as it neared him and the old man felt a strange familiarity wash over him. He squinted, staring at the figure's face as it came within a few yards.

"Twilana?" he said, his jaw slack. "Is that really you?"

Twilana stopped at the bottom of the porch steps and looked up at the old man. "Hello, Metatron," she said through ragged breaths.

Metatron's expression morphed from shock to joy as he rounded the railing encircling the porch and hopped down the stairs. He threw his arms around her, grabbing her in a big bear hug and lifted her from the ground.

Twilana draped her free arm over his shoulder and pulled him closer. Her cheek rubbed against his, the stiff stubble irritating her skin. She ignored it and closed her eyes, enjoying the embrace.

"How have you been?"

Metatron placed her on the ground and pushed away, his hands still gripping her shoulders. He looked her up and down, examining the evident fatigue on her face. "Better than you, it appears. Have you been to the Angelic High Military again?" He laughed at the joke, but as their eyes locked he sensed a lack of amusement in her.

Twilana lifted her arm and dipped her chin toward the Blade. She watched as the smile melted from Metatron's face.

"Well," he said, the word lingering in the air as he groped for the right follow up statement. Finding none, he offered a pleasantry. "How about some tea?"

*   *   *   *   *

Twilana sat on the raggedy floral couch, a knitted afghan draped over her legs. She cradled a teacup in her hands, holding it close to her chin so that the wisps of steam floated over her face. Sipping the tea, she closed her eyes and savored the taste of the fresh Earl Grey as it lingered on her tongue. She looked up and focused on Metatron, watching as he stared at the side wall, shaking his head.

"I can't believe Belial returned," he said, turning to face her. He lifted his teacup to his lips and slurped loudly. Smiling, he looked into her eyes. "The things I've missed, huh."

Twilana chuckled. "It was...not fun."

Metatron nodded, staring into the swirling tea. He leaned back in the old, wooden rocking chair and rocked back and forth. Memories played in his mind, thoughts of his time with the Grigori, the celestial group tasked with watching and recording the most important events in the universe. He'd thought a lot about the past in the early days of his retirement, unsure if he'd made the right decision to leave his post. But after everything that happened with the AHM, with Michael nearly killing three innocent people while ignoring the bigger, universe-destroying plot and the destruction of the Ocularium, he felt his time would be better spent taking care of himself. Regardless of that, as he pondered the events Twilana related to him, he found himself deciding how he would word the official report.

Twilana leaned over and placed her cup on the coffee table. Looking up, she watched Metatron as he sat transfixed, his eyes glazed over. She cleared her throat and his head snapped toward her. "I need your help."

He tilted his head. "Anything for you, my dear."

"I need you to take the Onyx Blade."

Metatron leaned back in his chair, his shoulders bristling. His eyebrows shot skyward and he nearly lost the grip on his teacup. "Me? Why me? I'm just an old man. I can't protect it."

"You don't need to protect it. You just need to keep it hidden. You've come out here to your quiet little space, away from the madness of humanity and the angels. I can't think of a better place to hide one of the most powerful weapons in the universe. And also because I trust you. Trust you to do the right thing. Trust you to listen to your morals and not be corrupted by its power."

Twilana watched as Metatron's eyes misted, touched by her words. He nodded.

Flipping the afghan to the side, she rose from the couch and strode toward the front door. She grabbed the hilt of the sword peeking up from the brass umbrella stand near the entrance.

Pulling it from the can, she turned back to Metatron and held the Blade out to him. He lifted his arms and she gently placed it in his hands.

"I will see that it's safe."

"I know you will," she said. "I should be going now. Thank you for the tea." She took a step back and nodded to the Blade. "Would you mind...?"

Metatron stared at her for a moment. He looked down at the sword with a jump, surprised to find himself holding it. "Oh, yes, of course." Rising from the chair, he grabbed the Onyx Blade with both hands and lifted it, struggling with its heft. Lacking any skills as a swordsman, or any combat training at all, the Blade was a cumbersome weapon to wield: dense, long and heavy. It took Metatron a moment to find his balance. Closing his eyes, he focused his mind, channeling the Blade's energies. He slashed downward, slicing a rift in space.

"Take care, Metatron," she said. She gave him one last smile before jumping into the nexus. Placing the tip of the Blade on the floor next to him, he leaned to the side, watching the rift as it healed itself behind her.

"Take care, Twilana."

EPILOGUE

Nathaniel strode through the long corridor, his boots echoing in the tight space. The white paint on the walls was old and yellowing, chipping in places and left to disrepair. He clasped his hands behind his back as his jet black wings twitched behind him. He dreaded this meeting and had tried to avoid it for weeks but the time had come.

He thought back to the battle with Belial, to the decision to rejoin the fold of the Angelic High Military. Lamechial granted him a pardon for his previous crimes in exchange for his service. After all, he had been a ranking officer during Michael's tenure and knew quite a bit about how to run the organization. But he still questioned his decision. He counted Lucifer as a friend and he felt terrible about turning on him the way he did.

Nathaniel's heart skipped as he thought of Michael. His hatred for him ran deep, ever since the first battle against Belial when Michael abandoned him, costing him his wings. But that's not to say he didn't respect him. And Michael deserved that respect, especially the way he gave his life to protect Twilana. Despite all of the things Michael had done through the years, he deserved a proper memorial, and Nathaniel would ensure that he received one.

As he rounded the corner, he came upon a stout, uniformed angel seated behind a small desk. As he spotted Nathaniel, he leaped to his feet, back rigid and placed his hand at his forehead.

"At ease, angel," Nathaniel stated and the officer relaxed. "How have they been today?"

"Snarky and sarcastic. But overall, not bad."

Yep, that sounds like Lucifer, all right. "I should just need ten minutes with them."

The officer smiled and sat in the chair. He pulled the keyboard closer to himself and clacked away at the keys. A moment passed and a loud *buzz* filled the room. The barred door behind the desk slid open. Nathaniel nodded to the officer and passed through the gates, the heavy metal bars slamming shut behind him.

Nathaniel waited a moment as the reverberation of the clanging door floated away. He inhaled deeply before continuing down the hallway, his eyes darting from one iron door to the next. Composed, he walked the stretch before him, passing each of the cells. His heart raced and his hands grew clammy.

Stopping at the last door, he turned the knob and pushed it open. He waited in the threshold for a moment, his eyes absorbing the sight before him.

Lucifer sat at a round white table, his hands folded in front of him. He was dressed in a dingy orange jumpsuit. A glowing yellow halo encircled his neck. Designed by the Angelic security, the H.A.L.O., or *Hellfire and Alchemy Limitation Ovoid*, inhibited the use of any kind of magic. Lucifer had been powerless during his stay in Maximum Security, but still managed to keep himself together well. Despite a few bags under his eyes, he looked well for a prisoner. He peered up at Nathaniel and met his gaze, flashing him a smile.

"Nate, buddy," Lucifer said, rising to his feet. The chain around his waist held him securely, forcing him to squat awkwardly over the bench. He lifted his hand and extended it to the seat opposite him. "Please, sit. I've been hoping to see you."

Nathaniel stared at him cautiously. He glanced at the two angelic soldiers stationed behind Lucifer, their arms crossed over their chests, watching him intently. Satisfied, he stepped closer to the bench and lowered himself. He looked across the table at Lucifer.

"So," Lucifer continued. "It's been, what, three weeks since you sold us up the river? How's the new gig going for you? Looks like they gave you some new threads."

Nathaniel looked down at his tunic. The dark blue garb

signaled his rank in the Angelic High Military. If that weren't enough, the Wings of Generals had been stitched to the sleeve of his right arm.

He looked back at Lucifer. "Lamechial decided that leading an army wasn't his thing. Being the angel with the most battle experience, the Tribunal granted me with the task."

Lucifer's smile grew wider and he clapped his hands curtly. "That's great! A turn-coat like you being given so much power. That's not at all the biggest mistake the Tribunal has ever made."

"Look, Lucifer…"

"No, *you* look!" Lucifer snapped, slamming his hands on the table. He rose from the bench and leaned closer to Nathaniel. The two guards rushed to his side and clasped him by the shoulders. They forced him back down against the bench, holding him in place as his anger bubbled to the surface. He inhaled deeply and blew the air out through pooched lips. He raised his hands and nodded to the guards. "It's cool, guys. We're cool here."

The guards watched him uneasily before looking over at Nathaniel. The angel gave them a slight nod. They released Lucifer and floated back over to their posts.

"You're angry," Nathaniel said. "I get it. But to be honest, I don't care." He watched the rage flare in Lucifer's eyes again. Nathaniel leaned back on the bench and crossed his arms. "I did what was in my best interest. Surely you can understand that."

Lucifer glared at Nathaniel, the anger slowly subsiding. He shot him a smirk. "I can, actually. And to be fair, I'm proud of you. It shows that you've learned a thing or two from me."

"Let's not get out of control here."

Lucifer raised his palm to Nathaniel, cutting him off. "You understand that altruism is overrated. And that belief will make you successful in your new position."

Nathaniel couldn't help but smile. He knew this was the closest that Lucifer would ever get to wishing him 'good luck'.

Lucifer continued. "But if you think for a moment that I forgive you for putting me and Lauren in here, you're out of your mind."

The smile faded from Nathaniel's face. His eyes remained fixed on Lucifer. "I know I betrayed our friendship, Lou."

Lucifer closed his eyes and cocked his head to the side, a pained expression on his face. "It doesn't matter anymore, does it?" He opened his eyes and leveled his gaze on Nathaniel. "What's done is done. But I promise you this. I will get out of here. And when I do, I will be coming for you."

The H.A.L.O. around Lucifer's neck pulsed as he stared at Nathaniel from under his brow. Nathaniel sat in silence, watching as the hate seethed in Lucifer's face. He rose from the bench and looked at the guards, cocking his head to Lucifer. Turning, he strode from the door, feeling Lucifer's eyes burn holes in his back as he sauntered from the room.

*   *   *   *   *

Lucifer shuffled through the hallway, passing rows of heavy iron doors. The two guards followed closely, their hands on the hilts of their swords, waiting for him to make a move. But Lucifer was relaxed. His shoulders slouched and his hands were thrust in his pockets. He even had the strange urge to whistle.

He stopped at the last door and looked over his shoulder at the guards. The taller angel shouldered him aside and grabbed the ring of keys from his belt. He rifled through them, the metallic jingle echoing as he searched for the right key. He inserted it into the lock and opened the door. Grabbing Lucifer's elbow, he led him into the cell and slammed the door behind him.

Lucifer stared at the door and listened as the guards' footsteps slowly receded down the hallway. He waited for the *clang* of the closing gate before turning to his bed. Looking down, he smiled and sat silently.

"Sooo…" Lauren's soft whine bled through the thick concrete walls. Lucifer's smile faded from his face and he sighed exasperatedly.

"Yes, sister?"

"How did it go?"

"It went fine," he said plainly, lacing his fingers behind his head and leaning back on the wall.

The silence hung in the air, paining Lauren. She cleared her throat. "Did he…um…did he ask about me?"

"No, I can't say that he did."

Lauren's face scrunched up in annoyance and she hugged her knees to her chest. She flopped sideways on the bed and lay quietly. Moments passed, the two of them staring at their stark white walls, counting the seconds as they ticked by.

"Lou?"

"Yeah."

"How are we getting out of this one?"

Lucifer leaned over and wrapped his finger around the corner of the mattress. He reached down and pulled out a small golden ball. Sitting back on the bed, he bounced the ball off of the floor against the far wall, and caught it as it flew back to him. He listened as the *clack clack* reverberated through his tiny cell and died away before bouncing the ball again. And again.

He caught the Sphere a third time and, pinching it between two fingers, smiled.

"I have an idea."

The Onyx Blade saga comes to a conclusion in…

The Unwavering Resolve
Of The Human Condition

CHAPTER 1

Matt nosed the '98 Buick LaSabre from the paved road at the tree with the painted pig's face, just like the instructions in the email had told him to do. The previous night's rain left large puddles of water throughout the dirt, water that splashed up from the car's tires, muddying the windows and the doors. Matt grumbled under his breath about having just had the car detailed.

Aaron sat in the passenger's, ignoring his friend's mumbles. His concentration was fully engulfed in the screen of the computer on his lap, flipping between the email with the directions to their destination and a word processing program.

"There should be an old, run down cabin about 200 feet ahead," Aaron said, squinting at the Outlook message. "Make a left there."

"We passed three run-down cabins already," Matt huffed. He pulled the stick on the steering column and a jet of water flooded his windshield. He watched as the wipers cleared the muddy grime from his vision, leaving behind thick streaks of brown in their wake. "How are we supposed to know which run-down cabin it is?"

Aaron flicked his gaze out through the window, then back to the computer. "Uhhh…there's a red pickup truck half buried right beside it."

Spotting the bed of the pickup truck sticking out from the dirt, he cut the steering wheel to the left, jolting him and Aaron to the side.

Aaron consulted the email one final time. "Should be about two miles straight." He clicked the tab on the screen and brought the word processing program to the front before clacking away on the keyboard.

Matt stared through the grimy windshield, listening to the soft tap of the keys from the laptop. He tried to think about how they got to this place. Not physically, of course; he understood that he drove from New Jersey all the way down to Kansas, a drive that took roughly two days, given their need to stop every few hundred miles for more energy drinks and sugary baked goods. No, Matt tried to contemplate the series of events that led them to drive thirteen hundred miles to a backwater cabin in the woods to see some guy about a video.

The car rumbled through a puddle as Matt snuck a glance at Aaron. "You realize this is the craziest thing you've done since we got back, right?"

Aaron acknowledged his comment with a noncommittal grunt, never looking up from the laptop screen.

"I mean it," Matt continued. "Quitting your job, getting kicked out of your place and having to move in with me. This goddamn website thing that you started up. None of that compares to a road trip like this and…for what?"

Aaron huffed, slowly lifting his gaze from the computer to look at Matt. "What would you have me do, huh? After everything we've been through I should just pretend that none of it happened?"

"No, that's not what I'm saying at all." Matt cocked his head to the side and gripped the steering wheel harder, turning his knuckles white. "I just mean that maybe going about things this way isn't really the healthiest."

Aaron shook his head, turning his eyes toward the windshield. "Whatever. We're here." He closed the laptop and placed it on the backseat as Matt brought the car to a crawl.

Matt looked through the window at the old camper parked in the middle of the woods. Long tendrils of kudzu had grown up from the ground, criss-crossing itself along the rusted metal hull of the camper. Strings of Christmas lights were tied from the top of the door leading out to trees all around the entrance. Drying skins of raccoons and rabbits hung from the wires of the Christmas lights. Beside the camper stood a rickety wooden picnic bench and tabletop, the one-piece kind that they have at local parks and playgrounds.

Smoke billowed up from an old barbecue, filling the air with the aroma of charcoal and burning meat. A face appeared from the smoke, red-eyed and mustachioed. The man wiped the smoke from his eyes and fixed his gaze on the LeBaron, adjusting the green *John Deere* baseball cap that sat on his head

"Ironic, isn't it?" Matt asked.

Aaron pulled the handle and let the car door swing open. "What's that?"

"After everything we've been through," Matt said, putting the car in park and killing the engine, "that this is where we're going to die."

CHAPTER 2

The man flitted around the room, watching as the workers pounded nails into the sheet rock. His poured over their of the work intently, investigating each tiny nail-head, ensuring they were flush against the wall. The workers sighed each time he drew near, the man's obsessiveness being a distraction. With each wall, he would ask one of them to revisit the work, either pounding a nail further into the sheet rock or having them remove one to try again.

Glancing at his wrist, the man clasped his hands behind his back and disappeared into a small office, grabbing a leather-bound notebook from the desk. He flipped through it to a page half-filled with scribbles, pulling a pen from the elastic loop affixed to its spine.

"Cassel."

The man jumped at his name, the pen slipping between his fingers. He looked up at the door, recognizing the figure drifting toward him.

Nathaniel dragged his fingers through his dark hair as he strolled into the room. His dark blue tunic was freshly pressed, the creases of the garment as sharp as switchblades. Two white wings were stitched to his right sleeve. The Wings of Generals, used to denote his rank in the Angelic High Military. As General, he was the highest ranking officer, answering only to the Angelic Tribunal itself. His own black feathered wings fluttered softly behind him.

"I didn't mean to startle you, Cassel," Nathaniel said. "Just wanted to check in on the progress."

Cassel snapped the notebook shut and dropped it on the desk. "Not startled, General. Just surprised." He strode to the center of the room, extending his arm to the angel. Nathaniel grasped it and gave him a firm shake. "And I'm glad you came."

Nathaniel dropped Cassel's hand and looked around the room. "I must say, it certainly looks better than it did the last time I was here." Close to a year prior, Nathaniel's ex-friend slash boss, Lucifer, had devised a plan to sow chaos across the universe. A plan that required the use of the Ocularium and the Leviathan, a beast destined to usher in the Apocalypse. With the unexpected intervention of the angels and a few dimension-hoppers, Lucifer's plan crumbled under the weight of itself, leaving the Leviathan destroyed and the Ocularium in ruins.

Nathaniel's first order of business as General of the AHM was to rebuild the Ocularium. Part of the reason was to make up for his role in its destruction. But he also had a vision for the Ocularium going forward. A new purpose for it.

Cassel looked up at the walls, watching as a seraphim in a yellow hard hat and torn blue jeans hammered a row of crown moulding to the ceiling. "Yes, it was a wise choice going with the Romanesque style. It makes such a difference compared to the drab Gothic look of the old place."

Nathaniel nodded as Cassel spoke, not grasping a word of what he was saying. Clasping his hands behind his back, he turned to the Grigori. "Have you ordered the new oculuses yet?"

"I believe the proper pluralization is 'oculi' and I've done more than order them." Cassel trotted off across the room, hooking his finger at Nathaniel to join him. He led the angel to a large, shrink-wrapped shipping pallet. The plastic wrap held together twelve cardboard boxes, six stacked on six. Each box was about three feet tall and two foot square. Cassel tore away a section of the shrink-wrap and grabbed one of the boxes, gently resting it on the floor at Nathaniel's feet. "They've already arrived."

Nathaniel's eyes went wide. "Wow, that was quick."

Cassel closed his eyes and gave him a shrug. "Eh, I know a guy." He reached into his pocket and pulled out a small penknife. A smile stretching across his lips, he fixed his gaze on Nathaniel and popped the cap on the knife. "So, do you want to take one for a test drive?"

Stroking his chin thoughtfully, Nathaniel flashed him a grin. "Let's do it."

Cassel plunged the knife in the packing tape securing the box and slit the flaps down the middle. Placing the knife on the boxes on the shipping pallet, he pushed the flaps to the side and dug his hands in the carton. Slowly, he lifted a translucent glass sphere from the box. About the size of a basketball, the sphere was attached to a pyramid of granite, a base meant to hold the sphere in place. Cassel's eyes were glued to the sphere, gazing at it lovingly as he held it before Nathaniel.

"Gorgeous, isn't it?" Cassel edged his way to a small workbench set up against the wall. He placed the sphere and base on the table, taking a step back to admire it from afar. "Crafted from a new type of Talgonian glass. Developed by Ramiel half a millennium ago. They say that its focus is twenty times more precise than the oculi Metatron used."

"Don't be too hard on your predecessor. He did what he could with what he had. If the AHM had diverted some capital into the Watcher Division, he probably would have chosen to upgrade."

"Oh, no, no," Cassel said defensively. "I meant no disrespect. Metatron was my mentor. I have the deepest respect for him."

Nathaniel nodded, staring at the glass sphere on the table. He placed his hand on the orb, feeling a cold numbness run up his fingers. He looked over at Cassel. "What do you say we give it a try?"

Cassel's eyes went as wide as his grin. Like a child being allowed his choice of toy from the store, he grabbed the oculus and rushed it to the center of the room. Placing it on the pedestal, he stepped back, admiring it again with a contented sigh.

Hands clasped behind his back, Nathaniel stepped next to Cassel as the Grigori shot him a look over his shoulder.

"Where should we go?" Cassel asked.

Nathaniel shrugged. "We chose this model for a reason. Try to find trouble."

Cassel gave him a curt nod. Placing his hands on the sides of the sphere, he closed his eyes, clearing his mind of all thoughts. He focused his mind on the center of the sphere, concentrating on the structure of the glass. This particular glass, developed by the Talgonians, has a special property that makes it vibrate in conjunction with the universe, allowing it to pick up important occurrences in real time, in the same way the voice coil in a radio vibrates to produce the sound of a broadcast. As the Grigori have learned a long time ago, they have the innate ability to interact with the glass, being able to interpret the vibrations. To see the "visions" as if they were witnessing the events. This ability earned them the nickname "Watchers" and allowed them to strike up a partnership with the Angelic Military.

As Cassel's mind focused on the vibrating of the sphere, a picture came into view. Cloudy at first, but slowly coming in more clearly as he pushed the remaining distractions to the side. He saw a well-furnished living room with a classic floral-print couch. Expanding his view, he spotted an upended brass canister in the middle of the room.

"I think I have something," Cassel said.

"Walk me through it," Nathaniel responded.

"A house, it looks like. Quaint, but shows signs of a struggle." Realigning his vision, more of the room came into view. Two legs protruded from a side wall. "There's a body."

Nathaniel's back went rigid at the words. He clasped his hands in front of himself and stepped beside the Grigori. "What happened?"

"I'm not sure. I just see it slumped in the corner. Let me try to focus..." As Cassel moved his vision closer to the body, a shiver went down his spine. His eyelids snapped open and his breath caught in his throat. "No."

"What? What is it?"

"It's...it's Metatron, sir. He's dead."

CHAPTER 3

Lucifer emerged from the dark hallway into the bright light of the prison courtyard. Through squinted eyes, he looked out at the basketball court, watching as a group of incubi ran back and forth, tossing the ball to each other. One of them, a red-haired incubus, snatched the ball from a darker haired opponent, infuriating him. The dark-haired one rushed the other, inciting the guards into action. Lucifer chuckled as the guards picked the incubus up by the throat and slammed him on the ground as a crowd gathered around the melee.

"Neanderthals," Lucifer mumbled to himself, brushing the hair out of his face. The chains on his wrists rattled as he tugged on the H.A.L.O. fastened around his neck. Designed by the Angelic High Military, the H.A.L.O., or Hellfire and Alchemy Limitation Ovoid, was a proprietary device used to negate and suppress the use of magical abilities, specifically Hellfire, as is evidenced by its acronym. Unfortunately for Lucifer, whose primary source of power was Hellfire, this left him as flaccid as an octogenarian in a Viagra shortage.

But if Lucifer was anything, it's a cunning son of a bitch.

"Hey, Lou," the voice came from behind him. Turning, he found Lauren, his sister and longtime confidant, sidle up next to him.

Lucifer looked her up and down. In addition to the H.A.L.O. around her neck, she was dressed in the same orange jumpsuit that he was. But unlike him, Lauren had made a few alterations. Her sleeves were rolled up mid-bicep and the front was unzipped to show off just enough cleavage. Lucifer shook his head and her wardrobe adjustments.

"Good to see that you're getting comfortable."

Lauren glared up at him, snapping a wad of bubblegum between her teeth. She turned back to the basketball court, watching as the guards dragged the last couple of incubi back inside.

"Where'd you get the gum?" he asked.

"Shanked a guy for it."

Lucifer smiled. "That was you?"

Lauren nodded. Lucifer raised his arm and upturned his palm. Lauren's eyes flicked to it a couple of times before digging into her pocket. She pulled out a stick of chewing gum and placed it in Lucifer's hand.

"We need to get out of here," she said

Lucifer nodded, unwrapped the gum and shoved it into his mouth.

"Do you have a plan on doing so?" she asked.

He nodded again, his mouth making wet smacking noises as he chewed.

She waited for him to elaborate, growing more frustrated with each second that passed that he refused to go on. "Wanna share that plan with me?"

Lucifer cocked his head slightly. "No."

"Why the hell not?" Lauren shouted, throwing her hands up. "I'm gonna need to know eventually."

Lucifer fixed his glare on her. She dropped her hands, clasping them behind her back, and took a step backwards.

"Two reasons. Firstly, you're acting like a child and when you get this way, you tend to run your mouth and ruin everything. And secondly…" He looked around the yard before leaning in closer to Lauren, dropping his voice to a whisper. "Why would I detail my escape plan when we're surrounded by prison guards?"

Lauren looked up at him and blinked twice. The edges of her mouth tugged upward, fixing a smile on her face. She nodded her understanding before looking back at the now empty basketball court.

"Just understand," Lucifer continued, "that when I make a move, you need to trust me completely."

"I always have," Lauren replied. "Despite how terribly that's gone for us so far."

ABOUT THE AUTHOR

Shortly after receiving his Bachelor's Degree in Visual Communications, Michael Gary Wirth realized that his passion didn't lie in the arts but in writing. Looking to make writing his full-time profession, he self-published his first sci-fi novel, *The Non-Linear Flow of the Universal Tides*. He has since turned his attention to other works, including the completion of the Onyx Blade Trilogy, a children's book, and a detective story. When he isn't guiding his characters through battles with demons, bowling alley alternate dimensions, and saving the entirety of space-time, he enjoys his downtime with his beautiful wife, Lauren, and his stinky but cute cat, Pepe. For more information on his upcoming stories, visit his website at www.MichaelGaryWirth.com